Reckless Bond

Reckless Billionaires

Maxine Henri

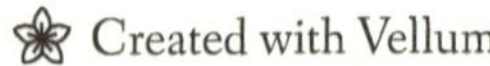 Created with Vellum

"Don't ever think I fell for you, or fell over you. I didn't
fall in love, I rose in it."
Jazz, Toni Morrison

Chapter 1

Finn

We look like the perfect power couple. In reality, I talked to her for five minutes and she was as dull as she was attractive, bragging about her number of followers while openly inspecting the brands I wore. Probably estimating the value.

I swipe my finger and smirk at another picture. Stupid paps and gossip sites. They had us engaged by the end of last night. Little did they know I drove her home, kissed her good night and left her pouting in front of her building.

Instead, I chased the thrill where I knew I could find it.

"Are we interrupting you?" The chair's voice slices through the air.

I jerk my head up, almost dropping my phone to

the floor. Seven pairs of eyes on me should provoke uneasiness, embarrassment perhaps.

But all these people are twice my age and thoroughly believe I'm a fuck-up. I don't think my spacing out during the board meeting will lower their opinion of me any further.

"No." I smile and nod. "Go ahead."

My father sits on the opposite side of the long conference table, glowering before he clears his throat and looks down at the paperwork in front of him.

These meetings are tedious on the best days, but after sleeping for only two hours, it's pure torture. The air is stale, the agenda is uninspiring, the participants are a bunch of dinosaurs or pussies and then, there is the chair. The leader.

Charles van den Linden, a man who continues to ride on the laurels of his past achievements. Loved and admired by many and feared and despised by more. Charles van den Linden, a business genius—former business genius if you asked me—and adulterer.

My challenge. My adversary. My father.

He, and the others, ignore me for the rest of the meeting and I try to stay away from my phone, because I might not have their support as it is, but I'm not pouring more oil into the fire.

They don't take my opinion seriously, anyway.

ıst their luck that today I don't have any capacity
fight.

ı should have gone to bed earlier, but the night's
events—I smile to myself—kept my adrenaline high, so
here I am enduring a day at work, running on fumes.
Fucking adrenaline sucks once it wears off.

I keep my phone on my thigh under the table and
every time my eyes start closing, I scroll for a moment.

When the meeting finally concludes, I'm the first
one to leave. I shuffle through the stuffy, dark corridor
to my office.

"Finn." My assistant, Reilly, stands up when he
sees me, and his face falls. "That bad?"

I hold out my arm to stop him from talking. "No
calls," I bark and he chuckles.

Besides my brother Caleb, Reilly is the only person
in this company I trust fully. The only person I can
rely on. The only employee who doesn't take my shit
and copes with my mood—which is usually sour when
I'm here—with enough perspective.

He'd better after I hired him. The only openly gay
employee and one of the few of Asian heritage in the
headquarters of Linden Enterprises.

And while my father believes I hired Reilly to piss
him off, I offered him the job because he was the best
candidate. Not that our outdated, prehistoric company
values would ever accept that.

I slam my door closed. Okay, one thing this stale behemoth of a company got right in the last century is the privacy of the management offices. None of that airy, open concept, glass walls bullshit. On days like this, it's heaven.

I collapse onto a large sofa by the door and close my eyes. But the peace is short-lived as my cell phone dances in my pocket. I groan and fish it out.

"What?"

"What's up your ass?" my brother snorts.

The buzz in the background suggests he's in a restaurant or some public place. He might be at work. Little brother is still going through mandatory on-the-job training, managing our flagship New York hotel.

He hates every minute of it, eager to come to HQ and start making changes. Poor bastard will have his dreams crushed fast. But before that he still has two hotels to manage, in Europe and in Asia.

Father is big on learning by doing, I have to give him that. My stint in our hotels was probably the best time of my life since I started working for the company.

"What do you want, Cal?" I cover my eyes with my forearm.

"Did you talk to him?" he asks me. "Thank you, I'll be right there," he says to someone else, multitasking.

"No." I sigh.

"Fuck, Finn, we agreed you'd prep him before we

ambush him together." The frustration in his voice pokes me the wrong way. I have my father to make me feel like a failure. I don't need my bro to join in on that delightful task.

"I haven't slept enough to go into it today. The management meeting was enough to suffer through."

"Jesus, do you always have to go and screw someone?"

"As if your dick didn't get wet last night." It's a reasonable guess and I won't admit my date was less than inspiring.

"Fuck you." He chuckles. "So who was the lucky lady? Just making sure we don't dip into the same jar." Now he laughs. Hilarious.

I sigh. This is the longest day ever. Then his words hit my cortex and I shudder.

"Jesus, don't even joke about that. We need to figure out some sort of system now that we live in the same city."

"Not the worst idea. So who was it?"

I run my hand down my face and close my eyes. Clearly my brother doesn't peruse the society sites. "No women. I was too stressed, so I—"

"Fuck, Finn, do you want to get killed? I know things are hard over there, but don't fucking do that shit. There are safer ways to release your stress."

"Any other words of wisdom? I don't get my life

managed and all my life choices criticized enough, so please do chime in."

"Sorry for being the voice of reason," he huffs. "Jesus. Talk to Pa and we'll force some sense into him together. Things can't continue the way they are. The stubborn bastard is proud, but not stupid."

I chuckle. My idealist brother. So like me when I joined the management team a year ago. Where even is that person anymore?

"Look, Cal, I'll talk to him, but don't get your hopes up."

"Thanks. Just suck it up there for two more years and then I'll join you, and together we'll breathe new air into that place. I mean some of your colleagues must retire soon. We can do this."

He's only three years younger, but a decade more naïve than me. Still, it would be nice to have a friendly soul slaving here with me.

We hang up and I finally have a moment to rest.

"The General! The General is coming!"

Reilly's panicked voice squeaks through the intercom, infiltrating the darkness that claimed me. But the code word works its magic and I jump up.

I don't make it far before Pa barges in. Casually, I walk around to take a seat behind my heavy mahogany desk—just one more thing I hate about this office, this building—and I smile at him.

"Pa." I nod.

He bangs the door closed, the pictures on the wall reverberate and I sigh because I know what's coming.

"How do you expect to gain the respect your status deserves if you keep behaving like an idiot?" my father bellows.

As if him yelling at me for everyone to hear is reinforcing my position here. At least this time he kind of has a legitimate reason.

"You were on your fucking phone, Finn. So disrespectful."

"Pa, I can recite everything that was said there." And I truly can. Because despite my father's disappointment, I know what's happening around here. And I ache to change it.

I would, but I keep hitting the wall. In the form of a man who is impossible to please. Currently looking at me with disdain.

"Don't be smart with me, Finn. You think you're better than any of them? When I was your age..."

Here we go again. I tune out and let him tell me, yet again, to value the opportunity, learn from the more experienced and show respect to my colleagues.

Not that I don't subscribe to those values. Fuck, what do I know anymore? At times, it feels like Pa is only pleased when I shut up and follow orders.

Not my jam, unfortunately.

"What do you have to show for yourself, besides headlines as the most eligible bachelor and party boy in town?"

I won't argue, because the headlines really aren't the best for our company's reputation, but I attract them whether I want them or not. And sometimes I do, the little boy in me craving the attention I don't get from the man in front of me. Pathetic, perhaps, but fun.

Pa sighs and shakes his head. "Finn, soon you'll be handed the reins. Grow up finally."

I swallow hard. This is news to me. This is the first time Pa has even mentioned that this management job is grooming me, not punishing me.

Based on his tighter than usual jaw—and that man can carve diamonds with it—he isn't happy about dangling that carrot in front of me. Encouraged by his slip, I get bold.

"Pa, since you mentioned the future, sit down. I want to show you the projections I ran on the refurbishing—"

"Finn, don't be ridiculous, I don't want to hear about your boutique hotels. We've been offering grand luxuries to our guests—"

I stand up. "My boutique hotels would offer top luxuries, but at the same time implement sustainable practices, switch to renewable energy sources and reduce our carbon footprint."

"Nonsense. These so-called sustainable practices are just buzzwords. Our guests expect certain standards and we've been successful because we stick to tradition." He shakes his head.

He's going to pretend that our dwindling hotel occupancy is just a seasonal discrepancy.

"Tradition is important, Pa, and I want to build on our legacy, but guests are increasingly concerned about the environment. We risk losing them if we don't adapt."

"Our customers come for luxury and opulence, not to be lectured on saving the planet." He smirks and turns to leave.

"We can still provide luxury and opulence while being environmentally responsible. And while the initial investment is high, we'll save in the long run. Let me show you the projection Cal and I prepared."

"Don't drag your brother into this. This is the real world, Finn. We have a legacy to maintain. I won't jeopardize that for your whims."

I can't help but chuckle. Fuck. A brick wall, this man. "A whim? If we don't change, our legacy will crumble."

His face reddens and his nostrils flare. "You're pushing your limits, son. I won't hear any more of this bullshit. Just do your job and keep your head down, so the board sees that you're the man for the job. And get a fucking haircut."

He storms away. Before I can stop myself, I tuck a strand behind my ear. My below-the-ears locks have been a point of pride. Not so much born from vanity as from the need to piss him off.

"Sorry, boss, he blindsided me." Reilly sticks his head through the doorway. "I overheard him flirting with Eleanor and only then realized he was coming here. Can I get you anything?"

"A new job would do." I spin in my chair and stare through the floor-to-ceiling windows.

The city is gloomy and pisses me off further.

"I can get you a coffee, or spike his drink so you inherit faster," Reilly muses from behind me. "Or I know this mobster—"

"Let's keep him on speed dial." I chuckle and turn. "Fuck, is it five yet?"

"Half an hour more and you can pretend to go for an off-site meeting with no one expecting you to come back."

"Some good news. Thanks, man."

"You need your beauty sleep."

"Get out of here."

He laughs and saunters away. I attack my emails, approving nonsensical campaigns and reviewing projections that are painting an eerie picture. Task after task to keep myself busy, just like the board and my father expect from me.

Soon you'll be handed the reins.

Maybe if I kept my head down, the soon would come sooner. And then I'd bring new people in, and along with Caleb we could finally bring Linden Enterprises into this century.

Or I can just say fuck it all and live off my trust fund. Frankly, on a day like this, that route seems more and more appealing. Women, cars, parties.

Why do I still need to please my father?

When I step onto Madison Avenue, I take a few breaths to enjoy the freedom. I imagine this is how it feels to leave a prison. It sucks when you have to do it every day. I yawn and dive into the closest coffee shop.

With the drizzle outside, the place is too busy for my frazzled nerves, but I order anyway. I need the caffeine and sugar kick if I want to make it home. God, I need my bed.

I stand to the side, waiting. My eyes roam and land on a... well, that's a nice ass. I let my gaze wander up and down her figure. If I wasn't this tired, I would totally approach her. Maybe I should anyway. I might be tired, but a good fuck would take my mind off things.

Aside from the outrageously purple hair, her body is definitely made for sin. I quickly check her ring finger. Bingo. I shuffle to the side to check her face. So far, she is a ten out of ten for me.

My phone buzzes and I groan inwardly at the interruption. I check the caller ID.

Shit, these people have been calling me nonstop. I should just talk to them and explain I have no interest. But something has been stopping me. Maybe I've grown into a coward under Pa's influence.

I took the meeting with our competitors one of those times when I was pissed at Pa. It's a great company. But I have my duties with Linden Enterprises. With our company. My family.

"Double shot vanilla iced latte for Finn," a voice announces, and I disconnect the call.

My coffee is a priority right now. And it comes right on time to change my vantage point and assess the beauty in front of me.

I step forward at the same time she does.

"I'll take it." She grabs my coffee and dashes out.

What the fuck?

"Hey!"

She glances back and her purple hair floats into traffic as she crosses the street. Did she just steal my coffee? No fucking way. I don't have the bandwidth for this shit today.

I march off the sidewalk, following her, and turn at the screeching breaks. An outraged driver honks and I almost flip the fucker off, but I don't want to get run over for real.

What the fuck are you doing, Finn? Just get yourself another coffee, you idiot.

I jump onto the sidewalk and spot her immediately. So, a thief with conscience, because she stopped running, hearing the commotion.

And now I can see her face. It's beautiful. High cheekbones, perfect nose, large eyes and kissable lips. Beautiful. And familiar.

This is rich.

She stares at me wide-eyed, and then glances at the cup in her hand and shoves it into someone's hands.

The haggard-looking woman pushing a shopping cart blinks a few times, grins, and takes a sip from my coffee. My fucking coffee.

I stare as she passes me. What the hell just happened?

I turn back to my little thief, my mood hitting a high for the first time today.

"Well, well, well, London Lowe, this is unexpected."

Her eyes widen for a brief second. I've known

London for years. We kind of move in the same circles, but for some outlandish reason, her little stunt just improved her attractiveness in my eyes.

"Oh, sweetheart, this is priceless. You stealing coffees." I step closer and her subtle scent, like a warm meadow, awakens something in me. It's an oasis of peace in the middle of the concrete jungle. During the shittiest day.

We stare at each other for a moment. The rest of the traffic blurs away, and it's just me and her on the street.

Snap out of it. This is not some chick flick. But I know for a fact that London Lowe is the same adrenaline junkie as me. Why don't we test our limits together? Suddenly, I don't feel as tired.

"You'll have to make this up to me," I rasp.

She bites her lip. "Maybe I can get you another drink?" She bats her lashes.

And we're on the same page.

Chapter 2

Paris

The last two hours have been liberating. Let's face it, pretending to be someone else usually has that effect. We've been laughing, talking, connecting on a level that frankly scares me a bit, because that's not what this is.

We ducked into a small bistro as the rain intensified and ordered a round of drinks. He took off his damp jacket and draped it over his chair. That was the exact moment my ovaries sent my brain on vacation.

I didn't expect him to take me up on the offer of drinks. Jesus. Pretending to be my twin is so high school. Back then it was our modus operandi, but now? I'm a thirty-three-year-old woman who is pretending to be her sister.

To get laid, no less. Because if that wolfish look on

the street was any indication, Finn, whoever he is, is not after a replacement drink.

I can't deny that the chemistry is off the charts. I'm so out of my element that I might redefine the charts. My ovaries are certainly on board with that.

"I can't believe you stole my coffee." Finn laughs.

"It went to a nice lady who couldn't afford it, so you should be pleased." I bite my bottom lip, grinning.

It's been clear he doesn't mind anymore. That he finds the whole situation quite entertaining. And somehow that makes him more attractive. Not that he needs any help in that department.

When I first snatched someone else's coffee, I truly intended it to be just that—a one-time item off my bucket list. It was the first thing on my adventure list, to challenge myself to live on the edge a bit.

That first time I casually picked up someone's coffee as soon as their name was announced, a jolt of excitement rushed through me before I even reached the door. I ran with that coffee like a madwoman, laughing.

I ended up giving it to a homeless person and that felt doubly good. I was like the Robin Hood of coffee. Okay, not really, but still, the exhilaration came with a side dish of craving.

The second time, I surprised myself. Since then, I

occasionally chase the high that comes with the silly prank.

Who knew my ludicrous coffee-snatching scheme would lead me here? Sitting in a bar with a ridiculously handsome man who was crazy enough to run after me. Based on the quality of his suit, he can afford hundreds of coffees.

His cheekbones and jaw are chiseled in granite. And his hair. Jesus, any woman would kill for those curls. A thick, longish, dark blond mane frames his face.

Even the dark circles and blood-shot eyes don't discount his attractiveness. If anything, they make him look more human. Because otherwise I'd be sitting here with a Greek god.

"It looked as though you needed a drink more than coffee." I wonder why he followed me instead of getting another coffee, but I don't ask.

He sighs and clenches his jaw. "Don't even get me started."

"Work?" He's wearing an expensive suit and we ran into each other on Madison, so I'm assuming he's an ad executive, perhaps. Though he certainly could model in his campaigns.

Finn nods, suddenly deep in thought while he continues grinding his teeth. The square of his chin is exquisite. Seriously, the man is unreasonably good-looking. And a bit familiar. No, that makes no sense, I'd have remembered him. That's not a face you forget.

"My father…" He exhales the word with a mixture of pain and something akin to respect. "He's always had high expectations of me. Growing up, it was a challenge I enjoyed."

He draws mindless circles around the edge of his glass. The moment stretches, but I don't want to speak because it feels like he's building up to find more words.

After another heavy sigh, he continues, "I kept trying to meet them. Only they grew bigger and bigger, and no matter what I achieved, it was never enough. I was never enough."

My heart squeezes at this admission. I want to reach for his hand, but I don't want him to think I pity him. I don't know this man, but he thinks I do. And he opened up.

Is it selfish to keep up this ruse? Most probably yes, but the moment is fragile right now, and I can't tell him I'm a liar. Not yet.

"Things got worse when I started working for him, but the pressure lately is just ridiculous."

He shakes his head slightly, as if to get rid of an annoying thought. A thick, shiny strand of hair falls over his eyes. It makes him look slightly more disheveled, more human amid the vulnerable admission.

"You work with your father?" Of course, something ridiculous comes out of my mouth.

He frowns. "I thought you'd know that."

Oh shit, just how much would London know about this Finn guy? Has she slept with him? That would be the next level fucked-up.

For some reason, I can't confess who I am. He just trusted me with his problems. I can't confess I'm a fraud now.

So I channel my twin sister. "Not every woman in this zip code is keeping tabs on you." I smirk.

He throws his head back laughing and touches his heart in a dramatic gesture. "You've crushed my feelings."

I giggle. "I'm sure you'll recover."

We stare at each other, and our smiles die in an intense moment that caresses every fiber of my body. Finn reaches out and tucks my hair behind my ear. His fingers linger and they might as well have a direct line to my core. The intimate gesture sets my heart into a gallop.

"Maybe he has something else on his mind. Maybe he's going through something?" I swirl the conversation back to his father.

Finn drops his hand and takes a drink. "Like a severe case of assholism?" His chuckle is derisive.

"Well, sometimes we act out to deal with our own insecurities." *Like me right now. Pretending to be my sister.*

"Insecurities? Have you met my father? Vulnerability of any kind isn't in his genetic code."

Shit. I need to stay away from topics that could expose me. Nothing good would come out of me confessing, anyway. It's just a one-night stand.

Lo wouldn't mind if she knew about it. It's not like either of us would kiss and tell. And Finn doesn't look like a guy who would call me the next day. He's definitely a player. More like a let's-get-her-out-of-my-bed-quickly kind of a guy.

"We're here to improve your day." I smile.

I'm shocked to discover I really want to make it better for him. And not even for charitable reasons. Purely because if his looks are any indication, making him feel better would be satisfying for me. My body.

His gaze locks with mine. If I thought he ate me up with his eyes before, he's devouring me now.

"You're right. I need to punish you for stealing my coffee."

Holy shit. Yes. Yes. Punish me. What's happening in my underwear is embarrassing. And so good.

"That's right. You do." I swallow, not even recognizing myself.

His eyes darken and glimmer with need and satisfaction. It makes me ridiculously happy that my answer pleased him.

Electricity zaps between us. The rest of the world melts into an inconsequential background as I, without thinking, lick my lips—yeah, the brain took a day off—and his eyes dip to my mouth.

I gulp down my margarita, breaking the moment. The intensity is too much.

I always knew this particular bucket list item wouldn't be happening without liquid reinforcements, but with this man, there aren't enough cocktails in this entire bar to cool me down.

"Thirsty?" He raises his eyebrows and the mischief on his face makes me relax. A bit.

I chuckle or giggle, or something that makes me sound like I'm twelve.

Great.

My stomach rolls with nerves, the good and the not so good ones.

Why did I put a one-night stand on my bucket list? I'm not a one-night stand kind of a girl. And definitely not ready for this predator of a man.

The whole idea of the list was to push myself to do

things beyond my comfort zone, but bungee jumping would have covered it.

Or stealing someone's coffee.

But here I am, having drinks with this more-than-fine male specimen who is God's gift to the female population. His only problem is he knows it, but who cares? It's only a one-night stand, after all.

"Pace yourself, sweetheart," he whispers darkly and leans in, grazing my thigh with his fingertips. "The night is young." His mouth by my ear sends goose-bumps all over my skin.

He doesn't lean back, just breathes beside my ear for a moment, tracing circles around the hem of my skirt with his finger. His aftershave might as well be a fountain of lust because it awakens the most sensual parts of me.

Pleasant shivers run through my body. Perhaps there is a comfort zone to be found in this situation.

"Maybe we need to move the party," I whisper. I like this Paris. This bold version of me is liberating.

He gives me a lopsided, satisfied smile. "I like your thinking, London. I know just the place."

God, I wish he didn't use Lo's name.

He pays and drags me outside. "Can you walk for two blocks?" He checks my heels, and before I can answer he pulls me under his arm and steers us into the pedestrian traffic. I guess he's deemed me ready to walk.

This is weird. It's not even dark yet. Though I'm not sure why it matters. In my mind, one-night stands happen under the veil of darkness. "Where are we going?"

"To my place." His hand on the small of my back gives me an unreasonable sense of safety. "It really isn't far, but we can cab it if you want."

"That's okay. Let's walk." I lean into him, relishing the feel of this man with my every fiber. I might as well go all in. Selfishly. Unapologetically. I only have him for a few hours.

"Apparently you can speed walk when in need of caffeine." He laughs. "What's up with that?"

We glide through the street in this half-embrace, and I can't not notice how well I fit against his solid body.

Here I go again, imagining things and making a big deal of something that is probably insignificant. *You hook up with someone and the following day you take care of their dry cleaning.* That's what Lo told me a while back.

Not this time.

"It's just a game. I did it once as a challenge... on my bucket list."

He stops and I chance a look up to meet his eyes.

There is that mischief dancing in them again. "Do elaborate." He's trying hard not to laugh.

I sigh, smiling like an idiot. Something about him is so easy, so freeing. It's like the angry man from before disappeared with the first sip of whiskey and he sucked me into this playful universe where everything is inconsequential, fun, and a bit reckless.

"I have this bucket list to challenge myself, and one item was to claim someone else's coffee."

He studies me for a moment and then shakes his head, laughing. A strand of his hair falls into his eyes again. Really, it's unfair how good he looks.

He mock-frowns. "And I fell a victim to your little challenge." He fails to look stern about it and we both burst out laughing.

"Something tells me you don't mind, Finn. You don't mind at all." I grin at him, joy coursing through my veins.

What is it about this man that somehow makes me feel different?

"You're right. And full of surprises, London Lowe, full of surprises."

His words are both a caress and a cold shower all at once. Yeah, well, London doesn't need a bucket list to be interesting.

* * *

"Hello, Joachim." Finn greets the doorman at a swanky high-rise building with a handshake. "Is the coast clear?"

"Nice to see you again, Mr. Finn," Joachim grins. "The place is all yours."

What? Was that some sort of a code? Joachim smiles at me kindly and I force my brain to stop thinking. There is no thinking needed—or beneficial—here. I'll have my one-night stand and that's it. *Thank you, brain, you can now retire.*

The elevator opens and Finn ushers me in. The moment the door slides closed, he pounces.

My back hits the wall while his body literally absorbs me. How is he this large?

The planes of his muscles are wonderfully solid under my palms as I hold on to him, because the explosion of raw, primal feelings is surprising.

And not unwelcome.

Not at all.

With one hand somewhere above me on the wall and the other in my hair, he captures my lips with an aggression and possession that should scare me.

And it does.

But it also spreads heat through my body.

Holy shit. This man.

I whimper against his lips and surrender. His

tongue claims me with such conviction, I let myself float on the moment. The hormones. The pure need.

He grinds his hips into me, and wow... do I have an effect on him. I push at his chest, not to shove him away, just to channel the influx of energy swimming through me.

He uses my move to grab my ass and hoist me up. Wrapping my legs around his waist, I fist his hair and he groans.

Stumbling, we hit another wall, this time with his back. He nuzzles my neck, and my eyes meet the gaze of a bewildered woman in the mirror.

I hardly recognize myself. I'm flushed and disheveled, but oh, I'm so alive.

Who even is this woman?

Finn bites my shoulder and jerks his pelvis. His hardness feels impressive even through the layers of clothes. What have I gotten myself into?

"I can't wait for you to scream my name, London."

London. That's right.

The woman in the reflection, the woman in Finn's arms is London. And London attacks life with abandon.

I can totally be her for one night.

Chapter 3

Paris

We stumble into the apartment. The place isn't large and it's only sparsely furnished with expensive items that don't seem to create a home, but rather are placed around functionally.

But I have no time to evaluate the decor as Finn drags me to the bedroom. Here, there is only one love seat and a king-sized bed. He kicks the door closed behind him and pins me against it.

"What am I going to do with you?" He nuzzles my neck.

"Do you really need an instruction manual?" I gasp as he bites me. Hard. Delicious heat spreads through me.

Finn whips me around and cages me with his whole body, my back to his chest.

"Smartass." He wipes my hair from my face and tucks it behind my ear as he leans down. His breath scorches the sensitive skin on my throat. "You stole my coffee. What does a little thief like you deserve?"

I'm game for double entendre, but this is so raw, so dirty, my mind misfires and goes blank. My body, on the other hand, is suffering from a completely different explosion.

"Hm, and she lost her words." He murmurs against my skin, gyrating his hips into me.

I can't move. I can't think. I'm completely at his mercy. I should be appalled by this, but instead my hips of their own volition arch into him.

Finn groans. "So what will it be, little thief?"

"I should apologize, perhaps." My breath hitches, I'm aroused and mortified at the same time. Why am I overthinking this?

Because I always overthink. It's my superpower. Fuck that, says my body.

"On my knees?" I rasp.

He hums his approval. "Isn't that a wonderful idea?" He steps back and I turn. My eyes clash with his hungry gaze, and being this desired is enough to shut up my brain.

He's still too close for me to lower myself down, just glaring down at me, panting.

And somewhere deep in my need, boldness blooms

within me. "Are you going to stare or take off your clothes?"

He smirks and loses his suit jacket and his pants faster than I can blink. He loosens his tie and undoes the first three buttons of his shirt, showing enough skin for me to salivate. My tongue darts out, wetting my lips.

Another reaction I didn't plan. Clearly around this man my body acts on pure instinct. It's the best feeling ever.

He kisses me roughly and walks away. Disoriented, I stumble and blink a few times.

Finn crosses the room, dropping his shirt and tie in the process and... Holy shit. How long does one train to get his body? He sits—sprawls—across the love seat.

"Your turn, sweetheart. Why don't you undress for me?" The darkness in his voice hits me so hard that I might just orgasm from being so overwhelmed.

I take a step, but he raises his arm and tsks. "Stay there."

It takes a second for me to comprehend his meaning, then my mouth goes dry. He wants me to strip for him? Me? I hate talking in front of people. I hate presenting. I hate eyes on me.

We stare at each other for a moment, or an hour, and in that time the hunger in his eyes, the patience and easiness in his posture slowly eat at my self-consciousness.

"No need to be shy, baby."

I pull out my phone and find a song. Finally, those dance classes will pay off in some form. I hope.

I drop the phone on the bed and lower my hands to the mattress, wiggling my ass as I smile at him seductively.

"Fuck." He groans.

Okay, I can feed off that reaction. Still bending, I find the hem of my dress with my fingers and slowly shimmy my hips as I trail the skin of my legs, showing him more and more of it and then stopping.

His Adam's apple bobs and there is no more hunger in his eyes. It's pure, raw need. It encourages me, and soon enough I lose myself to his desire and to the music and to the dance, and I undress for this man with no hesitation.

At last, I rake my hands through my hair, lifting it up, away from my neck. I jut my hip out and stand in front of him in my simple matching bra and panties that are, no doubt, visibly soaked. I've never felt this attractive. This comfortable in my body.

"Look at you. Beautiful. You're killing me here," he rasps. "But my little thief was going to apologize. Time to get on your knees."

I let go of my hair and take a step, but he stops me again. "Why don't you start there?"

My eyes widen, but the game steals all my reservations, and I drop to my knees and place my hands on the plush carpet. I toss my hair to one side, and without breaking eye contact I crawl to him, the music only adding to the wantonness of the scene.

Slowly, I enjoy every single jerk of his muscle, each twitch in his briefs, the tick of his jaw and the bobbing in his throat as I make my way to him like I'm a tigress. A goddess.

When I get between his legs, our gazes still fused, I hook my fingers into the waistband of his briefs and free him.

And that's when the game ends and he loses all control. "Fuck that, I need to be deep inside you."

He drags me up and to the bed, whips me around and bends me over. It takes only seconds—a foil tears, my underwear rips—before he buries himself deep inside me, groaning and murmuring dirty praises.

And in that moment, I adore the woman who holds the power in this bedroom. Who isn't afraid to be seen. Who made this man, who clearly isn't an amateur in bed, lose control.

I've never realized how vanilla my sex life was.

I stare at the ceiling, grinning.

Blissed. Happy. Ecstatic.

Finn is sleeping beside me. The light from the nightstand illuminates his glistening skin, giving me a perfect view of his muscles. One thing is sure. This man takes care of himself.

He works out, and thanks to that I got the workout of my life tonight. How does one recover from that?

He devoured me in the best and the most domineering way. I never knew I'd enjoy being manhandled, dirty-talked and possessed by someone like this.

But, shit, at one point I started counting my orgasms. Okay, they would suffice for fingers on one hand, but still... the man is a beast. An animal.

When I dared myself to do this more than a year ago, I assumed a one-night stand would be a fleeting connection of two bodies on a completely selfish basis.

Check.

Perhaps our liaison was so good because I was being truly selfish. I mean, it's not like I'd see him again. It's not like I need to care. So I didn't. Who knew you could gain so much by letting go?

What I didn't expect was to have the best sex of my life with a stranger. But while our bodies united in an incredible rhythm, other than that... I don't know who this man is.

Finn had a shitty day and chased after me when I stole his coffee. That's all I know about him.

And he believes I'm someone else.

I wish the sex was mediocre.

No, I don't.

But how do I move on from this? Even now, as I'm watching him sleep, I want to reach out and... Jesus. I'm overthinking everything again.

Time to leave. Keep the memories and cut my losses. This was a one-night stand. Nothing less and nothing more.

I turn and slowly push to a sitting position. Glancing at the love seat, the memory of me dancing and undoing this strong, confident man brings a smile to my lips.

The room is strangely naked. High-quality bedsheets, there is an air of wealth here, but not a full breath just yet.

"Why aren't you sleeping?" Finn rasps from behind me and I turn to meet his sleepy but still dazzling smile. He looks different now that he's rested a bit. Younger almost. The mischief in his eyes should concern me, but it draws me instead.

I don't resist when he pulls me to him. He props me on top of him and, for the love of God, the man is hard again.

"Hey." He grins at me.

"Hey yourself."

"Are you sore? Tired?" He jerks his hips up.

I giggle. "Wow. If I knew one-night stands required this much stamina, I'd have trained for it."

He frowns and studies me for a moment. Then he reverses us, so I'm on my back. He props his head on his hand and pins me with his leg. "Who says this is a one-night stand?"

I snort. "This whole situation does. Like you picked me up at a bar."

He kisses me, stealing my breath. "That's not true. I apprehended you on the street."

"Semantics." I grin at him.

He takes a strand of my hair and curls it around his finger. Avoiding my eyes? Thinking?

"If this was a one-night stand," he starts, "you'd have been at home by now." He looks at me now and the hunger is back in his eyes. "Now, be a good girl, spread those fine legs and make those sounds of yours."

"What's with my vocalization?"

He throws his head back and laughs. "Running the risk of ruining the night by mentioning other women, let me explain. Most women mew like stray cats when you just touch them. I hate the fake moans. It kills the mood."

"Oh." I run my hand through his hair. "Do women fake it with you a lot?"

His eyes go dark, and he flips me around so fast I don't even have time to react, and I'm on my stomach. He spanks me. It's a playful slap, but the heat spreads through me so unexpectedly, I moan.

To prove his point. Or to refute it. I don't know, because the sound is genuine and it screams *I need more.*

"See, your sounds, on the other hand, are driving me crazy," he whispers in my ear. "And you liked this."

His palm connects with my cheeks five more times in quick succession, and I immediately revisit my departure.

"Have you just moved in?" I draw mindless circles over his chest. I should leave, but maybe I don't have to just yet.

"I don't live here. I have a penthouse in Greenwich Village with my brother." He rolls us over, nestling himself between my legs while he nuzzles my neck.

"You live with your brother?" I shove him playfully.

He pushes onto his elbows, cocking his eyebrow. "Yeah, I was bored living alone." He nibbles my shoulder, his hand trailing down my stomach.

Who is this man-child? Living with his brother? I

grab his wrist, stopping him from reaching my center. My body screams at me in protest, but I don't think I have it in me to get another taste of his mastery. I'm too exhausted.

"So, what is this place?"

He smirks. "It's a fun pad."

I look at the sheets and shudder. This is his fuck cave? I've just slept in a bed where he fucks other women?

"Don't worry." He chuckles, following my train of thoughts. "The housekeeping at this place is superb, and it's not like I want to roll in my brother's junk." He shudders now.

Jesus. He shares this fuck pad with his brother. I slip down and pad to the bathroom.

"I need a shower." I shut the door and hear him chuckle again. Bastard.

Lowering my head, I lean against the sink and sigh.

What was I expecting? To be treated better? After I stole his drink and tried to seduce him? Okay, it wasn't hard to seduce someone who was game from the get-go, but still. Why am I annoyed by this?

This is actually good. I definitely won't get attached. Who cares about the best sex of my life if the sex god lives with his brother and brings women to his sex lair? Probably many of them, considering his prowess tonight.

I groan, and before I jump into the shower, I lock the door. While having another round with him would be arguably what I should be after, I need to keep my distance now and exit gracefully.

This is just a one-night stand.

When I emerge, showered and dressed, Finn jumps from the bed. "I had fun, we should do this again."

I snort and he eyes me, unimpressed. "I'll call you," he says as he finds his boxers and pulls them on.

"Famous last words after a hookup." I laugh.

Come on, Finn, don't make it hard on me. You're my one-night stand. No other ideas or feelings are allowed here.

"Well, sweetheart, I'm going to call you." He plops back in bed, crossing his hands under his head, rewarding me with the most blinding smile.

He's so casual, so confident, so free, I almost want to stay to soak up some of that attitude.

"You don't have my number," I deadpan.

"Are we pretending all those calls when you tried to pump me for donations never happened? Though I must admit, this uninhibited London is way more fun."

Shit, I forgot he thinks I'm my sister. I giggle, but it sounds a little manic. I look away, scrambling to gather my purse and leave. *Leave now, Paris!*

"Oh, and before you launch into professional mode..." He jumps up and leaves the room.

Jesus. I take a few breaths and follow to find him scribbling something.

"Here you go." He pushes a check into my hands.

I'm so stunned it feels like an indecent amount of time passes before my eyes leave the unfair beauty of his face and land on the piece of paper in my hands.

He filled out the recipient field with my sister's charity.

I literally just fucked for a good cause.

Chapter 4

Finn

When was the last time I woke up thinking of a woman? Never. Or yeah, there was that stripper, but my thoughts then related to my missing credit card, cash and the watch she stole after I fell asleep.

Last night, I dozed off thinking of London fucking Lowe, and I'm grinning right now as I wait for my coffee, almost wishing she would show up and snatch it again.

Snap out of it, idiot.

I scan emails on my phone, but my mind is set on returning to the purple-haired temptress from last night. There was something about her that turned me on.

It's almost like she was hesitant, pretending to be someone she isn't, but then she let go of any restraints and let me possess her in a way I haven't experienced for the longest time.

She submitted with abandon, and I remember now how satisfying it is to draw on someone else's pleasure. How empowering it feels.

It's not always that a woman can take me the way I need it, so I stopped looking for such a partner. And here we go, my little thief turned out to be the right woman for me.

And as if life rearranged around me, I feel new this morning. I even let her put her hands in my hair, which is usually a hard no with anyone else.

A good lay is just that, getting lost in the moment. But with London, the moment is stretching beyond the immediate act. It's amazing.

And fucked up. I didn't see myself falling for someone like this. Or ever. But here I am a few hours after she left, daydreaming about her. What the hell? Pussy-whipped after one night?

I jerk my coffee from the barista's hands, spilling some of it over our fingers. I growl and grab a bunch of napkins.

The girl behind the counter looks at me unimpressed. It's official, I'm in lust with London Lowe and it makes me behave like a jerk.

By the time I reach the office, I let the fantasies bubble inside me, and lo and behold, my mood improves. Is it too soon to text her? Maybe if I got another shot of her, I'd snap out of this lust.

"Well, someone is in a better mood than last night." Reilly greets me and follows me to my office. "Who made you this cheerful?"

Now he's going to pry until I spill the beans. I'm not telling him anything. I don't need his ridicule.

"Why do you assume someone is involved? I can manage my mood just fine by myself." I plop into my chair, lying through my teeth and grinning like a lunatic.

"Sure, sure, if that's the line we're going with." Reilly rolls his eyes. "Well, whoever she is, I'm glad you found her... on the street last night?"

"Stop fishing. A gentleman never shares—"

"A gentleman doesn't, but you could. Come on, Finn, I've been alone for months now. I need to live through you vicariously."

"TMI, man, TMI. I don't need to know you don't get laid." I shudder. "I don't want to think about you getting laid. And you shouldn't care about my sex life either. What would Rosie in HR say?"

We both burst out laughing, because if HR should concern themselves with anyone's conduct, it'd be my father's.

"This is not a pub." Pa's voice slices through the air and the mood shifts.

Reilly scurries away, past my father standing in the doorway and looking at me with an expression like he is going to throw up. He stands there for a moment, and then he shakes his head and leaves.

Now, my father is predictable. No matter what I've ever achieved, he found something else to criticize me for. I grew to never expect his satisfaction. Not that it stopped me from seeking it, like an unattainable beacon of light that would make my life shine brighter.

But him leaving without another spout of verbal abuse is weird. Shocking. I walk out of my office and watch him retreat to his wing, his head down. This is not the proud man I know. What the hell is going on?

"That was unexpected." Reilly stands beside me. We stare into the empty space. How fucked-up is this scenario that we are weirded out because we *weren't* yelled at?

Maybe he's going through something.

London's words suddenly ring a bit truer. The thought propels other images from last night and I feel better instantly. "What's on the agenda, Reilly?"

I return to my desk, but Reilly's phone keeps him from following me.

While I wait, I decide to go with the flow. Last night was the best thing that's happened to me in a while, so why not ride the wave?

Confession: I can't stop thinking
about last night.

LONDON LOWE

Okay? Are you sure you wanted to
share that with me?

No, I'm not. I've actually never called
a chick after a hookup, so enjoy being
the first:-)

LONDON LOWE

I would, but I'm happily committed.

What? She's with someone? Is that why she was
shy and hesitant at first? Did she sleep with me to keep
me from exposing her kleptomania? To shut me up?
Did I completely misread it all?

Are you really going to fucking
pretend nothing happened last night?

LONDON LOWE

A lot of things happened last night,
but not with you. What the fuck,
Finn? You're texting the wrong
"chick."

Fuck. I check my contacts to confirm I'm texting
London Lowe. Who I most definitely fucked last night.

Is this some sort of a game?

LONDON LOWE

Fuck off van den Linden.

I stare at my phone, stunned. Pissed. And annoyingly deflated.

"What's wrong?" Reilly frowns from the door.

"Nothing." I shake my head. "Just..." I stare at my phone. "My hook-up from last night is pretending nothing happened between us."

The bark of laughter that leaves his mouth has my jaw clenching. Fucking Reilly.

"Finn van den Linden, the master of ghosting, is getting a taste of his own medicine." Reilly doubles over. *Nothing is that hilarious here, dickhead.*

I throw my phone on the desk. No. First, I'm fucking deleting London Lowe from my contacts. She'd better think twice before ever asking me for a donation again.

"Stop it, Reilly, this is a place of business," I snap. Great, now I sound like my father.

"I'm sorry, boss." He inhales sharply, biting the inside of his cheek to stay composed.

The adrenaline running through my veins right now is not the exhilarating kind. I need to break something. "What's on the fucking agenda today, Reilly?"

His face falls immediately. He goes from laughing like a maniac to someone who is about to offer me condolences. "That was your father's office calling just now."

Pa was here a moment ago. This day is going from weird to outright bizarre.

Reilly closes the door and comes to my desk. "You have a meeting with the advertising agency in"—he checks his watch—"ten minutes, and then your father requested a lunch meeting."

The words leave a sour taste on my tongue. I raise my eyebrow. "Pa wants to have lunch with me?"

Reilly nods.

"Today?"

He nods again.

"Why?"

"I didn't ask."

"It's your job as my gatekeeper."

"Finn, with all due respect, that's not a question that would go well. When the General summons you, you don't ask questions."

"You're right." I sigh and stand up. "I better go meet with the ad guys. Come with me to take notes."

He blinks a few times but doesn't question me. It's not common for me to drag him to my meetings, but today I doubt my head will be in the game.

Fucking London. Fucking lunch with Pa.

I arrive at the restaurant half an hour before my meeting with Pa. We're meeting in a popular Italian place, which might be a good thing.

If he wanted to lecture me on family legacy and business operations, we'd meet in our hotel. That restaurant is stuffy and dark, though the food there is good.

I have to give it to my father—he always hires the best chefs. He's equally responsible for them not staying long enough. After each of their innovative ideas is squashed, they give up.

Somehow we still stay profitable enough to placate the shareholders, but we won't ride that wave for much longer.

Can this meeting be about that? Does he want me to finally present him with my projections for necessary changes? Shit. I should have brought the presentation with me, and fucking Reilly should have found out the reason for this meeting.

I pull out my phone and call Caleb.

"Hey, what's up? I hear you got a taste of your own medicine." Caleb greets me cheerfully.

Wait? What? And then comprehension sinks in. I'll kill Reilly and his big mouth. It would be easier and cleaner than firing him.

"Why did you talk to my assistant?" I growl.

"I needed to check your calendar, so we can go shopping for Mom's birthday present together."

I smirk. "What, are you aiming for the son of the year award? Since when do we shop for Mom's gifts?"

"Since she's turning sixty this year. It's a big deal, dickhead."

"Isn't her birthday in like two months?"

"Yeah, and I'd rather do it now. Not at the last minute. So, who is the woman who endured your tiny dick and is now claiming amnesia?"

Hilarious. Reilly is dead. Dead.

I ignore his jab. "For the record, my cock is unforgettable. Have you spoken to Pa?"

"Wow, whiplash anyone? Why would you mention your cock and Pa so close together? Jesus. I haven't spoken to him for a week. Not long enough, if you ask me."

"I'm having lunch with him." I sigh.

"When?" The slight panic in his voice shouldn't please me, but it does. Especially after he enjoyed the dirty little secret about London ghosting me.

"Now."

"Fuck, you're coming here?"

Now I understand the panic. "Chill, you idiot, that's the weird part. We're meeting at Modigliani's in SoHo."

"I like that place. Ever since they got a new owner, their milanesa is divine."

"Focus." Is he for real? "What does Pa want? I can't be blindsided. It's enough to deal with him when the cards are on the table. Call Mother."

"Oh, no, no, no, I'm not snooping with her. She'd get me into some sort of charity event, or worse, set me up on a date. That's a hard no. Just wait and see."

"Thanks for nothing."

"Sorry. For what it's worth, Mom might have no clue. I'm sure this is about work. Maybe he's going to fire you."

That actually wouldn't be all that bad, would it? On the other hand, being ignored by the first woman that interested me in the longest time and getting booted from the family business in one day would not help my self-esteem.

Fuck. My. Life.

I look up. "Shit. He's early." I disconnect the call and stand up as if a drill sergeant has just entered. Straight up, just short of an army salute.

Pa walks as he always does, like he owns this place. But today there is a slight drag to his step. Is he in pain?

Or is he just dreading the meeting?

He *is* going to fire me.

"Son." He nods and pats my shoulder before he takes the seat across from me.

I collapse into my chair, observing him for any signs of where this is going. But I'm pretty sure it's a termination of my stint with the family company.

I don't feel relief, however. I always thought that being freed of my duties, of his expectations, would be liberating.

And suddenly I regret I didn't try harder to please him. To see his way of business. To do more. To learn more. To follow more. I've become disillusioned way too soon.

My plans for the company have always been squashed. But they are good. They are my legacy. They're what I'm meant to do. I don't want to be the first van den Linden who didn't grow the business.

The waitress takes his drink order. *His* because Pa doesn't consult me and gets whiskey for both of us. It's fine—I need a drink anyway.

Between the morning fiasco with London and this summons, I'm going to blow a gasket before Pa even gets a chance to talk.

I push my hand against my thigh to stop my leg from bouncing. He hates that. He abhors fidgeting.

"Finn, I let something slip yesterday..." He takes a glass of water and places it to his lips, taking his time. Is he searching for words? My father never searches for words. He hurls them at everyone like grenades.

Wait? What? What did he let slip yesterday?

"You'll be taking over the company sooner than I originally planned." He puts the glass down and picks up the menu.

Come again?

I blink and follow him, holding the menu in front of my face so I can replay what has just happened. I'm not getting fired. I'm being promoted?

"Why?" I lower the menu. Fuck the meal.

"A plethora of reasons, including some health concerns."

He is sick. I open my mouth, but he waves my attempt away with his hand.

"And when I thought about it," he continues, "strategically, we need to have you voted in now when the board is still..." He shakes his head, annoyed. "Some of the members will be retiring soon, and God knows what happens then. We should get you in while we have unanimous support."

"Because otherwise I have no chance," I snarl and lean back. Firing me would have been a morale boost. Fuck this.

"Don't get your panties in a bunch, son. I'm just being realistic here."

The waitress returns to take our order before I can comment or process what is happening. My father asks about seven questions, grilling the poor server, before he settles on the special of the day with five modifications.

The waitress smiles at me. "And for you, sir?"

A new life.

"I'll have tuna steak with a side salad."

She pours water into our glasses before she leaves.

"I always hoped you'd want to give me the job because I deserve it, not because it's the last chance I might actually get it."

"Finn, you're always so sensitive. Of course you deserve the job. You're my firstborn. It's your legacy."

Not my drive, my ideas, my capabilities and experience. Just my birthright.

He looks at me with a dash of exasperation. "It's just a question of when, which leads me to the point of this little occasion here." He gestures between us.

"Me being voted as the new CEO is not the reason for this meeting? There's more?"

He clears his throat and sighs with annoyance. "It's related. Look, Finn, I let you have your fun and put up with your irresponsible way of life."

Have you now?

"But answer me this." He leans back, folding his arms across his chest. Looking at me down his nose, he asks, "Do you want the job?"

"Yes, of course." I answer before I can even think

about it, surprising myself. And him, if his face is any indication. I didn't even know how much I wanted it.

All my life I've believed I needed to do what he expects of me. And I kept hitting a wall or failing outright. But this is the chance to prove myself. To really make a mark and finally show him I'm worth the name van den Linden.

"If you want the job, you need to settle. You need to prove to the board"—his gaze bores into me with a significant pause—"and to me that you're ready. My condition is simple. Marry and settle down. Take life seriously."

Stunned doesn't even start describing how I feel. "You want me to get married?"

He nods.

"Because with a wife I'd be a better leader of the family business?" I'm saying the words and processing his answers, but if this wasn't my father, I'd expect a hidden camera.

"Yes, you settle down, the embarrassing pictures in the media cease. You demonstrate how serious you are about the business."

"Pa, you're joking!" I grin.

"And this is what I'm talking about. You think everything is a joke. The responsibility of having a wife and children would force you to mature. At thirty-three is the best time."

"How does Mother influence your ability to lead the company?"

"She provides a much-needed foundation. Anyway, Finn, find a wife and the company is yours. The sooner, the better."

Our meals arrive and we stay silent. He has nothing else to say to me. And I... I feel the weight of my sentence deep in my stomach.

"Why are you not eating?" Pa chews on his steak. "I don't blame you, though. Ordering fish and salad, like some girl." He chuckles and continues to gnaw.

"You should try it, it's better for you." I spear a tomato aggressively and shove it into my mouth.

He scoffs. "You sound like my doctor."

I snort inwardly, as if the invincible Charles van den Linden went to a doctor. Wait a minute.

"What health concerns, Pa?"

He wipes the corners of his lips with the linen napkin and downs his whiskey. "My cardiologist is a bit uptight. Probably eating fish like you." He makes a dismissive sound I'm accustomed to and sucks on something between his teeth. "Anyway, I need to manage my stress." His tone suggests the whole thing is a nuisance. "Nothing to worry about if you do what I say."

I push my chair out. "I'll be right back."

I stumble around to find the bathroom.

What the hell? This is rich. The biggest adulterer I know is preaching about the need to have a family in order to become a leader. And apparently now I'm responsible for his heart health. Fuck.

I pull my phone out and dial.

"Anthony speaking." The accented voice on the other side sounds sleepy.

"Set up a race for tonight," I snap.

"Finn?"

"Don't test me, Tony. You know it's me." I rake my hands through my hair, staring at the reflection in the mirror. A man on death row.

"Are you okay?"

"Tonight," I growl.

"Man, that's not how it works. I need to check who patrols the streets and there is—"

"I'm signing up with 30K and you get 10K for the trouble. Get it fucking done."

Chapter 5

Paris

I pace the small bathroom. Please, universe, don't be an asshole to me now. I went out there and grabbed life with abandon, pushed my boundaries—I should be rewarded.

Inhale.

Exhale.

Looking down at the stupid white stick, I close my eyes, but when I reopen them, the situation remains the same.

Not the reward I expected.

On autopilot, I get dressed and shuffle downstairs to the kitchen. I press the button on the espresso machine, and the grinder comes to life. The aroma of the freshly ground beans churns in my stomach.

I watch the liquid drip into the tiny cup, my mind blank. I should feel something. Joy? Anxiety? Excitement? Sadness? But I don't think I'm feeling any of it. I'm just stunned. This was not the plan.

This can't be happening. My hands shake as I pick up the cup, my heart beating in my temple. Panic. Yes, panic.

Jesus, that's not the feeling I want right now. The coffee's aroma hits my nostrils and I gag.

I dump the espresso into the sink and let the water run.

"Not in the mood for coffee?" Andrea's voice comes from the door to the patio.

"Fuck, you scared the shit out of me." I lower my head, but don't dare to look at him. My current predicament is surely written all over my face.

"Sorry, you know I live here. *You* live here with me." He jokes and kisses my forehead.

I volunteered to babysit my stepbrother during his post-rehab recovery, but right now I wish I was at my place. Alone. With enough time to compose myself.

"I can move out, but Gio would kill me. I promised I'd stay for a month at least."

"Oh, yeah, Gio and his brotherly love."

I turn and find Andrea sitting on the island, taking a bite of an apple. The juice rolls down his chin and he wipes it with the heel of his palm to his lips.

My stomach protests. I can practically feel that apple fermenting inside me.

"You look horrible today. What's up?" He's relaxed and looking suspiciously happy. Which should make me happy, but today is not the day for that.

"Well, thank you very much. I guess I'll just hide in my office all day. I have to go to work and then I have a few errands to run. Will you be okay?"

He shakes his head. "Sure, Mom. I have to head to school soon." He jumps down and ambles through the arched opening to his sitting room.

"Okay, please call me if—"

"Jesus, sis, do your thing. I'm fine." He plops onto his couch, taking another generous bite of the apple.

I never considered apples gross, but... I groan inwardly. "Are you sure?"

"I'll text you every hour and pee in a cup if you want," he deadpans.

I sigh, and suddenly tears prickle in my eyes. Oh no, no, no.

"Jesus, Paris, sorry. I'm grateful you're around. Okay?"

"Okay." I sniffle. "I'm going to go."

My car is only half a block away because I got lucky last night and snatched a good spot. Today I wish it was at least half a city away because walking would do me good, but I have a client meeting to get to.

I take a deep breath. *You can do this, Paris. Pretend nothing has changed.* For one day. Then I can collapse.

Who am I kidding? I can't do this alone. I pull out my phone.

Can we have lunch today?

LO

Sorry, I have plans. Coffee later?

Yuck, coffee? The idea of sitting in coffee-infused air causes me to gag again.

3 pm?

LO

The usual spot?

Me: Great.

Okay, the idea of sharing my current predicament with my sister should carry me through the day. I get into my car and try not to think on my drive to the office.

"Good morning. Are you okay?" Shayna, my receptionist, greets me.

Great. I feel like roadkill and apparently I look like it also. "Good morning. I must have eaten something last night. Do I have time to look at the Woodfield project before Mrs. Rodriguez comes in?"

I walk through the open concept and nod my greetings to my employees with Shayna following me, her heels clicking loudly on the birch floors.

"Mrs. Rodriguez is not coming alone today."

This stops me in my tracks. No. I don't have it in me right now. "He's coming as well?"

The Rodriguez remodeling project has been a never-ending process. We went through it once and then she changed her mind and we restarted from scratch.

It's not my most favorite project because usually I take pride in helping someone realize their dream home. In this case, the Rodriguezes contribute to my bottom line, so I indulge them.

Besides, I get challenged by designing the same room a thousand different ways.

"Not that you want my opinion, but the problem is that you're too nice to them." Shayna's heels click behind me.

My offices in Greenwich Village are large but simple. An open concept full of natural light from the floor to ceiling industrial windows on one side. It's my creative oasis, but today the usual thrill doesn't come.

She's probably right, though. Those two need therapy, not a regular argument in their interior designer's office. "They are my clients."

"But that doesn't mean you have to cater to all her whims and then endure his tantrum."

"Look, she's lonely and this keeps her happy. Or content, at least. And the fact that from time to time he needs to put the reins on her budget is understandable. What should I do? Fire them?" I shake my head.

"I would." She shrugs.

"They pay your salary," I snap and Shayna steps back. And now I'm snapping at people. Great. "Sorry." I reach my desk finally and drop my bag on a cabinet behind my desk.

I often joke I have a corner office because my large L-shaped working space is in the corner with a view over a charming street with coffee shops and small boutiques.

I love to people-watch when I work. While I'm designing someone's house or apartment, I love the connection with the outside world to remind me how each home fits within its environment.

Today, I look around and I wish I had an actual office where I can close my door and process.

"At least you should stand up for yourself. You can't be friends with everyone, Paris. People take advantage of you."

I sigh and take a seat, booting up my computer. "Could you clear my calendar for the afternoon?"

"You have a meeting with Chrysal at four. Do you want me to reschedule?" She taps her fingernails on my desk.

"Hey, Paris, could you come and look at this?"

Barry, our in-house architect, stands up from his desk, his short figure barely visible behind the huge monitor.

"I'll be right there." I smile at him. "Who is Chrysal?" I walk to the small kitchenette to get a glass of water. A day without coffee sucks. My life sucks.

Shayna follows me. Have her heels always echoed like this? Maybe I need a new policy for work attire. Rubber soles only.

"The visual artist who started making furniture."

Her words slice through me like an insult. *He makes furniture.* "Oh." I blink away tears. Since when am I this whiny? "Yeah, reschedule him." I fidget around, not wanting to face her. *Go away, Shayna.*

Chrysal has been trying to meet about a collaboration for several weeks now. Professional me wants to broaden the service and product range I offer my clientele. They are looking for trendy and unique, after all.

Petty me is avoiding him because... well, I'm jealous. A new designer on the block is yet another reminder of what I am not.

Chrysal started as a painter, similar to my brother Andrea. Violet Mathison, a SoHo gallery owner, discovered him. In fact, I think he was the one who really helped her get into the art dealing business. And now he's designing furniture.

Everyone is willing to take the leap except me.

"Are you sure you're okay?" Shayna frowns at me.

I force a smile. "Of course. You better go out there, so the Rodriguezes don't stand there, waiting."

She eyes me, unimpressed, but thank God she doesn't pry anymore.

"Paris," Barry calls again, and I finish my water and my micro meltdown and with a fortifying smile I step back into the open space. Ready to attack the day and accomplish some work. Hoping it will take my mind off the disaster of my life.

Two hours later, I finally have a moment to myself, and without even thinking I head to the elevator. Three years ago, I rented another space in the attic of this brick building.

"I'll be upstairs. Text me if there is anything urgent," I say to Shayna before the elevator closes.

She knows that once I come up here, to my workshop, I need my space.

The large skylights illuminate my wooden workbench, the small dust particles shimmying in the cones of light. Magic.

I put on an apron and my noise canceling headphones. On my phone, I open a playlist and start the music.

With the first tones of Alicia Keys's "Girl on Fire," I'm already feeling on fire.

I open the drawer and take out pliers and wire

cutters. I examine my work in progress and plug in the soldering iron.

Even on a day like this, calm washes over me when I'm here. When was the last time I even came here? Not often enough.

When I first designed this space, I thought it would be a new beginning. But then my brother Gio was accused of sexual harassment, and by association I lost several clients.

It forced me to refocus on saving my business, and the workshop became just a hobby. An outlet. I come here to build pieces that bring me joy. Mostly lamps.

They could one day illuminate and bring warmth to someone's home. But they remain on the shelves here. Decorating my workplace, and instead of shedding light, they remind me of my shadows.

I put on my safety glasses. The wires and metal plates might not yet look like a base of a tall standing lamp, but I can already sense its shape under my fingertips. It's clear and vivid in my mind.

I get to work and lose myself in the process. Molding, shaping, cutting and attaching are like meditation for me. A place where I forget.

Today though, I work on autopilot. The joy of the craft lost, I mechanically execute each step. Hopefully, with the next song, the flow will return.

What will I do? What will I do?

Fuck. Fuck. Fuck.

Searing pain jolts through my hand.

Screaming, I drop the iron. The tool clatters onto the wooden surface, its red-hot tip hissing against it.

I gasp and recoil, cradling my throbbing hand. Damn it. I'm usually so careful.

The scent of scorched skin turns my stomach upside down and I gag. Yet again.

Tears of pain and disappointment roll down my cheeks. The burn hurts, but it's not too bad. The last thing I want today is an emergency room visit.

I unplug the tool and with my good hand I place it carefully on its stand to cool properly. The medical kit is downstairs, so I leave the mess behind.

There is a much more urgent mess I need to address.

"I'm pregnant." I don't wait for London to sit down. I so desperately need to say it out loud that I dump it on her before she even orders her drink.

She raises her eyebrows and drops into the seat across from me. "Congratulations?" she asks, because yeah, it's unclear if this is a reason for celebration.

I sigh, my eyes welling up.

London stands up, rounds the table and scoots

beside me. In a very uncharacteristic gesture, she freaks me out when she wraps her arms around me. This is really bad if London is showing sympathy openly in public.

With deep understanding, she sums up the situation with a succinct, "Fuck."

I giggle through my tears. "Fuck I did, and now everything is fucked up."

We both lean back and sit in silence for what feels like an eternity. A bleak, shapeless eternity.

I don't know what I feel.

Blindsided. Overwhelmed. Shocked.

Yeah, that's it. I wish I could move past those paralyzing emotions and finally accept the truth.

How do I feel about becoming a mother? This baby wanted to come into this world, and not even condoms or the contraceptive pill could have stopped it. I should have gotten the IUD. Argh.

"Who is the father?" London addresses the air in front of her.

I'm grateful for her closeness and practical aloofness. It's easier to talk this way.

"Five weeks ago, I checked another item off my bucket list." I sigh.

I more sense than see her head turning to me. "The one-night stand?"

For a millisecond, I'm pleased she remembers

what's on my list, but that joy dies immediately with another bout of nausea.

"This was not on the list." I swallow around the lump in my throat.

"Okay, can you find the father? Or was it completely anonymous?"

Oh, Jesus. I haven't even accepted that I'm about to have a baby, let alone thought about that clusterfuck of the situation. "I guess I could try to find him."

"Or you don't have to. First, how are you feeling about this? Do you want to keep it?" There is hesitation in her question, like she understands it needs to be asked, but she wishes it wasn't the case.

"I'm just so shocked right now."

A guy with a hundred-watt smile saunters toward us. I groan. I know that look. We've gotten similar offers before.

"You're twins?" he drawls.

Yeah, genius.

"Fuck off," London snarls and several people turn their heads. For a second, it feels like even the coffee machine quieted.

The jerk snorts and raises his arms in surrender before he leaves. Thank God. But his presence reminded me that my twin sister knows the father.

The father of my baby. This sounds so strange.

I always thought I'd find a guy, fall madly in love

and move to the suburbs. The white picket fence and all. With a dog and cats and…

Not happening anymore.

But I need to tell her.

I open my mouth, but she beats me to it. Turning to me, she smiles. "You take your time figuring out how you feel about it. For what it's worth, you will be an amazing mother, Paris. You're caring and generous, and just crazy enough, and the baby is blessed to have you."

I blink away the tears, but they roll down my cheeks. Enough with the waterworks. Jesus. "It should be a joyous occasion."

"Oh, please, stop with the *shoulds*. Should have, would have—those are your worst enemies. It is what it is—there is no point beating yourself up over something that is in the past. Is the situation ideal? No. Can you change it? Also no. You're rich and you have a family larger than most. You're not alone, and that's before the father of my niece or nephew is even in the picture. Stop overthinking it."

"But that's what I'm good at." I smile, and for the first time today it's a genuine smile. A sad one, but still. "Thank you."

We sit in silence, staring into space. Lo didn't even get her coffee, but she doesn't complain. She sits there, keeping me company in my state of... I don't want to define it.

The coffee shop is bustling with the afternoon rush, but here at our table the world is still while I continue sorting through the fog in my head and my sister squeezes my thigh.

"What happened to your hand?" She beckons to the white bandage.

"I burned my palm with a soldering iron."

She gasps. "On purpose?"

I giggle. I actually giggle. "I'm clumsy, but not that nuts."

She rolls her eyes, but the corner of her mouth quirks up. "I guess you will have to put your bucket list on hold for a while. Stop with the stripper classes." She snorts.

I sigh. "Don't call it that. You know better. It's a dance class." My defense comes out louder than I intended, but I'm way too emotional to deal with her teasing judgement.

"Okay, sorry." She bumps me with her shoulder playfully. "I really thought you wanted to see me because Andrea is driving you crazy."

"He's actually doing okay. Fragile and defeated, but you know him, he's hiding it well."

"As long as he's not hiding it at the bottom of a bottle. Do you think he's good enough to see me?"

Now that shocks me. "You want to see Andrea? You haven't spoken to him for years."

"Well, technically, he hasn't spoken to me." She shakes her head, annoyed. "I realized that all my life, I've been regretting that I didn't spend the last days of his life with my childhood sweetheart, and here I am going through my life ignoring a person who is still here."

I stare at her for a beat, a wave of dread and realization washing over me. "I think I need to find the father, don't I?" My hands instinctually go to my stomach.

She sighs. "You don't have to do it today, but he needs to know."

We sit in silence again while I try to formulate my next statement and tell her the father believes he slept with her.

"Are you excited about the fashion show?" Lo asks, and the coward in me welcomes the turn of the conversation. Because delaying my admission will make it easier. I groan inwardly.

"I was excited and a bit scared. Frankly, I think I should call Nora Flemming and cancel."

The charity fashion show is in a couple of days. Walking the catwalk is an item on my bucket list, and this is my opportunity to cross it off, but I doubt I would enjoy it now. Fuck the bucket list.

"Don't. You need a distraction. I'm not a fan of that

list of yours, but modeling is something you've dreamed about since we were little."

Her phone rings.

"It's the hospice, sorry." She answers and listens for a moment to one of her colleagues or employees. London runs a charity and the hospice is one of her endeavors. "Okay, I'll be right there."

She turns to me with an apology, but I know someone is probably needing her more. I've always admired her work for people at the end of their journey. "It's okay. Go."

She kisses my forehead. "I'm guessing we're keeping this a secret for now?"

I nod and let her go before I admit she is the best person to help me find the father. Because he doesn't even know I exist.

Chapter 6

Finn

Anthony unbuckles me and pulls me out of my car. "You fucking idiot. What do you think you are, a daredevil?"

I groan, pain cutting through my left side. Fuck, I hope my ribs aren't broken.

"Are you able to stand?" He supports me for a few steps before I can lean against a tower of tires. The air is pungent with burned rubber and the smoke coming from my car.

The ground swirls around me. "Sure, man. I can stand." *Can I?* I pat his shoulder.

He snorts. "Are you trying to get killed? This is not good for business, Finn. I can keep the police away, but not if we cause trouble."

He doesn't care much about me then, just about the business. Story of my life.

No patrol ever ventures to this abandon complex of warehouses in South Bronx. There is nothing to steal here. No drugs or other illegal activities on NYPD's radar.

That's why the place is ideal for this. Not that there is anything legal about the races, but Anthony makes sure we can race without prosecution. Or at least without being officially discovered.

It's perfectly safe. Minus the occasional crash.

"Can you save her?" My custom-made yellow Porsche steams from the hood in a pile of old tires.

"Maybe." He shakes his head in disapproval.

I wipe my forehead, blood smearing my fingertips. Fuck. I take a few steps. Okay, not too bad. I'm banged up, but still in one piece. "Get her fixed as soon as possible."

"I'm not letting you race. You've been here several times a week for a month now. And your head is not in it."

The fucker is right. Not that I'd ever admit that. "Don't fucking forget your entire little operation thrives thanks to my patronage."

"Yeah, you idiot, but there's a difference between chasing adrenaline and being insane. I'm not going to jail if you get yourself killed." He flicks his leather gloves over my shoulder.

"Don't be such a drama queen." I wave him off, trying not to wince.

"Look at your car, and thank God everyone else avoided you. Fuck, Finn, I don't know what your problem is, but get laid or find a different hobby. If you want to die, jump from the fucking Brooklyn Bridge like any other idiot. Don't drag *me* into it." He turns his back to me, throwing his arms out in frustration.

His silhouette against the backdrop of my steaming car resembles an action movie set. He's right though. I'm not a daredevil, and while I'd like to change a lot right now, I don't want to die.

I limp away, leaving him behind to deal with the wreck while I take the wreck of my life with me.

I've been spending too much time here. Usually, the speed, the recklessness, the acceleration, all blur in tunnel vision and give me perspective. It's just me and the engine and a lot of exhilaration.

The potent cocktail of fear and excitement, ironically, despite the breakneck speed, pumps me with a sense of control. A sense of calm amid madness. Something I need to carry with me into everyday life where everything is ruled by my father and his unreasonable expectations.

Behind the wheel, I'm in charge as my feet dance between the pedals. For many, racing is about the competition, the thrill of winning, the battle of skills, but for me it's about pushing myself beyond the mundane. The normal. The expected.

It's about losing myself in the speed and adrenaline, so I can cope with the outside world. But as much as I've tried lately, racing is not helping.

I'm certainly nowhere close to finding a wife.

Or getting my father to sign-off on any of my business proposals.

Or even getting laid.

Fucking London Lowe ruined me for other women. And it's been weeks.

I get an Uber and struggle not to fall asleep on the way to my penthouse. My left side hurts like hell, but if I'm careful, nobody should notice it. I just need to sleep and forget about my father's condition.

I wave at the night doorman and limp to the elevator. There is something wrong with my knee. Goddammit. I really should have been more careful. I chuckle inwardly. As if that was ever my jam.

The living room light is off, but a video game is playing on the large screen.

"Where the fuck have you been?" Cal doesn't move his eyes from the screen, jerking around with the controllers of the gaming console.

"Out." I turn the corner to the kitchen and get a bottle of water. "I'm going to sleep."

"What happened to you?" Cal jumps from his seat.

"Fuck, man, I thought you were banging some chick, but you've been racing again."

I consider telling him I got into a fight, but the lie feels like too much effort. "I raced *tonight*." Okay, not really the whole truth, but the last thing I need is the only person who is on my side to criticize me.

He shakes his head. "You better get yourself into tip-top shape. We promised Mom we'd accompany her to the fundraiser tomorrow."

"You promised Mother, and I don't see why both of us need to go."

"It's a fashion show. Socialites are parading down the catwalk for a good cause. Nora Flemming is organizing it. I've been attending every year, enduring Mom's matchmaking. This year we share the burden."

"I went once." I remember attending the charity event. It wasn't actually that bad. But back then I was looking for a hook-up, not a wife. Fuck my life.

"That's why you're going again. Look at the bright side, you may find your future missus among all the willing society ladies." He chuckles.

Maybe he's right. If all the racing hasn't solved my problem, Operation Wife needs to start. A charity event is as good a place to pick a woman as any other.

* * *

"You look tired, Finn. Is Pa working you too hard?" Mother pats my lapel and I lean in to kiss her cheek. "What happened to your face?"

"You look lovely." I don't bother responding to her question. She never expects an answer, and I don't need to feed into her patronizing style of communication.

"Why, thank you, darling. I have a new hairdresser." And she's already forgotten about the bruise on my forehead that I'm barely covering with my hair.

"We should find our seats." Cal offers Mother his arm.

"I love having you both here." She threads both her hands through ours, her eyes roaming around. Always on top of society's news and gossip, she thrives at public events like this one.

The journey from the lobby takes us an indecent amount of time because Mother networks like her life depends on it. She offers compliments. Mostly fake. She asks questions. Glossing over the answers. She instigates gossip.

She works the room like a pro. Cal and I trudge behind, Cal assessing every glimpse of ass and cleavage in our vicinity, and I try to breathe without breaking a sweat.

I took several painkillers, but they did little. I'm in full survival mode, counting the minutes till this shit show is over. I should try to socialize like Mother does. But there is nobody I want to talk to.

"Do you know Samantha Pierce, Finn?" Mother's voice brings me out of my stupor. "She's on the board of the Creative Arts Foundation."

The young woman in front of me is beautiful. Like any other woman here. Come to think of it, they might as well be mass produced. Same makeup, similar hair, a different version of the same dress.

"Nice to meet you, Samantha."

She smiles shyly. "Call me Sam." Her hand is smooth in my sweaty palm. Sam is getting a painkiller-subdued version of me. Not that I care much.

"Samantha should be out there on the catwalk, shouldn't she, Finn?" Trying to supplement the conversation I'm clearly failing to steer, Mother pokes my ribs playfully.

The air whooshes out of me as I try not to grunt. Fuck the painkillers. Fuck this evening. Fuck my life.

"She certainly would outshine all the ladies there," I grit through my teeth, and Cal snickers. The fucker is having the time of his life.

Mother looks at me, her eyes shooting daggers. She clears her throat and widens her eyes, but whatever she is trying to communicate to me is not coming through the fog in my head.

She huffs and turns to Samantha. "Finn will call

you. The two of you should go out soon. He's been a prominent supporter of arts."

I swallow and nod. "I can't wait." I wink at her, but my eyelid stays closed for a beat too long. I finally un-glue my eye open, only to meet my mother's scowl and Samantha's unsure smile.

Cal snickers again, but at least our small party finally moves forward.

"Sammie would look good in your honeymoon bed," my brother whispers to me.

"As soon as I'm in charge, I'll fire you."

The idiot chuckles.

We finally find our places, right in front of the catwalk. I settle into my seat, relieved the pain seems slightly less persistent when seated and if I lean slightly to the right.

My relief is short-lived. I look to my right, to the row of seats perpendicular to ours, along the longer side of the stage, and my eyes land on London fucking Lowe.

She is laughing at something. Her hair is shorter and no longer the ridiculous purple color. It's dark, like I usually remember her.

I watch her for much longer than appropriate, my blood boiling. She looks so fucking happy and content. A big part of me agrees to ignore her. Just like she ignored me. It's not like she's the only woman in the world. Her loss anyway.

But I still stare. I haven't seen her for over a month and I'm shocked at how different she looks. It's still her, but her gestures are off. Everything about her body language feels completely different.

The woman I remember was more refined, gentle, somehow alluring. Fuck, my mind is playing tricks on me.

A man in an expensive suit saunters in and she smiles at him. The smile is bright, but there is something off about it. It's not the smile I remember and picture while fisting my cock in the shower.

Before I realize it, I'm walking toward them.

"London," I growl.

She blinks a few times and stands. "Finn, how are you?"

"I'm fantastic, but you owe me an explanation."

I'm sure once my drug-induced high wears off I'll regret this little tantrum, but right now that voice of reason gets squashed.

She smiles, shaking her head. "Explanation? I don't think I do." She's eying me like she's expecting a punchline.

"What's going on?" The Suit stands up and wraps his arm around her waist. "I'm Dominic Cressard." He extends his hand. "Lo's boyfriend," he adds, marking his territory, the fucker.

She doesn't look one bit guilty or worried about me exposing her. Just perplexed or amused by this exchange.

"You have a boyfriend? That's rich." *Cut your losses and go, idiot.*

"Watch your tone, asshole," Dominic's voice is low and menacing, breathing the words right into my face. He moves to stand in front of her. "Or better, never talk to her again. Do you understand?"

"Don't fucking threaten me," I spit. I don't even know what pisses me off right now. How could I have read her so wrongly? I peek at her above the boyfriend's shoulder and wonder who the woman is.

Fuck. I took too many of those pills.

"Finn, let's find our seats," Cal says from behind me, tapping on my shoulder. The energy of our exchange must have carried back to him.

I leave the two *lovebirds* standing there and shuffle behind my brother.

"What the fuck was that about?"

"None of your business," I snap, and he stops.

With a smile that I assume is a show for the onlookers, he pats my arm. "You looked like you were going to punch Cressard. It seems like you're doing everything to prove to Pa you're out of your mind and completely incapable of stepping up. Get your shit together, Finn. Charles's exit strategy hangs on you, bro. Stop harassing happy couples and let's find you a wife."

I grind my molars for a moment. "You're right. Fuck them. I'm game. I'm walking out of here with a date."

"That's my man." He goes to poke me, but my expression stops him. "Sorry, I forgot." He raises his arms in surrender.

"Let's go before Mother loses her cool."

"She wouldn't. Not here, but I think we're already in for a good scolding once we're behind closed doors."

We both chuckle, memories of all the mischief she's ever had to address solidifying our bond. Judging by her tense smile, we're in for an earful.

The lights blink a few times and the fashion show starts. The stunning Nora Flemming opens up the event with a speech that I care little about, lost in my own thoughts.

I'm so pathetic that I continue stealing glimpses of London. Yes, I'm hurt that she didn't want me as much as I wanted her, but it's something else that I can't shake off.

It's like the woman I spent the night with was a completely different person. I can't put my finger on it, and it bothers me.

It shouldn't though, so I force myself to focus on

the socialites and business-women promenading them-selves for a good cause.

The third model comes out and my jaw drops. What the actual fuck? I stare at the beautiful woman who I know. Her hair isn't purple. It's silvery white, perhaps a wig, but...

My eyes dart to London and back to the stage. Her full cleavage, the hips, the legs, the entire package.

She's perfect. As she strides toward me, I'm mesmerized by the energy she emits.

Her almond-shaped eyes look sad, the mischief I remember missing, but this is her. This is her. This is... I swipe my eyes back to the couple to my side again. This is not London.

The model gets close. She's wearing red lipstick, and on those full lips it's a fucking vision. My mind immediately conjures the memory of her on her knees with those perfect lips around my cock.

She twirls around and steps to one corner of the walkway, away from me. The dress she is showcasing reveals too much skin if you ask me. I make fists, but as soon as she steps to the other corner of the stage, right in front of me, my anger melts.

She smiles and looks down at the audience and our gazes meet. Her eyes widen and her smile dies, but she recovers quickly. Still, she doesn't look away, and for a moment, it's just the two of us.

Me taken by her beauty and confused by everything else. Her boring her eyes into me with a plea on her face. What is she asking?

The music changes and she jumps, then turns to make her way backstage, hips swaying, and my cock twitches.

To make sure my mind isn't playing tricks on me, I glance back to where London sits and this time our eyes meet. She holds my gaze and then she looks up at her doppelgänger. Or rather, a much more alluring version of herself. She smiles and looks back at me.

That smile is telling. Knowing. As if she's just pieced a puzzle together. I wish I had all the pieces as well.

* * *

"Are you waiting for someone?" Mother asks impatiently.

The cocktail reception has dragged on for an eternity. Like a whole twenty minutes has passed and some models have already joined the guests.

Where is she? And more importantly, who the fuck is she?

"Who would I be waiting for?" I snatch a champagne flute from a server who beams at me suggestively. *Yeah, sweetheart, any other night I'd get your number.*

"You're fidgeting, sweating and ignoring Samantha," Mother hisses, all the while smiling for the others.

"Who is Samantha?" I keep looking around, and before I realize it, my glass is empty. I probably shouldn't be drinking on top of all the drugs I took today.

"Finn, focus. I'm trying my best to help you find a wife. Your father needs to rest and you're his firstborn, so get the job done. You're good-looking enough to charm any of these women. The clock is ticking." She walks away.

My mother just told me I'm failing them all, and somehow that doesn't seem like the biggest issue of my life at the moment. I don't even know why I'm so focused on finding her and... then what?

Fuck it. My body hurts, my mind is foggy, and frankly, I'm done with everyone's expectations.

I don't even bother to say goodbye to Mother or Cal as I storm out of there. This isn't my kind of party, anyway.

Nora Flemming organizes a lovely event to support some cause, all the ladies get to play models for a night, and the who's who of New York's society gets to dress up and pretend we can save the world.

Fuck that. Fuck them all. Fuck my parents. Fuck all the expectations.

I turn the corner. The hotel lobby feels empty compared to the ballroom, just a few tourists, some businessmen and... Well, look at that.

London Lowe and my mystery lover seem to be arguing beside the large piano. My feet move before I even decide to join them.

"He certainly looked at you like he more than knew you," says London with her back to me.

The brown-green eyes of her companion meet my gaze, and she gasps.

London turns and when she sees me, she narrows her eyes. Then she turns to the other woman who is looking at me with such desperation that I want to reach out and console her.

London sighs. "Fuck, Paris. Is he the father?"

Chapter 7

Paris

All the cowardice of my life has culminated in this moment. My mouth goes dry, my heart hammers in my chest and the world seems eerily quiet, making the pulse in my temple too loud.

Walking the catwalk was an item from my bucket list. I wish it wasn't.

I've spent three nights since I found out about the unplanned consequence of my other bucket list item imagining how this would go down.

I'm a pretty imaginative person, but not in my wildest fantasies, did I see both my sister and the father of my child finding out this way.

"Fuck," London rasps. "I'm sorry." She looks at me, fully comprehending how her blurting out just complicated an already complicated situation.

My smart sister put two and two together and figured out Finn thought I was her. Now I can't even be mad at her.

The last piece of the puzzle set in just as he approached us. And now my sister stares at me with disdain and a dash of regret.

And Finn? I don't know, because I'm too scared to look at him. A coward.

The silence stretches and we stand there frozen. I wish time travel was on my bucket list. Or just an achievable form of dealing with fucked-up situations. Situations I caused. Betraying my sister and the stranger beside me.

A stranger who gave me a memorable night and will now stay connected to me forever.

London fidgets, and that's telling because she's always composed and commanding. Right now, I think she'd like to kill me or shake me. Or give me a piece of her mind. All of it I deserve.

"Well, obviously the two of you need to talk. Or at least start a conversation, so I'll leave you to it."

My eyes dart to her. *Please don't leave me here,* I plead, even though I know I'm being ridiculous. I created this mess and I need to own it. The thought makes me whimper internally.

"I'll wait at the bar." She sighs and walks away.

Lo and I are not the kind of twins who are attached

at the hip. We don't have premonitions about each other. We don't have a special connection, but right now I feel like a shield, an integral part of my defenses, has left.

"Father?" Finn croaks, and I finally meet his eyes. They burn, and not in the hot way.

Lying in an anthill would be more comfortable. "I was going to contact you—"

"Really?" He snorts.

I guess he won't make this easy. "Look, Finn, I didn't plan on this, but it happened—"

"Is it mine?" The aloofness in his voice sends shivers down my spine.

I can't even be offended by his question. It's a fair one, given the extent of our acquaintance. "Yes," I whisper, and swallow around the lump in my throat.

The commotion in the lobby continues unperturbed. Nobody here has any idea of my life unraveling right here, right now. No one could sense the freight train running toward me.

"Are you sure?"

He puts his hands into his pockets, straightening up and wincing a little, but still towering above me with all the power and dominance he carried when we first met. The only difference is, there is no playfulness in his eyes.

His tone carries so much venom, I snap out of my self-pity party. Who does he think he is?

"Yes, I'm sure. Why would I lie about it?"

"I don't know. Why did you lie about who you are?" He steps closer.

I deserve that. Fair enough. But also, enough enough. I don't need this treatment from him. I feel like shit without his direct help.

"Look, Finn, it's late and I'm tired. Let's talk tomorrow. I'm sorry—"

"About which part are you sorry?"

His breath fans over my face and I'm enveloped in the scent of him.

In the last week, my body has been feeling like a steamroller flattened me, and that's during the best times, when I'm not nauseous on top of everything else.

Right now, every single cell in my body blooms with recognition and need. It's like he planted a seed that grows inside me and by default made my body crave him, crave to be owned by him.

It makes no sense. Not to my brain, anyway. My hormonal body, on the other hand, is perfectly comfortable and attuned to him.

I close my eyes briefly to collect my thoughts. There must be a functioning brain cell somewhere in the haze of the pregnancy, my lust, or his anger.

Swallowing hard, I look up. I lick my lips and hope to find my voice. His eyes immediately drop to my mouth, his gaze darkening.

He looks at me like he's going to devour me, but he's disgusted by the idea at the same time.

I finally find my words. "I'm sorry about a lot of things. But look, Finn, I'm still trying to process all of this, and maybe we need to cool off before we talk."

His nostrils flare as he continues glowering at me. Several beats of time merge into one long pause where he's probably planning my death, or considering bending me over and fucking me in the middle of this lobby.

Please let it be the latter.

What?

Okay, it's official, the pregnancy brain is a thing. And it's making me lustful and utterly stupid.

He steps back suddenly, and I almost lose balance at the loss of his warmth. He shakes his head a bit like he's annoyed. With me? Or with himself?

"Give me your phone." He stretches his hand out to me.

I dig into the pocket of my maxi skirt, unlock the phone and give it to him.

He types quickly and hands it back. "Now you have my number. You have forty-eight hours to *process,* and then we talk."

The way he throws the words at me finally awakens some sort of gumption and dignity. "I'll call you when I'm ready. You have no right to boss me around."

For a second it looks like his head might burst, then he takes three deep breaths. "I think you lying to me, ghosting me and then betraying me..." He glances at my belly and then he leans in close to my ear. Too close. Invading my space and my common sense. "It gives me some rights in this situation, *Paris*."

He says my name with so much spite that I flinch. At the same time, my ovaries scream for attention. I heard pregnant women might lose interest in sex. Of course, I'm not that lucky. I clench my core.

I also raise my chin, because while he's right, to an extent, we do need to talk, and without his ultimatum I'd probably chicken out. But I will not cower.

He shakes his head again. "Forty-eight hours," he bites out, then storms away.

* * *

"How did it go?" Lo asks me as soon as I slide into a seat across from her.

The lobby bar is quiet and empty and I'm grateful for the lack of an audience to my humiliation. Not that people would eavesdrop, but the bit of privacy in this public space is definitely welcomed.

I look pointedly at the two cocktails at the table and raise my eyebrow.

"I got you a virgin mojito. Fuck, Paris, I'd be mad at you if you didn't have bigger problems right now. What were you thinking?"

"I... he thought I was you, and it felt so liberating that I went with it." I sigh and she shakes her head.

"First, you don't have a one-night stand with someone in your zip code. Second, don't use my name if the person actually knows me. Dominic almost punched him earlier." She leans back, a ghost of a smile on her face.

"You would have enjoyed that, wouldn't you?" I take a sip of my drink.

"He can still beat the shit out of him if he doesn't man up." She shrugs and I snort. The beat of lightness feels so good. But it dies quickly.

"I don't know what to do." I sigh and gesture for the server. I'm starving.

I order a burger with fries, because apparently the calories I can't get in due to morning sickness are happy to get in late at night.

"What will I do?" I whimper, sagging in my chair.

"I'm no expert here, so maybe consult Bianca or

Sydney, but I think you're good for a few months before you need to get the nursery ready." A smirk plays on her face.

A part of me is grateful she makes fun of the whole situation, but her mentioning our stepmom and older sister douses the lightness. I'll have to tell the family that I'm pregnant, by someone I don't know.

"Who is he?" I utter the most embarrassing question.

Because let's face it, what I know about the father of my baby can be summed up in three qualities: he's talented with his tongue, his hands, and his cock.

"Jesus." London condenses the level of fucked-up into that one word. "Finn van den Linden, the hotelier family."

"Oh." My face falls. "I know his mother. She's on the board of the Creative Arts Foundation with me. She is not nice. Pretentious."

"Yeah, she's a bitch." London nods and takes a generous sip of her drink, gesturing for another one as she does.

I groan. "Where is Dom, by the way?"

Lo stopped drinking because Dom doesn't, but she enjoys a cocktail when he's not around.

"I sent him home in case you needed me. So how did Finn take it?"

"He hates me."

The server brings my food and I attack it like a hungry wolf.

"Pace yourself, gobbler. He doesn't hate you. As I was waiting for you, I remembered he texted me after *our* night together. At least you didn't tarnish my reputation." She is grinning now, enjoying my downfall with every inch of her being. Give it to London to lead with sarcasm.

"I'm sure Dom would love to hear about your rep," I deadpan, wiping burger sauce with the back of my hand as I lean over the table.

Lo eyes me but doesn't comment on my un-ladylike manners. Frankly, table etiquette is the least of my worries.

"Do you want to see the text?" She cocks her head.

I nod. But do I? She clicks on her phone a few times and passes it to me.

FINN VAN DEN LINDEN

Confession: I can't stop thinking about last night.

That makes two of us, Finn. Or I used to until I peed on the stick. Somehow, the new situation erased the memories. But they're still there, and they came rushing back in the lobby when his presence ate up all the oxygen.

I scan their conversation and close my eyes. No wonder he hates me. For weeks he thought I ghosted him, and now... now he's found out... everything.

"You could have been nicer to him. He donates to your cause." I'm not even sure why I chose this turn of the conversation. Perhaps to share at least a small bit of guilt? Not that it's working.

Lo snatches her phone. "Fuck you, sis, I didn't know what he was talking about. Remember, it wasn't me he couldn't stop thinking about."

"He ordered me to contact him in forty-eight hours." I pick up a fry and pop it in my mouth.

"I guess he's pissed. But he's pissed at the situation, not at you. You can't blame him. He's right, you need to talk. Not so much about past mishaps, but about the future."

"I don't even know how I feel about the situation. What I think about it all. How can I discuss it with him?"

"Paris, this is something you need to figure out together. He has a right to be involved. As much as he wants."

"And that's the problem. What if he wants to be involved? How am I going to co-parent with someone I don't know?"

"Well, at least you'd get laid at the pick-ups and drop-offs." She shrugs, chuckling to herself.

"I'm glad someone is amused by this situation. I wish he didn't know yet. I wish I had more time to think about everything before talking to him. I wish I had the opportunity to tell him once I know what I want."

"You're right. You need to overthink it." She rolls her eyes. "Cut the wish list right now. You don't have more time. You have eight months maximum before another person will depend utterly on you, so you better figure it out. If he wants to be involved, you need to let him. I think all of us would be just a little more fucked-up if Bianca hadn't met our dad. If they didn't work together to give us a home and support. And that baby deserves all you can give her. Even if it means allowing a stranger into your life."

The truth of her words rings loud in my head. "It's all... That's not what I wanted."

"Shit happens. You can't change that anymore. You can't hide, Paris. You've been hiding from your talent, postponing the home accessories business launch for years. You shy away from corporate clients because private homes are easier, safer. You're hiding behind your bucket list so you don't have to truly leap into any adventure. Just grazing it on the surface. This is the biggest adventure of your life, and you can't hide anymore."

If I wasn't down already, give it to Lo to shower me with a sobering dose of reality.

I gulp down the sweet mojito. There really is no point to cocktails if they have no alcohol. I push the plate away, avoiding Lo's eyes.

I'm not hiding. Am I?

"I'm done with words of wisdom." She sighs. "But I'm here for you. If you need to talk, to destroy the van den Lindens or just blow off steam somehow. If you need to cry, better go to Sydney. I'm not good with that shit."

I chuckle at that, and we sit in silence for I don't know how long. There is no silence in my head, for sure, but at this point I'm so tired I don't recognize where the truth ends and where the fantasy starts.

The finality of life as I knew it infiltrates every pore of my skin. And as much as I want to fight it—hide from it—I don't have that luxury anymore. I palm my flat stomach and rest my hands there.

"I always thought I'd have a husband and four children in the suburbs," I utter in a farewell to that vision.

"I know, I know." London nods. "You still can."

But right now, it doesn't feel even remotely possible. I'll be a single mother in the middle of this large city.

And suddenly the bucket list feels like the death of my dreams, not its instigator.

The thought hurts like hell. Not only because I lost something, but because I'm gaining something new. Something that feels so much bigger, more important, more profound.

I look at my hands covering the part of me where new life blooms. Someone I already love.

Chapter 8

Paris

"Good morning." I step out of the elevator with a smile and Shayna blinks a few times before jumping from her seat.

"Good morning, boss. You haven't been this perky for days now. Is everything okay?" Her heels click behind me.

"Yes, everything is okay." I walk into the kitchenette, drop the portfolio and my bag on the table and rise on my tiptoes to reach for a teabag.

It's been only three days since the charity fashion show, but I spent them soul searching, dream burning, vomiting a bit, but mostly falling in love with my new world. Falling in love with the baby I'm growing. With my baby.

I didn't call Finn. Not to hide, but to give myself this time. The time I needed to reconcile this new—

wonderful—turn my life has taken. It's not what I planned, but it's what I got dealt, and I'm slowly but surely accepting it.

I'll give myself a few more days to enjoy it and then I'll talk to him. And tell my family. This new plan finally brings some comfort.

"You're drinking tea?" Shayna puts her hands on her hips as if my choice of morning beverage offended her somehow.

"As you can see." I refill the kettle and take out a cup. "What's on the agenda today?"

"Why?" She observes me with suspicion.

"What do you mean why? It's a workday like any other. You're in charge of my calendar and this is how we usually start the day."

She shakes her head, short of rolling her eyes like I'm the one acting weird here. "Why are you drinking tea?"

Jesus help me. "Because I quit drinking coffee and I like a cup of tea to start my day."

"Are you now?" She's watching me like I'm an experiment about to go wrong.

"What's on the agenda for today?"

She finally consults the notepad she's been clutching to her chest. "You have a call with the Italian marble importer at eleven, lunch with your brother Gio at twelve thirty and..." She consults her notes again.

"Mr. van den Linden called saying that you owe him a meeting. Should I schedule that? Is he a new client?"

My blood flow takes several different turns at the same time, mostly redirecting to my face and my temples. Of course he found me. It's not that difficult once we learned each other's names. I pinch the bridge of my nose.

Come on, Finn, give me a day or two to enjoy this by myself.

Suddenly I'm mad for not loving the pregnancy from the moment I found out. For letting the circumstances taint the moment. I'm being selfish, but everything about this went wrong. Can't I have a moment to readjust?

"I'll call him myself."

"Which van den Linden is he? I hope he'll come in person. Both brothers are so hot."

I frown at her. "How do you know that?"

She looks at me like I'm from a different planet. "They get photographed a lot. You really live under a rock." She shakes her head. "Enjoy your tea." She gives me another suspicious glance and waltzes out of the kitchenette.

Has she always been this nosy? I don't need her scrutinizing my drinking habits. Especially not in the morning when my stomach is wobbly at the best of times.

But to be honest, I'm more annoyed about her extensive knowledge of the van den Linden brothers. Apparently, there's more than one of them. Something I would have known if I dated Finn before he knocked me up.

The good morning vibes gone, I dive into my work with all the effort I can muster. My newly found joy is challenged at every turn. My body and mind are exhausted. Who knew growing a person, however tiny, required this much energy?

And why would Mother Nature make it impossible to eat for the part of the day when I need all the extra energy I can get?

I close the next quarter projections and stand up, afraid I might fall asleep.

The bustling street below me is fluid and undisturbed by my own personal challenges. Even the curb looks like a suitable bed.

"What are you looking at?"

I whip around, and two binders from a cabinet along the windowsill fly to the floor with a loud thud. Several heads lift from behind their screens.

"You scared the shit out of me, Shayna." I put my hand to my chest and lean against the cool glass.

"Sorry, I didn't mean to." She narrows her eyes, and I realize that while one hand is on my chest, trying to contain my galloping heart, the other went to my stomach protectively.

I move both hands to clutch the windowsill behind me. "Did you want something?" My tone is a bit more annoyed than she deserves.

"Finn van den Linden called three more times, demanding that I put him through. I kept telling him you'll call him and he became hostile."

I close my eyes briefly. "I'm sorry. I'll deal with it. Don't answer his calls."

Not the most mature solution, but I need to deal with work first. *You can't hide from this.*

Shut up, London, I snap in my head.

I grab my phone and scroll through my contacts.

I'm in meetings. Stop harassing my staff.

FINN

Who is this?

Oh, please, what a jerk. But then, he saved his number in my phone. Not the other way around.

It's Paris Lowe. Feel free to lose the number.

I hit send before I think better of it. I shouldn't be poking the bear, but it's not like he's respecting my space.

FINN

It's been three days. Forty-eight hours is only two days. Basic math. I better take charge of our child's education.

What? Is he kidding? Or is he just this obnoxious by default? And is this just a case of verbal sparring or is he making a commitment to be involved? Oh, for fuck's sake, I need to talk to him.

I guess my days of untainted joy are over.

I needed more time. I'll call you at the end of the day.

FINN

I won't hold my breath. At least I know where you work.

Is that a threat?

FINN

And I know your name now. What a delight.

Okay, I guess it's just sarcasm.

I sit through my call, slightly absentminded, but it's just a preliminary scouting call to see if we can do business together. Their business focuses on bigger projects and that's where I'd like to move my firm, but I guess I'll be focusing on other endeavors now.

I wrap up the call with a noncommittal promise to keep in touch.

"I thought we were going to pitch the remodeling of Quaintique hotel chain," Barry says after the call. Apparently, my chief architect expected more commitment from me during the conversation with the Italian supplier.

Shit, my mind is not in this. I can't commit to such a large project at this moment. But seeing Barry's fallen face makes me feel like a traitor. Is taking another year before we expand to commercial projects something my closest colleagues would forgive? I bailed out before.

"Yeah. I need to think about it."

He says nothing, just leaves, but his silence is telling. I'm letting these people down. Putting breaks on all the projects before they have a chance to grow. Staying with the familiar. With the comfortable.

"I hope you don't mind that I'm joining you." Mila, Gio's fiancée or a girlfriend only right now—I can't keep up with their dynamics—stands up and smiles at me.

The Madisson Club's restaurant is humming with

the lunch rush of business deals, lunch meetings and casual conversations.

"Of course she doesn't mind," Gio growls, and kisses my cheek before he sits down with a slightly annoyed countenance.

Mila shakes her head and squeezes his hand as soon as she sits. It melts away the lines on his face as he looks at her with adoration.

Another reminder of what I don't have. Jesus. I mean, I wish Gio all the happiness, especially since his default state is a brooding grump. Mila changed him, but some habits die hard. And yet, they have so much more... Will I ever experience it?

I won't ever be completely free anymore. Another jolt of affection for the life growing inside me hits me unexpectedly. Maybe I'm past romance, but love is definitely in my future.

I have lunch with Gio once a month at his club. He advises me on my investments and I pry into his personal life. My part of our meetings has shrunk significantly since his personal life is under control, while mine is...

"Did you enjoy the fashion show?" Mila starts the conversation, and I'm grateful she's here because I wouldn't be able to keep this going for an hour. And Gio certainly isn't the chatty type.

"I did. It was fun and scary." And not only because

walking in front of all those people is nerve-racking. Meeting the gaze of the outrageously handsome man who is my baby's daddy knocked my anxiety right off the charts.

Though that look. I didn't get the chance to ponder that in the aftermath of the event, but it is still seared into my mind. Yes, there was shock and a dash of loathing, but there was some uncensored want brewing under it all. Not that he embraced that feeling later.

I can't blame him. I blindsided him. A part of me really doesn't want him to want me. It would complicate things. But there is a big part of me that can't deny I'm attracted to him. What a nightmare.

"I can imagine. No one would get me to do that. I'd probably trip and rip the dress." Mila laughs. "So, what's next on your bucket list?" She crosses her legs and leans in, wiggling her shoulders.

When did all my life become nothing but the bucket list and its items? "I think I'm done with that." My list will now contain baby formula and diapers. Shit, I should get that pregnancy book right after this.

"Are you?" Gio asks, raising his eyebrow. That's the problem with my brother—he's way more perceptive than one would think. I've been tackling the items on that list for over a year. I'm sure he'd be surprised once he finds out where the list led me.

I fidget, but the server saves me. We order our

meals and Mila dives back into the conversation. "So did you accomplish all the items?"

No, but free diving and wild water rafting might be off the table for a while. "Yes, I have," I lie instead. "The idea was to push my boundaries, and I think it's time to apply the experience in real life."

"Doing what?" Gio meets my gaze. He used to stare into his phone during any conversation and I'm almost shocked by the X-ray qualities of his eyes.

"I think it's time to pitch a larger commercial project," I blurt, surprised by voicing a commitment I haven't even made to myself or my colleagues yet. And buying strollers. I keep that one to myself.

He perks up. "That's great. Do you need some help to get your foot in?"

His offer to help isn't patronizing. It's genuine, even though I know he feels guilty about destroying that chance for me once before.

It wasn't his fault our family was slandered by association in the aftermath of accusations that couldn't be further from the truth.

"I think our first project will be Quaintique. I mean, if we get the business." I say the words with way more confidence than I actually feel, and suddenly the idea resembles a plan. And a jolt of excitement courses through me.

"You know I'll support you in any way I can. I owe

you this one. But I also know you'd rock that project. I might start booking rooms there after you're done with them." His gaze is heated now, devouring Mila.

"Okay, I don't want to even imagine what you would do there. Jesus." I shake my head.

Mila chuckles and swats at him playfully, and we all laugh.

"How is Andrea?" Gio asks when our meals arrive.

"He's reasonably well. Some days he stays in his room, but he's been teaching and coping decently. He doesn't want to go to his studio. He claims he'll never create again." I sigh, because our brother's belief he can stay sober only if he doesn't set foot in his studio is just heartbreaking.

"That would be such a shame," Mila says.

"I didn't know you liked his art?" Gio growls, and Mila and I both giggle. Andrea kissed Mila at his last exhibition to piss Gio off, and I guess the sentiment is still alive.

"He's very talented," Mila says, biting her lip.

"He's none of your business," Gio grunts and channels his frustration into the piece of steak in front of him.

This time our laughter is full on. "Seriously, love, your jealousy is misplaced."

"I'm not jealous." He rolls his eyes, winning himself another round of laughter from the two of us.

"What's so funny?" A familiar voice freezes me on the spot. I don't even have to look behind me. I don't want to look.

"Finn." Gio stands and shakes the hand of the man who I've been ghosting for longer than either of us deserve. It's bizarre that I'd never met him before and now he's everywhere.

"These two are ganging up on me," Gio jokes and sits back.

Finn towers above our table, probably glaring at me, but coward that I am, I don't lift my eyes. *Really mature, Paris.*

"Do you need—" Gio starts, and Mila gasps when Finn sits down.

"What the—" Gio starts again.

I finally look up, pushing into the back of my seat, hoping I can disappear. He's just sat down, but it's like he already owns the surrounding air. And he's poisoning it with his anger.

Why didn't I call him yesterday?

"Paris." He nods his head briskly in my direction. I think he's not strangling me on the spot only because there are witnesses. And he doesn't want to lose his membership here, probably.

"Finn," I croak and reach for my water. I take a generous gulp, but no amount of water can flush down the lump in my throat.

Hiding from things is so much easier.

Gio leans back, folding his arms and darting his eyes between the two of us, a grin ghosting his face.

"I thought we were going to meet." Finn somehow found a level tone and sounds almost amicable.

I swallow.

"What do you two have to meet about?" Gio muses. Having siblings is annoying.

"None of your business," Finn snaps and Gio bristles.

"Finn, don't—" I plead. I'm not even sure what I'm asking him. This whole situation is my fault. I wanted to steal a few more days to grow into this new reality. But really, I was probably trying to avoid it.

"Don't what?" Finn raises his voice and I flinch.

"What the fuck is going on? Don't talk to her like that." Gio pushes his chair back. Oh, no.

Finn snorts. "I'm just glad I get to talk to her at all."

I lick my lips. "Let's take this conversation elsewhere."

He looks down at where my hand touches his arm. When have I even reached out? Something softens in his eyes while energy passes between us. A glimpse of calm. It doesn't last.

"Good idea." He stands up. The chair behind him balances on two legs before it descends back to the floor with clang.

"Are you sure?" Mila's eyes dart between me and Finn.

I nod and stand up.

"Here, some suggestions for your stockbroker." Gio hands me a folder.

"Thank you. Sorry, guys, just pressing business. I'll catch up with you later." My voice is several octaves higher than usual. I sound like a madwoman, tripping over my words.

Finn grabs my hand and barrels through the dining room of Gio's club, leaving the shocked faces of my brother and Mila behind. I look back and try to send them a reassuring smile.

And just like during our night together, while my brain is appalled by his behavior, a dark hidden part of me enjoys the Neanderthal.

"Hey, what's with our lunch?" A man stands up from a table to my right.

Finn stops and I bump into him. He grabs me with both hands to steady me and assesses me with concern. I'm not sure what is behind the gesture, but I'm pretty sure his touch burns my skin even through my sweater.

We stare at each other for a beat. Or longer. I don't know because the light contact of his hands consumes all my awareness. Our eyes communicate something we're not willing to say out loud or to accept.

Care?

Attraction?

Lust?

"Finn?" the man urges, breaking the moment.

Finn shakes his head, snapping out of whatever dimension we've just traveled to. "Cal, just fucking eat alone."

He turns and drags me behind him. He is not fast though, certainly not at the pace his long legs would allow. Is he making sure I can keep up? For my benefit? Or just to avoid more fuss?

By the time we reach the elevator, we are more or less walking like a normal couple. We step into a full car and stand in silence.

My heart hammers inside my chest. What am I going to say? What is he planning to say? Why is this such a shit show?

But it's his touch that steals my breath and bits of my sanity. He hasn't let go of my hand. To an outsider, we probably look like we belong together. The truth is different, but for a moment I let myself bask in the idea.

The fantasy isn't living up to the reality because the nervous energy seeping from the man beside me is frightening. Or it should be.

Somehow, I know I don't need to fear his temper. If that look he gave me when I collided with him is anything to go by, I'm safe.

I hope.

We march outside the building and Finn stops. It upsets the flow of pedestrian traffic, but the New Yorkers adjust quickly and start floating around us.

"Talk," he orders.

I chuckle. "This is where you want to talk?"

"I have to seize the opportunity since you continue avoiding me." He puts his hands into his pockets, relaxing his weight to one side.

In that moment, someone bumps into me, shoving me forward, helping me make my point.

I stumble into his chest and Finn grips my elbows, keeping me upright. The solid muscles, his scent, the air around him. Jesus.

Why did I even think I could stand my ground around this man? Two minutes in and I've collapsed into his arms. Twice.

And a part of me wants to be protected by him. It feels too good to ignore.

"Fuck," Finn growls and ushers me closer to the building before he walks toward a corner coffee shop.

I should be annoyed by his caveman routine, but I'm not. I'm just relishing the fact someone else is in charge. For now, I can enjoy the moment.

If only he didn't open the door, and I realize it's the same freaking place where I stole his coffee. I guess the realization hits him at the same time because he smirks. I hesitate at the door he holds for me.

"After you." He bows his head. "Let's see what you steal from me now."

If I ever thought this could be a friendly conversation, I was already high on pregnancy hormones. I'd better snap out of it quickly. And I do, because as soon as the coffee aroma hits my nostrils I gag.

I cover my mouth with my hand, but my lunch is balancing, undecided which way to go. "Oh, God."

"Are you okay?" The bully disappears and Finn searches my face with concern.

"Coffee makes me sick," I mumble through my palm and gag again.

"How ironic." He smirks, but turns to leave.

We step outside. "There is a deli there." I point across the street.

When we get inside, the animosity, frustration and strange attraction is simmering within both of us. Well, it is within me.

I plop down at the empty corner table. Finn looks around and moves his chair, assessing it like he's never sat on a plastic chair before, but then he sighs and sits down. "Do you want something?"

"Water," I whisper. He stands up and gets two bottles of water.

"So…" he starts, but doesn't continue, just stares at me, his jaw ticking.

I take a fortifying breath. "Let's start from the beginning. When you thought I was London, I felt… I don't know, it was somewhat freeing. I don't think I would have ever gone through with it if I was… just me." I shrug and giggle, but he doesn't find my confession amusing.

If his scorching eyes and rigid jaw are any indication, I'm pissing him off even more. I study his face for a beat, trying to decide how much I need to bare myself to him. Or if at all.

"What happened to your face?" I reach to trace his eyebrow. There is a scratch there and a bruise. How did I not notice that before?

"What happened to your hand?" He glances at the antiseptic patch on my palm.

"I found out I'm pregnant," I whisper and sag in my chair.

"That's right. Let's get back to the topic at hand." He leans back. Even on a plastic chair in a dingy deli, he looks aristocratic, almost royal. The confidence oozes from him.

Me? I'm trying to deflect. I'm good at that.

"Look, Finn, none of us planned for this. Frankly, I don't know how a one-night stand turned into a life-long commitment, but I can't change that. I'm not holding you accountable. You don't need to worry about anything. I can take care of this baby."

My hands go to my stomach like so many other times in the last few days. As if the contact can really solidify reality in my mind.

He follows my hands and shakes his head. "Are you kidding me right now?"

"I don't know what you want me to say, Finn. I'm giving you a way out." Isn't that what he wants?

He jerks his head and grinds his teeth for a moment before he speaks.

"We should get married."

Chapter 9

Finn

She blinks a few times. "Are you for real?"

Is *she* for real? I've had enough of these games. "Of course. We should get married."

"I don't fucking know you." Paris flails her arms in frustration.

She sags further into her chair, if that's even possible. She's looked like an adopted puppy that doesn't trust its new owners since I saw her at the hotel. It's infuriating how she's trying to escape this whole thing.

Especially since it clearly makes her miserable. I don't want her to be miserable, but for fuck's sake, she can't ignore the situation. However unexpected the turn of events is.

"We'll have to overcome that pretty fast. What do you want to know about me?" I should rein in my tone, but the woman draws the worst out of me. It's like I exhaust all my control on managing my situation with Pa, and when it comes to Paris I have none left.

Do I want to argue with the mother of my child?

I do.

And that's the stupid part. I know I shouldn't, but I want to. She just pushes all the buttons.

It doesn't help that I'm so fucking attracted to her. Or is it just the fact she goes out of her way to avoid me? Is Reilly right? Am I just annoyed she ghosted me? Fussing because I'm not used to rejection?

"Excuse me?" She glares at me.

"You heard me. What do you want to know?"

Her eyes widen. "You're joking. It's not a twenty questions first date kind of a situation, for fuck's sake. We missed all those steps already if you didn't notice." Her eyes shoot daggers, but her voice hitches with the last sentence, laced with regret.

She probably had some romantic idea about becoming a mother. I want to console her, but at the same time I'm pissed about her excluding me. "Tough shit. You're pregnant with my child and I'm going to do the right thing."

She chuckles. "To bully me into marrying you? No way. It's enough I get this screwed up version of my happy ending. I'm not making things worse."

"What is so horrible about marrying me?"

She fucking rolls her eyes.

"I'm rich, accomplished, an Ivy League graduate with plenty of resources, and a business to inherit that can take care of several generations. And we are compatible in bed."

Out of all my options, Paris is actually the perfect candidate to marry. In fact, much better than any of my other options—mostly orchestrated by my mother.

I mean, if I have to marry, at least it would be with someone fun and sexy. Though it looks like she's forgotten how to be fun.

"Impressive," she says, but her tone suggests she's far from impressed. "But the answer is still no. If you want to be involved, we'll figure out a co-parenting agreement."

Pa's face crosses my mind. If I uttered the phrase co-parenting agreement in his vicinity, I'd certainly give him that heart attack we're trying to avoid.

"Any other woman in your situation would be thrilled by my proposal," I huff. Not the best card to flop at the table, but yeah, here we are.

And it makes her laugh. "Do you have much experience with this situation? Are there other little Finns running around?"

I fell right into that one. I grit my teeth, breathing. Even I'm aware of my flared nostrils, but whoever suggested breathing would calm you down has never met Paris Lowe.

"No, and don't deflect again. You lied to me, you're avoiding me, and if I wasn't at that stupid fashion show and happened to overhear your sister, I probably wouldn't know about…"

I trip over my words, not able to say it. I have been so focused on the betrayal and rejection that I haven't even fully accepted the reality of becoming a father.

"So forgive me, Paris," I continue, "if I don't trust you enough to have you raise my child alone."

She opens her mouth, but closes it and sighs. She plays with the water bottle for a moment, probably phrasing another rejection in her head.

Her silver hair is darker at the roots. She hasn't colored it again. I wonder what's up with that constant hair change. Or what her real hair looks like. Even with the outrageous dyes, she is quite stunning as she chews on her lip.

"Why do you want to marry me? Do you really want to spend the rest of your life with a stranger?"

Her statement is filled with disillusion, broken dreams and regret. The hunch of her shoulders elicits the familiar pang of rejection my father has been cultivating in me.

So I rebut. "Don't be dramatic. We wouldn't be strangers for much longer."

She flinches. I'm an asshole. A pissed-off, dejected asshole.

"And what if we hate each other? If our recent interactions are any indication, we would probably kill each other soon. Call me naïve, but I want love, not hate."

Her words hit me in the chest. "I don't hate you."

"So let me get this straight. You got her pregnant, she ghosted you, and then you tried to bully her into marrying you?" When Cal puts it like that, I hate the situation even more. Paris called me a bully as well. Fuck.

I want love, not hate.

Her words took up residence in my head. She didn't mean it as an accusation, but it felt like one. Like I failed this woman with a strange taste in hair color, kissable lips and a penchant for stealing and lying.

A woman that infuriates me but equally intrigues me, and definitely turns me on. The mother of my child.

"And by the way she looked when you dragged her from the Madison Club," Cal continues, enjoying himself a bit too much, "she must have been thrilled by the whole act." He takes a sip of his whiskey and fails not to laugh.

I glare at him and slide my empty glass across the dining room table to him.

"You're such an idiot." He pours two fingers of golden liquid into my tumbler and pushes it back to me.

I force a gulp down. Getting drunk is what I need to forget for a moment about the clusterfuck this situation is. "What would you do?"

Not that I'd admit it to him, but I can see that I'm too close to this shit, too emotional, to know what's what.

"First, do you want to spend your life with her? Like is she reasonable enough that you can have a decent life?"

Wow. When did my little bro become this cynical? I guess with parents like ours it shouldn't surprise me. "I spent one night with her. She ghosted me. What do you think?"

"Well, the length of your dick will always be a problem—"

"Fuck you," I snarl and walk to the glass door of our patio while the idiot chuckles. Why am I even confiding in him?

The city flickers with lights of life and fun. Our lights are off, bar the small reading lamp in the corner. We sit in darkness, discussing the darkness of my life.

"Okay, but seriously. Why do you want to marry

her? Is it the right thing to do? Or a convenient thing to do because of Pa's ultimatum?"

"I guess both. I mean at least I know we can have fun together, unlike with Mother's uptight acquaintances." I shrug, annoyed by the sense of compromise my words carry.

I can't even be sure Paris is fun. What if she's right and we ended up hating each other?

Do I want a relationship akin to my parents'? The problem is that just a few weeks ago I wasn't even thinking about my future in this way. About a wife, kids, settling down. It was nowhere on my radar.

There has been no one I wanted more than three dates with.

I wish the one woman I wanted the second date with—okay, a night with—didn't attract me this much. Though it's unrequited, because Paris Lowe decided never to see me again before she even slept with me.

The minute she told me she was London, she must have known she was in for one night.

I don't think I would have ever gone through with it if I was... just me. What did she even mean by that? As if she was less than London? Does she feel inferior to her sister?

That's just fucked up. And another thing I don't know about her. Though I really want to. I should have listened better.

"Okay, well then, why are you trying to scare her?" Cal joins me by the window.

"Scare her?" I turn to face him.

"She probably had some romantic plans for her life. You didn't plan on it, and it's not really your fault, but you ruined that for her." He shrugs and sips his whiskey. "Maybe you should try to win her over, not coerce her into marriage."

* * *

"Take her on a date. Just dinner, where you can talk and get to know each other," Reilly suggests, tapping his pen on his chin.

I don't think I've ever spent so many hours in my office not working. But then, Operation Marry Paris will result in me taking the helm here, so it kind of qualifies as work.

At least my father's expectations to keep doing what they've been doing for decades require very little involvement on my part. My lack of focus will go unnoticed for sure.

"But is that enough? I'd have to go out with her for months, and I don't have that much time." I throw a bouncy ball against the wall, catch it and throw it again.

"Oh, you can't date her for more than three dates." Reilly sounds horrified.

I snatch the ball and frown at him.

"She would discover your personality and run." He shrugs, feigning innocence.

"You're fired." I throw the ball again.

"You can't speed these things up. You can't force her to fall in love."

The ball thuds to the floor, bounces a few times, loses momentum and rolls under my desk. "Fall in love?"

For the first time since I've known him, Reilly doesn't look his usual smartass self. He looks genuinely puzzled. "Why else would she marry you? From what we know, she is independently wealthy and professionally successful. Why would she need you?"

I sit up straight. "What the fuck, Reilly?"

He chuckles. "Don't be so sensitive. I just think that sending flowers, thoughtful gifts or wining and dining her might not be enough."

"You literally just suggested I take her to dinner." Why am I even discussing her with this idiot? Between Cal and Reilly, I'm more exasperated by the situation than sure of my next move.

Paris pleaded for more time when we talked yesterday. *Let us digest the situation more* were her words. Well, shit, I might get indigestion if we don't act soon.

What good is it going to do if we think about this shit separately? We need to think about it together.

"My brother met this girl at work, and they went out like three times and decided to go on vacation together. Literally, three weeks after meeting her, they boarded a plane and spent ten days together somewhere. Before he left, our mom says to him, 'I thought you liked this girl,' because why would he force them into a twenty-four seven situation this early in a relationship? They came back so in love, they married a few months later and have been together for years now."

"Where is this story going, Reilly?" I tap my fingers on my desk, the nervous energy cruising through without an outlet. I can't race and I haven't gotten laid in like... Fuck me. I haven't fucked anyone since Paris. Other than my hand.

The realization rocks me to the core. I guess all the racing took my mind off other things. And I have been preoccupied with Pa's games, his health, and the ongoing, slow downward spiral of our company. That must be it. Fuck.

"Maybe you need to take her away. Somewhere exotic where you're forced to spend time together. Though I can't imagine her falling in love with you if she spends more time with you. I mean, I'm with you every day—"

"Get the fuck out of here, Reilly, because I will fire you for real." I pick up a stapler to mock throw it at him.

"Promises, promises..." He chuckles and saunters away.

But maybe he's onto something. If she couldn't avoid me. Couldn't run away. Couldn't hide. She would have to listen. She would have to consider our future. We would have to talk about it.

If we were somewhere alone for a few days and I unleashed my charm, Paris Lowe would see our future more clearly.

And I know just the place.

Chapter 10

Paris

I swipe through all the messages and sigh. Finn van den Linden doesn't give up easily. And I'll have him in my life forever. That one fact is painfully obvious. I'm not even sure why I'm resenting it so much.

The choice was taken away from me. I guess I made the choice of sleeping with him. But the consequences were... what, a one percent chance? The universe is fucking making fun of me.

"Did you work from home today?" Andrea kisses my head and ambles toward the espresso machine.

I move to the sitting room with my tea. Not only am I tired, but I can't stand coffee. Pregnancy sucks. "Yeah, I did. I'm leaving for my dance class soon if you want me out of here."

It's been four days since my meeting with Finn

and he has been sending flowers to my work. And since I haven't found the time to see him again, I suspect it's only a matter of time before he shows up in person.

So I didn't go to work. Not proud of myself, but it's too hard to maintain my sanity around him.

And sure enough, he showed up, and half of the office fell in lust with him immediately based on the call from Shayna.

"He's so dreamy. You'd be stupid to reject him, but I'm happy to step in if you do," she gushed into the phone. "He brought flowers, all dressed up in an expensive suit, full of smiles and winks—"

His relentless pursuit would be so damned romantic if it were for the right reasons. If he wanted to date me for me. But that ship sailed before we even found where it was docked. I groan.

"Is everything okay?" Andrea leans into the opening between his kitchen and this room.

I feign a smile. "Yes. I've just been busy."

He narrows his eyes but doesn't push it. "Okay then, sis. I'm going back to school, anyway."

"It's almost six. Do you have evening classes now?"

He stops on his way to the door. "Chillax, Paris, I'll be on my best behavior." He gives me a lopsided smile and leaves.

I eye my laptop and consider working instead of

my dance class. I've been so tired lately that I spent my time working from home by mostly napping.

I still didn't get that pregnancy book, but based on my internet search, fatigue is normal in the first trimester.

That seems like too long of a time to just fake-work. Especially now when I want to pitch Quaintique renos. I should go to my class.

According to some mommy sites, it's important to continue doing everything as before, and my body, and my soul, need to get lost in the movement and music.

If only standing from the couch didn't feel like an inhuman effort. I sigh and push myself up. Before I reach the door, someone knocks.

I roll my eyes, throw my tot across my shoulder and swing the front door open. "Did you forget your keys—"

My heart rate spikes when my eyes land on Finn's.

The vein at his temple is going to pop any minute now. Either that or he'll need enamel replacement if he doesn't relax that chiseled jaw.

I blow a raspberry. Not at him, just at the situation.

"It's you." I smile brightly, not fooling him. Not really reacting in a mature way, but his testy nature is tiring and I'm tired already as it is.

"Who was that?" He balls his hands into fists.

"Who?" I suspect he saw Andrea leaving, but

being reasonable doesn't seem my jam today. I wonder what it is about him that makes me bitchy.

Paris, you're too nice to everyone. Hard pass when it comes to Finn van den Linden.

"Who do you live with, Paris?" he growls.

"Cool down your caveman routine, Finn. It's my brother," I deadpan. "How did you find me?"

"I went to your house and found all my flowers on your front steps, and when your receptionist confirmed you work from home, I called my PI." He jerks his head, raking his hands through his disheveled hair. "Sorry."

I guess he didn't plan on admitting that part. It's kind of hot though. He hired a PI to find me. A rational person would be upset about breached privacy and all that.

A hormonal person has butterflies exploding and her core clenching at the gesture. Goddammit.

I sigh. "Your PI found me fast, but still fire him because he should have told you who this house belongs to. Not that I approve of you spying on me like this." Okay, I approve a little bit.

"You live with your brother too?" He's practically shaking with nervous energy. The man needs some yoga.

"My house is being fumigated." I glare. I have never told as many lies as I keep telling him. He just draws reactions from me that are not the good, polite, putting-others-first Paris.

"Fumigated?" He cocks his head, narrowing his eyes.

"That's what I said."

"That's what you said." He keeps assessing me like a dangerous object. Or one he fears would poison him.

"You don't have to repeat everything I say." I adjust the strap of my gym tot.

"Well, then don't say things that need to be repeated to believe them." He quirks an eyebrow, unimpressed.

"Are you suggesting I'm lying?"

My indignation is so misplaced right now, but here we are. Finn van den Linden is a threat to my morals. And my underwear, because how this interaction makes me hot for him is beyond me.

He shakes his head, not denying, more like shaking off the entire exchange. He looks above my shoulder into the house and back at me. "How many brothers do you have?"

I sigh and step outside, locking the door behind me. "Enough to beat the shit out of you, so behave."

He chuckles. "Yes, ma'am." His shoulders relax. Just slightly.

And I do too. He looks tired, but I can see why Shayna almost peed her pants. We stare at each other without the usual tension, and it feels good. Probably because it's a relief after all that barking.

A smile tugs at the corners of my mouth, and his gaze softens. It's like an intimate conversation is happening between us without words, where we vow to bury the hatchet and try to move forward in a more respectful way.

Or at least that's what I hope for. Because I enjoy being looked at like this. Like I matter. Like he wants to be looking at me.

"Are you going somewhere?" Finn asks finally and I snap out of my stupor.

I turn to take the few steps from Andrea's brownstone and Finn follows me down the street.

"A dance class. I'm parked one block down there." I point in the general direction of my car.

"What kind of dance?"

He seems genuinely interested, but something tells me he would judge this particular class the same way London pokes at it.

I sigh and redirect. "Why did you come, Finn?"

"To take you on a date."

"Now?"

He looks at me sideways, and in that moment he doesn't look like either the bully or the confident player. His face is soft with hope and my heart swells.

I owe him this. I owe us this. I owe our baby this.

"I'd ask you on a date, but you've proven to be very bent on avoiding me." He shrugs.

I might owe him, but he won't make this easy. Why should I? "I have a dance class."

"I'll wait for you. We'll go out after," he announces, like I have no say in this. Jerk.

And I'm not having him come to my dance studio. "I have a business call after."

"Why do you have a call at night?"

And the peaceful coexistence is gone. "There are time zones around the world," I bite out.

"You shouldn't work that hard." His tone is a tad too authoritarian.

I'm back to being annoyed. "I'll ask for your opinion when I'm interested."

Finn sighs and takes a deep breath. "Okay, sorry. Tomorrow?"

"I have a photography class."

I love that class, but just talking about my schedule makes me exhausted right now. Jesus, I need to adjust my agenda for the next few weeks to include more napping.

"What are you, a professional hobbyist?"

We reach my car. "Go away, Finn." I unlock my Mini Electric and throw in my bag.

"Is this your car?" He eyes my ride with suspicion.

"No, I'm breaking into someone else's."

"You need a bigger and safer car."

This man.

"Do I now? And I should work less. Thank you for chiming in on my life."

"But you need a better car."

"Fuck, Finn, I want a small, electric car. Stop organizing my life."

"Where will you put the car seat?"

Shit. He got me there. "It'll fit."

Tears prick behind my eyes, and suddenly I'm overwhelmed by the whole situation. By how unprepared I am, how much I don't know, how this was not supposed to be on my to-do list. How shitty I feel for all those thoughts. How freaking emotional I am.

I want to turn away and hide before he sees my untimely meltdown, but the tears roll down before I can act, and Finn sighs and pulls me into a hug.

I bury my face in his chest, and as much as I try, I can't stop it anymore and let go. Stupid hormones.

He wraps one arm around me and strokes my hair with the other as I sob into the lapels of his expensive suit.

"Don't cry, Paris, you don't have to get a new car," he whispers, and it only propels more tears.

"It's not that, it's everything..." I bawl. "I didn't even think about a car seat, and I'm so exhausted all the time, and I made the commitment to expand my business. And I keep thinking about how I don't need this right now. How this was not supposed to happen. How this…" I look at him, my vision blurry with tears. "It was supposed to be a one-night stand. And now… this. And then I feel like the worst person in the world because I already love the baby. I love him or her, so how can I feel regret at the same time?"

Another sob rakes through me and Finn wraps me tighter, kissing the top of my head. "You're not the worst person in the world, and this baby is fortunate to have you. Let me help you."

I smile through my tears. Even if he's just saying that to comfort me, it's nice not to feel so tragically alone for a moment.

He lifts my chin with his finger and wipes one of my cheeks with his thumb. The touch is light, but so significant. Because at this moment, right now, I feel more connected to him. And I don't even care that it might be hormonal.

He leans in and kisses my forehead gently. It's so unexpected from the man who owns the air around him and dominates with confidence. So tender and genuine, I sob again.

He groans. "Please don't cry. Let's go on a date. I want to know how many siblings you really have."

I chuckle. "Seven."

"Wow. You see, seven siblings only begs for more questions about your family. I think we need that date."

"Okay." I nod.

He opens his mouth, ready to retort, and then jerks his head back. "Really?"

I nod again, giggling through tears.

"Yes," he shouts, gaining himself a few eye rolls from passersby.

"I have one condition..." I shake my head. I can't condition this. "Suggestion."

"Tell me." He tucks a strand behind my ear, our gazes playful on each other.

"Can we not discuss the future and just have one date pretending it's just a date?"

Chapter 11

Paris

"We're here," the driver says as he stops the car at a large, abandoned parking lot near the Hudson. I might regret this date before it starts.

"Are you going to sell me to the mob?" I whisper and Finn laughs.

His driver opens the door and Finn gets out, reaching back for me.

"Where are we?" I duck my head, but don't take his hand.

He chuckles. "Trust me."

Trust me? The two words feel loaded.

When Finn picked me up tonight I had anxious butterflies in my stomach, despite our agreeing we wouldn't discuss the pregnancy and future. Or maybe I had them because of that.

I have no reason to trust him. But I have no reason not to. Since he's learned about the pregnancy, he's been trying to do the right thing.

And while we may have very different ideas about what the right thing is, it's time I lean into this adventure. However messy it might be. I take his hand and get out.

I'm wearing a skirt that flares from my waist to just above my knees and high heels. The cool air sends shivers up my legs.

"Have I told you that you look amazing?"

I touch my light blue hair, suddenly shy. "Thank you."

He offers me his arm and I snake my hand through it. This is nice. More than nice. I can do this. I can pretend it's just a date.

But when I look at the abandoned warehouse, my steps falter. "Okay, now I'm sure you're selling me to the Mafia or killing me. Nobody would ever find my body."

"Watching a lot of movies, are you?" He takes my hand and pulls me forward.

We enter what is clearly an old factory and I gasp, stunned by the mesmerizing transformation of this forgotten industrial space. The air is heavy with history, but the current purpose is contemporary, light.

Dining tables are scattered throughout the

cavernous expanse of the factory at the most unexpected places.

A couple shares laughter at a table perched on a scaffolding's platform. Another group eats behind some rusty machinery, inside an old railway car.

The hostess leads us under the soft glow of Edison bulbs around the wall of bricks, weathered and worn. I spy a few more tables, all set up for an intimate dining experience.

We take a curvy metal staircase, Finn letting me go in front of him, guarding my each step on the uneven surface.

We get to an old freight elevator where a table is set for two. Its metal surfaces gleam under amber lighting, the space made cozy with large potted plants in the lift's corners.

I smile at Finn. "Wow."

"I thought you'd appreciate the design." He winks. "And hopefully the company as well."

I'm stunned into silence. The creator in me doesn't even want to sit down. I want to roam around and discover more details in this place.

"Very good choice, Finn. How did you even know about this place?" I take the chair he moved for me.

"I can't tell you, or I'd have to kill you." He sits across from me.

I laugh. Our server comes with water and recites the cocktail selection, but Finn stops him.

"We won't be drinking."

"You could have something," I protest.

"That wouldn't be fair. Besides, I don't need booze to enjoy the evening."

I swallow, my throat painful with emotion. God, he plays the game well. Really well.

The server asks about allergies. "The dinner is a tasting menu at the discretion of our chef, so we need to make sure there are no dietary limitations," he explains.

When he leaves, I try to dive into the familiar topics from our first meeting, hoping we can rekindle some of the intimacy from before. "How is work? Have things with your father improved?" I put the napkin on my lap.

"And here I hoped for a light conversation." He chuckles humorlessly.

"Sorry. We don't have to talk about it."

We remain silent for a moment, the air filled with awkwardness. Shit. We can't do this. Why is it so hard tonight, and so easy when we first met?

"Me and my brother, we'd like to make many changes that are desperately needed, but Pa defends tradition at all costs. The problem is many of our processes, designs, and services are not traditional, they are simply outdated."

"Why don't you apply your ideas somewhere else? It sounds like you're not appreciated, so why stay?"

He regards me for a beat and then releases a loaded sigh. "As much as I wish to just break free, I care about the company. I don't want to jump ship because things are tough right now. I care about our heritage. Even more now when..."

He swallows and takes a sip of his water. *When he's about to have a family of his own?*

The desperate passion behind his words sheds new light on the man. Having built my own company, I can't imagine how it would feel if someone were constantly derailing my efforts. And yet, he perseveres.

"I guess it's going to be hard to avoid the elephant in the room." I rub my stomach, hoping we can keep this light. Lighter. "You seem close to your brother."

His face brightens, no longer marred by the shadows of his father. "I'm close with both my siblings. Though I don't see Saar often."

"Oh, I didn't know you have a sister. The media only features you and your brother."

"They feature Saar way more than us. But people on this side of the pond don't connect us. She's a model."

"Oh, that Saar?" I know of the European beauty,

but apparently she isn't European. "How is it possible the media doesn't make the connection?"

He shrugs and I get a feeling he's happy about it, protective of his sister. "It's boring since she isn't here much, and she makes sure her life is as private as possible."

"That must be hard in her position."

He shrugs again. "But you've been checking on my coverage." He doesn't seem annoyed by it.

"I didn't say that. But frankly, all the attention you cause isn't something I—"

"Paris, the paps are always around the most frequented clubs and occasionally I go out, so I end up being photographed. I'll keep the attention away from you, don't worry."

His confidence and candor shock me. "How? And why?"

"How? For starters, by picking discreet locations like this one to make sure you're not harassed when you're with me. I don't need to go clubbing if that helps."

I stare at him, not sure what to make of this commitment. Is he playing me? Is he really ready to change his lifestyle? For me? "I don't understand. You've always been a playboy."

His eyes pierce me. It does things to my core, my heart, my stomach. I don't look away because his gaze consumes me completely. And as much as I wish I didn't like it, I do. Oh my, I do love it.

And then he speaks. "I only want to play with you."

My breath hitches. I'm almost sure the lights around us dimmed. God, he's good at this, and my hormone-dazed brain is eating it all up.

I'm sweating while goosebumps cover my body. My mouth is dry, but I keep swallowing. I don't know how long we sit there, staring.

I don't know what he's thinking about, but I envision swiping everything off the table and climbing over to straddle him.

"Let me present your starters." Our server jerks our attention away and we both fidget as if he truly caught us doing what I just pictured.

He presents the dish to us, but I don't hear half of what he says, desperately trying to compose myself.

"So," I try to get back into our conversation. "Your sister..."

"She's five years younger," Finn jumps in quickly. Is he as affected by our brief moment as I am? "Our parents sent her to a boarding school in Europe and she stayed there, choosing her freedom over the family."

There is sadness but also pride in his tone and his expression. "Freedom?"

He waves his hand. "My family comes with a hefty

dose of unreasonable expectations. Tell me about yours."

I accept he doesn't want to dive deeper. "My family? How long do you have?"

"All night. To start with." His voice is serious, laced with promise and seduction, but also with commitment.

And again, we gaze at each other. This time, our eyes try to fill the gaps we're not ready to address with words yet. And I'm trying not to think about crawling across the table.

Focus, Paris. "Okay, Finn, but pay attention because I will quiz you after. Do you know Casa Cassi?"

The server is clearing the plates and gives me a stern look. I bite my lip and Finn barely stifles a laugh.

"You want to get us banned by mentioning the competition? Of course I know Casa Cassi. I can get us a table there, too."

The confidence in this man. "I'm sure you can, but I don't need your help. Casa Cassi belongs to my step-brother, Massi."

"Massimo Cassinetti is your brother? He's one growly son of a bitch." He jerks his head, realizing his words, and I laugh.

"You're not wrong. Obviously you've met him."

"My father wanted him to work in our flagship hotel here in New York."

"I see. Well, you know Gio, and you saw Andrea who I live with, they are Massi's younger brothers. And there is Baldo who lives in Europe. Bianca Cassinetti met our father, they fell in love and the families merged."

"What happened to your mom?"

I sigh. "She died."

"I'm sorry."

"Don't be. We can't change it, and we were fortunate to get a second mom in Bianca. I miss Mom sometimes, but unfortunately I don't remember her much."

"But you said seven siblings. Four Cassinettis, you and London, that's still only six together."

"We have an older sister, Sydney, and a younger sister, Brooklyn."

"Please don't tell me your parents named you based on the place where you were conceived." He makes a face like he's bracing himself for an unwelcome truth.

I snort. "I'm pretty sure they couldn't have conceived me and London at two different places."

We both laugh.

"Have you thought about..." He swallows, glancing toward my stomach, and an awkward pause descends. "The names."

"God, no. I'm still getting used to the idea."

"Me too."

Again, we stare, the air filled with many unresolved topics and a lot of attraction. Equally unresolved.

We're not ready to resolve the first, and we definitely shouldn't act on the latter. Or should we?

Chapter 12

Finn

"I had a great time." I help Paris out of my car in front of her brother's place.

"Me too."

We grin at each other and then I glance up the steps. Okay, can I make a move? Am I going to piss her off? Though she lives with her brother...

I step closer and dip my head, our noses almost touching. Her meadow scent infiltrates my senses and I remind myself to tread carefully, but I still don't step away.

Paris is gazing at me, a smile lingering on her lips. Those lips.

"It's a shame your house is getting fumigated," I whisper. Shit. Am I fishing for an invitation?

She chuckles. Thank God.

I put a strand of her hair behind her ear, brushing my knuckles across her cheek. The intimacy of my move and how it spreads tingling heat down my spine is enough to sober me up. I jump back and she blinks a few times, mirroring my action on wobbly legs.

What's wrong with me? What the hell do I want from her? That's the problem. I want her to help me get my inheritance, because if we're having a child, it's a practical solution for all parties involved.

But the conversation tonight and the moment we just shared, and many other similar or more intense moments tonight... those aren't part of the plan.

"I'd like us to go away together," I blurt. Yes, I need to speed this thing up and close the deal.

Her eyes widen. "And you had to spoil a lovely evening. I don't know you well enough to go away with you."

Fuck. "Look, it's not like we have a lot of time. I thought going away would help us get to know each other."

She eyes me with disdain, or... something. Definitely not the sweet, hot gaze she rewarded me with all night. It fills me with regret. The familiar taste of dejection. And suddenly all I want is for her to go back to being soft and lovely. What is wrong with me?

"Look, Finn, it's late and I'm tired. Turns out

growing a person takes up a lot of energy." She turns to the stairs.

I walk up with her, making sure she's okay. "That wasn't a hard no."

She sighs. "I'll think about it, Finn. Good night."

* * *

"Finn, you're finally here." Mother dashes into the foyer as soon as the housekeeper closes the door.

"Mother." I dip to kiss the crown of her head. "Am I late?" I thought dinner was in fifteen minutes. I always come just early enough, but I guess I got the hour wrong this time.

Mother pulls me toward the sitting room, and the minute we cross the threshold I understand the warm welcome.

Fuck. Me.

"Hello, Finn." The woman Mother introduced at the fashion show stands up. "What a pleasant surprise." She smiles.

I'm sure it's pleasant for her, but a goddamn surprise for me. What's her name?

"I didn't know we'd have guests tonight." I would have had two more whiskeys.

"Samantha just stopped by to drop off a few things

for our board meeting," Mother explains, both of them smiling at me like I'm their dinner.

"Okay, I'll leave you to it then. Is Cal here?" I pivot but don't get far.

"We've just finished. Why don't the two of you catch up? I was telling Samantha about the new chef at our hotel. Maybe you should take her sometime soon."

And the award for subtlety goes to my Mother.

"Why don't I walk you out, Samantha," I offer. No need to play this game.

She perks up and I feel like an asshole, even though we are both innocent victims in my Mother's schemes.

"I have time next week if you want to have that dinner." Samantha doesn't waste time.

"Samantha, I'm sure you're perfectly lovely company, and any man would be happy to spend an evening with you, but I'm kind of involved at the moment." And it's so complicated.

"Oh." She sighs, keeping her red lips in the O-shape for a beat too long. She's beautiful, if a bit fake, but I'm about as interested in her as I am in a presentation on the history of beige. She blinks a few times and I almost recant. Almost.

"If the situation changes, I'll call you." It's a shitty thing to say, since we both know I won't call her.

Would I have been interested in her before Paris

came into the picture? Not likely. I open the door for her and come face to face with Cal.

"Hey, assho—" he starts. "Hello, Samantha." He smiles and kisses her hand. Of course he remembers her name. And why does that irk me?

"Caleb, Finn, enjoy your dinner." She blinks rapidly and practically runs to her car.

"Did you make her cry?" Cal digs his elbow into my side and I cough, my ribs on the mend but not ready for his abuse. "Shit, bro, you should get that checked."

I groan and turn to join our parents, with Caleb in my wake.

The dinner is a silent, boring affair until dessert is served.

"How is everything at the hotel, Cal? Is the holiday season booked out?" Pa asks.

Cal and I exchange a look.

"Eighty percent booked," my brother says.

"Well, do better. By now we should be at full capacity, sold out." He puts a large piece of carrot cake in his mouth. "Isn't that marketing's fault?" Chewing, he glances my way.

"And as I've been telling you, we need to make some changes to stay competitive." I try to keep my voice level. "But even without those, the marketing budget was cut by thirty percent—"

"Then get creative," Pa bellows. "At the rate our revenue has been declining over the past two years, we had to adjust the budgets. We don't grow money on trees."

I take a deep breath—not that it ever helps in my conversations with him—but before I can respond, Cal jumps in.

"Pa, talking about being creative, Finn and I, we've identified areas for improvement that would definitely increase our revenue. We can test these changes at my hotel and then roll them out to others."

"Your hotel?" Pa raises his eyebrow.

Cal groans. "You know what I mean. We would start by renovating the members only floor and then we'd adjust the membership program to—"

"And who do you think will pay for that? Do you really believe we can present the board our bleak projections and ask for approval to take out another loan at the same time? It's embarrassing." He stands up, his face red. He yanks his tie loose.

"Charles." Mother stands up, but he doesn't look at her.

Panting, he shakes his head. "I'm still in charge, and I don't want to hear these risky propositions. When Finn is in charge, he will understand being responsible for over two thousand employees around the world. Until then, just do your fucking job. Both of you."

He storms out with Mother on his heels.

I let out a long breath through my cheeks and sag in my seat. Cal stands up, brings the crystal whiskey decanter over and pours us both an ungentlemanly amount.

"Fuck. Why doesn't he see what's happening? How did he run the company for decades?" Cal takes a generous gulp.

"Beats me." I spin my tumbler.

"You really fucking have to marry Paris, and soon, before we lose the company." He stands up and paces the room.

I chuckle. "How do I do that? I can't force her."

Three days have passed since our date, and Paris remains adamant that this is not the time for her to leave and ten thousand other excuses. At least she's answering my phone calls and responding to my texts. That's a step in the right direction.

We have another date this weekend, but that's five days of not getting any closer to resolving the situation. Not even thinking about the fucking boner I'm sporting every time I speak to her.

And my Porsche is still on the hydraulic lift in Tony's garage. Fuck. Who knew chasing Paris Lowe would be so challenging?

"How hard can it be?" Cal whips around. "She's already pregnant."

"Who is pregnant?" Mother's voice slices through the air.

Chapter 13

Paris

"Are you serious? You want to leave now?" Barry flails his arms. His exasperation isn't unwarranted, so I let him have his moment. "We need to brainstorm the Quaintique project and get cracking on that."

"And we also need to tend to new clients that are actually going to pay the bills," I respond.

"Quaintique is a new business." He paces around the boardroom.

Shayna studies her nails while the other employees burn their notebooks with their lowered gazes.

"Quaintique is an important business opportunity. I'll be gone for a few days. I can sketch some ideas while flying, and when I'm back we'll get things done, Barry."

He stops, glaring at me, his chest heaving, and then he nods.

I smile. "Good. Everyone knows what they need to do. Go and create the magic." I dismiss the meeting.

"You're way too nice," Shayna says.

"You've been telling me. I'd like to dash out early to get packed. Is there anything else urgent on my agenda?"

"Take me with you," she begs, batting her fake eyelashes at me.

"And who will make sure everything runs here as it should?"

"It's not fair you get the hot van den Linden chasing you, and now you get a client on a private island." She pouts.

"That's why I'm making the big bucks," I deadpan.

Her mentioning Finn only intensifies the guilt Barry instigated. I shouldn't be going away at this time. I need to cancel the date with Finn, and I have a feeling he'll go all ballistic on me.

I've been rebuffing his trip offer, and now I'm going somewhere in the Pacific. But the offer from a secret client who has been dealing with us through his agent has been too appealing to refuse. I mean, a private island? Unlimited budget? And potentially meeting a celebrity?

If I'm honest with myself, my eager acceptance of

the clandestine assignment also relates to my current situation. Finn has been swoony, slowly chipping away all my defenses, which would be a great thing in our situation.

But at the same time, I can't trust myself right now. Not with the raging hormones, my work stress and everything else.

And then he comes up with some stupid proposal, like marriage—as if—or the trip. And my doubt about his motivations to spend time with me blossoms.

For all I know, he's just chasing after the heir, not necessarily me. As things stand right now, I'll never know. The baby is his reason for it all.

Can I imagine marrying a man I don't really know for the sake of our baby? Yes.

Can that man be a playboy with a fuck pad he shares with his brother? To my dismay I'm torn about that one. That's just a recipe for heartache. But my brain has been hovering on the edges of sanity between lust and fatigue.

Welcome to my life!

The long flight and some island paradise are just what I need to think this through. To gain distance. When I'm back, we'll iron out the co-parenting agreement and I'll cut my losses and move on.

Well, move forward, because I don't think I can move on for the next two years. When can I date again? I imagine it's not the easiest thing for a single mother. Would I schedule my dates on the days when the baby is with Finn?

The idea leaves a bitter taste on my tongue, but my mind goes all in, envisioning Finn getting married and my baby having a stepmother. Oh my God. Why is this so complicated? It's like I'm in the middle of a divorce before I've even had a third date.

I park my car and fish my phone from my bag.

> I'm sorry, but I'll have to cancel our date. Something came up at work. I can grab a coffee later today.

I should be able to squeeze him in before my flight. That way he won't go all military strike on me.

FINN

> Shame, let's catch up next week. I'm swamped at work as well.

Hm, that was easy. And strangely anti-climactic. It's like I'm already attuned to his irritated responses, craving them. I'm so out of character around this man, it's scary.

I trudge home and find Andrea on the sofa. "You don't have classes today?"

"Don't worry, *Mom*, I'm not skipping school." He

doesn't stand up. Shit. Maybe I should stay home. "Aren't you flying out today?"

I hesitate at the bottom of the stairs. Should I ask Syd or Gio to stay here?

Andrea jumps up and folds his arms across his chest, answering my unspoken question. "I'll be okay."

With a sigh, I go to pack my things and let him help me to the waiting cab. "Are you sure you'll be okay? Andrea, it's okay to—"

"I promise to call Gio on my way to the nearest bar." He winks at me and gives me a hug before I get into the back seat.

I'm leaving for a few days, please check on Andrea.

GIO

Okay.

For a man who is always on the phone, that wasn't a reassuring answer, but I know he will be on top of it.

The water brightens from turquoise to crystal blue, the beautiful contrast peaceful from the air as the chopper takes me to my destination.

The flight was long, but I got work done reviewing materials from this client, so I'm excited to see the property myself. My smile comes easily because I slept for a good ten hours of the flight, courtesy of the bedroom on the charter flight I had all to myself.

An attendant waited for me at the airport and led me to the helicopter. I've been playing a game, guessing who will be waiting for me on the other side. An athlete? An actor? Or a politician? A business tycoon? Oh, did Gio recommend me for the job? I should have asked him.

A small island with white sand and palms around the perimeter of a large bungalow comes into view, and I can't help but wiggle my shoulders. How exciting is this? I might schedule an extended visit to oversee the renovations here. Just to enjoy paradise.

I lean to the side, watching the remote beauty opening up in front of us. The house looked different in the pictures the agent sent. I'll have to rethink my ideas, but I can do that on the fly. It wouldn't be the first time.

We circle the island before we descend at the farthest end of the heliport. The pilot helps me get out and takes my luggage.

"There is nobody waiting," I yell over the roar of the blades.

"I'm sure they saw us coming in. I have to hop back to pick up another client." He points toward the beautiful ocean and I nod, stepping aside.

I try to hold my hair as the bird lifts, and when the wind and roaring finally disappear, I shade my eyes and look around at the beautiful, vast sea.

I bite my lip and laughter escapes me. This is just what the doctor would prescribe, if there was a doctor to deal with the current mess of my life.

An engine hums softly behind me. I whip around and my momentary bliss erupts, leaving all the good feelings in ashes at my feet.

The golf cart stops in front of me and Finn smiles, cocking his head. "Surprise."

* * *

I pace the spacious veranda back and forth while Finn watches me, leaning on the banister. To his credit, he's not talking and letting me stew in my rage.

"For the record—and do remember this one well— do. Not. Ever. Surprise. Me." I put my hands on my waist. I need to calm down. This is not good for the baby. I look around and sit on a rattan egg chair.

"Duly noted."

The swaying churns my stomach and I hoist myself up, back to pacing.

"What is this place? Is this some sort of a fuck pad?" *Yes, Paris, this is the right inquiry.*

Finn shakes his head and rolls his eyes. He fucking dares to roll his eyes.

"I can assure you I've never brought a woman here before." He folds his arms across his chest.

I snort. "Oh, yeah, I forgot. You have the perfect condo for that in the city."

"You didn't seem to mind the first time." He flinches at his words as if realizing too late he said them out loud.

I pace some more. I'm so mad that I can't even see through my rage to recognize what really pisses me off about the situation.

How dare he blindside me like this? My mood is so at odds with the breathtaking scenery, I feel like an intruder.

Which makes no sense at all. Nothing makes sense anymore. I snap my eyes to Finn and I wish I didn't, because he stands there, calm and so rested. His dark blond hair is all messed up, playfully waving in the wind.

He's wearing a white V-neck tee and low hanging Bermuda shorts, and God help me, he's so fucking gorgeous I lose my train of thought. As if he knows the effect he has on me—great, Paris, just carry your thoughts written all over your face—he straightens up, his gaze embracing me.

The man could truly be royalty. It feels like the sun

moves with him, so he's now casting a shadow over me. Like he can command nature. Like he owns my body already because I'm mad at him, but my ovaries are high-fiving each other, hoping he steps closer.

No. Way. I step back and almost trip on a large potted plant. Finn leaps forward and grabs my elbow, steadying me.

He smells of ocean and sun and something carnal. My skin tingles as I meet his eyes. I swallow, painfully aware he senses my body is at odds with my mind. The odds so great that my panties are wet already.

It doesn't help that I've been horny for days now. Thank you very much, pregnancy hormones.

I look away, but he's too close, and I end up staring at his chest. The T-shirt he's wearing is almost transparent, the fabric so soft and thin. My looking away from his face did me no good, because the planes of his defined muscles erase all rational thoughts.

Okay, not all, because I push past him and make my way to the other side of the veranda that stretches along the entire front of the house. As far as possible.

Finn sighs and bows his head, giving me a view of his chiseled back, and I'm so screwed. Jesus.

"So this entire island is yours?" Talking is the safest way to have him piss me off again. And I need to maintain that anger. To stay strong.

I'm attracted to the father of my child. That should

be a wonderful concept. Not in our case though. We need to iron out that co-parenting agreement before Finn van den Linden steals my sanity.

"Well, technically, it belongs to my father." He turns to face me. "He bought it years ago when he was dating a stripper and Mother couldn't stomach the idea, so he hid her here."

"So it's your father's fuck pad?"

That is so fucked up. By the looks of it, Finn thinks the arrangement is perfectly normal. I try to think of something to say to that, but this is more of a several-hours-of-therapy issue.

What kind of a relationship do his parents have? What a shitty example to give your children.

I want to do better for my kid. Will I be able to, since it's not even the size of a bean and I'm already failing him or her completely?

He sighs. "Don't worry, the sheets are new."

"The whole bed should be burned, for fuck's sake." *Good job, Paris, because that's the problem here.*

He bows his head, shaking it. Is he exasperated? Annoyed? Am I spoiling his vacation?

"You really thought that bringing me here where your father hides his mistresses is the best plan to, what... to get laid?" I put my hands on my hips.

"No." He looks at me, taken aback. But then a smile tugs at the corner of his lips and the playful boy from our first night is back. "I mean, I wouldn't mind if that happened."

I scream and dash down the stairs. I run to the beach, which is only a hundred feet away, so my escape is widely unsatisfactory. I jerk off my sandals and step into the balmy water, the waves soothing around my ankles.

This was supposed to be my getaway. To clear my head. To enjoy creativity in a new place. To organize my thoughts.

I sense Finn's presence behind me and the war in me intensifies. I could spend a day here with him, but the growing attraction would only complicate things further.

"I'm leaving." I turn to him, and he jerks his head as if I slapped him.

We stare at each other, the space between us crackling with my indecision, with his insistence, with my hiding energy and his unearthing one. So at odds, yet so connected.

"You can't leave." It sounds like an order. Even his posture feels larger somehow.

"Excuse me?" I put my hands on my hips and realize I'm mirroring his stance.

I don't know what's going on in his mind, but the war brewing there is evident. He keeps it under control, but he's ready to explode.

But he doesn't.

And in my twisted mind, it pleases me. As unconventional as our practically non-existent relationship is, he's trying. Whatever his motivation is, he's trying.

"There are no flights."

"I'll get my brother to send a plane for me." Both Gio and Massi have private planes. Lo has as well. It's Dom's, but I'm sure they would rescue me.

"First, you need a helicopter, and there is a storm in the forecast, no pilot would take off now. They warned me when you were arriving. You almost didn't make it."

"What a bummer." I snort and look around. Bingo. "I'll take your boat." I gesture to the cruiser docked at our side.

Finn raises his eyebrow. "Into the storm?"

I huff and my stomach growls. Loud.

"Let me cook you something. As soon as the weather clears, I'll get you a ride," he offers, eyeing me like I'm a bomb and the timer is approaching single digits.

I sigh and start back toward the house. "You know how to cook?"

"Let me surprise you." The relief in his tone is too pronounced. *Don't be too happy yet, mister.*

"There have already been enough surprises for a lifetime."

"Sorry. Wrong choice of words. I'll prove to you I can cook, and we'll have another opportunity to get to know each other better over a good meal."

I chance a look at him, and the boyish grin sends a shock wave through my body.

Oh, boy, this is going to be a long day.

Chapter 14

Finn

"What the hell? What happened here?" Paris stops in the doorway.

When I arrived and found a construction zone instead of the luxury paradise this place used to be, I almost burned it to the ground.

Turns out my father's last mistress, or the one before, started renovating the house, and then they broke up. Shit.

A large plastic sheet hangs from the ceiling, covering half of the room. At least the kitchen is intact. And the view provides a decent backdrop.

"Sorry about that. I didn't know my father was renovating." I move to the kitchen and open the fridge our housekeeper stocked for us before I sent her away.

This getaway hasn't started auspiciously, but I can charm my lady dragon.

"Where is my room? And the bathroom? I'd like to shower after the flight." She stands by the entrance, part petulant child and part strict teacher. I wouldn't mind role-playing the latter later. Fuck. Focus, asshole.

The next surprise won't make this evening any better. I'm suspecting the opposite, but shit, it's not my fault.

I will fucking kill Reilly, because I told him to book us a resort and he came up with this isolation idea.

At the time, the idea of trapping her without an escape route seemed like an excellent opportunity. Being here proves how deranged my assistant's ideas are. Why did I listen?

So here we are. She is so desperate to not be near me that she wanted to fly a plane from the States to save her. Like spending time with me is such a pain.

I'm fucking desperate, and I need to make sure she stays. The lie about the weather will probably backfire, but that's a problem for another day. Now let's face the issue at hand.

Paris glares at me, tapping her foot.

"Just down the hall. Let me help you with your suitcase."

I step outside and grab her luggage. She follows me around the plastic sheet, to the other wing of the house.

"At least the renovation wasn't a lie." She chuckles

humorlessly. "But sending me fake photos, that's next-level deceit. I spent the flight sketching suggestions."

Shit. "I'm sorry. In my defense, my assistant freelanced on that one and took it a bit too far. He has a tendency to exaggerate."

"It suits you well, our third date is happening in a construction zone. Not scoring any points here."

She tucks a strand of hair behind her ear and a smile ghosts her face. I should be glad she's relaxing, but I know what's coming.

The next fight is about to start. I open the door to the guest room and Paris stops in her tracks. She narrows her eyes at me, and I swear her look physically cuts me.

She assesses the other doors, all covered with plastic sheets, and then looks back at my things strewn around the bedroom.

The only bedroom usable in this fucking renovation nightmare of the house.

"Is this the only room?" Her voice could freeze the desert.

"Yep." I smile my best let's-have-fun smile, but it doesn't work on this woman.

She groans, snatches her suitcase, and slams the door in my face. Okay, that didn't go that poorly.

I let the air out through my cheeks and lower my head against the white polished wood of the door.

A stifled scream on the other side has my hand on the door handle immediately. "Are you okay?"

"Go away, Finn."

Okay, she's pissed, but it's not my fucking fault there is only one bedroom. It's not like we haven't slept together before. The image of Paris on her knees flashes through my mind, and my cock stirs.

"I'll be in the kitchen. The fresh towels are in the bathroom."

I better give her time. And myself. I glance at my half boner. Fuck.

Half an hour later I set the table outside. The chicken is in the oven and the water is boiling for the pasta when Paris saunters in.

She's wearing a pink sleeveless summer dress, falling in a large skirt down to her ankles. Her light blue hair is still damp and she is barefoot. With the sun shining at her from behind, she looks almost angelic.

"It smells good." She climbs on the stool on the other side of the island. As she hoists herself up, her cleavage shifts, giving me a glimpse of her bra. It fucking matches the color of her dress, and for some reason it's the most arousing thing.

"It's penne with chicken parmigiana. I hope you'll like it."

The scent of my shower gel wafts toward me and I snap my eyes to her. She used my soap. She smells like me. Okay, not exactly, but somehow it grows the hope in me.

Snap out of it, idiot, she used the only soap in the bathroom. She probably didn't even want to unpack her shit, so as to be ready to leave as soon as possible.

"I'm not sleeping in one bed with you, Finn. Let's get that out of the way so we can have a decent evening."

Decent evening? "The idea of sleeping with me repulses you so much?" *Shut up, idiot.*

Paris closes her eyes and takes a deep breath before she looks back at me. "I'll take the sofa or the hammock." She points toward the beach at the back of the house.

"Okay." I'm not letting her do that, but I won't argue that now.

She watches me as I chop the tomatoes and cucumber for the salad and put the pasta in the boiling water. Even though we are at odds in all the important directions of our lives, having Paris watch me cook has an air of peace.

Of this strange domesticity. And I don't mind it at all.

Minus the unresolved issues.

"How come you know how to cook?" She breaks the silence.

"When my parents shipped my sister to boarding

school in Europe, we would visit her during the breaks because she didn't want to come back home."

"And that led you to cooking?" She cocks her head and a few drops of water from her hair land on the soft skin just above the swell of her breast. I almost bobble the knife.

I clear my throat, grateful she can't see my hard-on from where she sits. "It wasn't completely voluntary. At the beginning of every summer, the three of us would suggest what we wanted to do for those two weeks and then play poker. The winner's idea went. One summer Saar got really good—I'm pretty sure she cheated somehow. Unfortunately, that was the summer she wanted to go to a cooking school in Tuscany."

Paris smiles. "And you obliged her. What a great big brother you are."

I bow theatrically. "Thank you for recognizing that. Cal bailed the second day after he almost burned down the kitchen."

Paris laughs and the sound pleases me unreasonably. We stare at each other for a moment.

It's like she forgot she was mad at me and looks at me with different eyes. Softer. Curious. Open.

The kitchen timer dings, taking me away from the moment of truce between us. I turn to the oven.

"Dinner will be served in five outside by the pool." I take the dish out of the oven.

She slips down from the stool when her phone rings. She fishes it from some hidden pocket in the flowy skirt and her shoulders sag when she reads out the screen.

"I'll be outside." She slides the screen door open and sneaks out to sit at the table.

I strain my ears, only marginally focused on plating our meal.

Outside at the round table by the closed pool—this place really is less than ideal at the moment—Paris puts her phone down and hits the screen.

A male voice comes from the device. I can't hear what he is saying, but I don't like how she reacts.

Scooting her legs up, she hugs her knees and lowers her forehead to them. What the hell is going on? I pick up our plates.

I should let her have the conversation in private, but I'm not that noble, so I use my elbow to open the screen door and step outside.

"But if the job isn't happening, why don't you return and help us work on Quaintique? This is really the worst time for you jet-setting around the world."

"It's not like I took vacation, Barry. Believe me, I'd like to be there with you"—I wince at her words—"but it's just not possible right now. I can't command the weather."

"And what happened there? Why isn't the new client biting?"

"We'll talk about it when I return, Barry. In the meantime, make sure that the Rodriguezes are happy, and the team does all the research for Quaintique while taking care of the ongoing projects."

"I don't like it, Paris. I don't like it at all that you're bailing again when the shit is getting real."

What the fuck? Who is this asshole? How dare he talk to her like that? I stride to the table and Paris jumps.

"Don't talk to her like that," I bark.

"Who is that?" the man on the other line asks.

"I have to go, Barry." She taps the screen to disconnect the call. "What the hell?"

"He can't talk to you like that." I put the plates down.

"And you shouldn't listen to a private conversation." She retreats from the table. Embarrassed? Annoyed?

"I overheard, sorry. Who was that asshole?"

"My colleague. And I don't appreciate you barging in. Or you constantly giving me your opinion about my life."

Is she for real? "Your colleague? You mean your employee? He crossed so many lines. You can't let people walk all over you like that."

She sighs and sits down. "Let's eat before it gets cold."

Fuck. This is not going well. Not at all. But for fuck's sake, Barry the asshole should get a grip.

Paris picks up the cutlery and attacks the plate like she hasn't eaten in a month. I watch her for a moment. I never thought that watching a woman wolfing down a meal would be this satisfying.

"I let them down before. After they dragged Gio through the mud with the false sexual harassment accusations, I lost a few clients by association. It scared me and I stepped back from the planned expansion into commercial projects. Barry is just excited about the Quaintique pitch..." She looks up with her fork halfway to her mouth.

"It's okay. If my father has his way, Quaintique is going to outgrow, outperform and outlive us. It's a great company to work with. Based on my research." I shrug.

She considers me for a moment, her eyes softening again. "I really want to get it." She bites her lower lip, excitement-laced vulnerability seeping through. God, she's beautiful.

"You will. But maybe you should put Barry in charge instead of letting him bully you." I'm not sure if Barry is qualified for a promotion, but it seems he's eager enough.

She takes another bite and chews for a moment.

"That is actually a good idea. I trust him, and it would please his ego."

"And he'll treat you with the respect you deserve."

A shy smile blooms into a grin on her face. "Thank you."

"You're welcome. Do you want another serving?" I point to her almost empty plate.

"Oh." Her eyes widen, red coloring her cheeks. "I didn't even realize I gobbled it down already. This baby makes me act..." She stops, as if broaching that particular topic is scandalous, or forbidden.

"Paris, you're having my child. We need to move on from the cat-and-mouse dynamic. We need to talk about this."

She lowers her head. "I know."

The short admission carries so much heaviness that the hair bristles on my nape. Why is she so fucking stubborn? Doesn't she see I can make all her worry go away?

"What were you thinking when you orchestrated this?"

Okay, that's a fair question. But it's not like I can change the circumstances anymore. "I was hoping you would see what a good catch I am." I wiggle my eyebrows and she rolls her eyes.

"I'm serious, Finn. What were you hoping to accomplish?"

"I thought if you were forced to spend time with me, you would relent and accept my proposal." I shrug and push my plate away.

"What proposal?" She snorts.

Not sure what's so funny. "To marry me."

Paris jumps up and stares at me. She opens her mouth and closes it again, fisting her hands.

"Jesus fucking Christ, Finn, grow up. First, you try to bully me into marrying you, and then you practically kidnap me. Whatever happened to getting down on one knee with a huge diamond?"

I stand up, which might not be a good idea because she flinches, and now I'm towering above her and she steps back. I'm someone she needs to distance herself from. "Is it jewelry you want?"

She screams, stomping her foot. "That's not the point." Her words echo with frustration. People on other islands probably heard her.

No one has ever driven me this crazy. Not even my father. "Then enlighten me. What is the point? Because I'm fucking trying to do the right thing here."

"That's it, that right there is the point." She wiggles her finger in front of me and starts toward the house. "That you don't even know what you're doing wrong."

She barges inside and I follow her. What is her fucking problem? Sure, the situation isn't ideal, but we need to fucking move on from here.

Entering the bedroom, she starts opening and closing cabinets. "I specifically told you I'm not ready to go away, and you just went on executing your will. This..." She swings a finger between us. "This thing between us would never work. You pointed out that I let Barry bully me. Well, it's time I stop letting *anyone* bully me anymore." She jerks linens from a closet. "I'll sleep on the couch."

Fuck. "Don't be ridiculous. Take the bed."

"I don't want to sleep in your father's filthy bed." She marches out of the bedroom.

"Fine," I snap, and slam the door closed.

Chapter 15

Finn

I toss and turn, unable to sleep. A lot of the things she spat at me earlier rang true. The woman makes me act desperate.

What is so repulsive about me?

Not even my own father can accept me.

And with Paris? I never seem to do the right thing. No matter what. She's like a spark too close to my fuse. I should talk to her. In the morning, first thing.

I'll apologize for this stupid idea. Note to self: never listen to fucking Reilly.

Then, I'll get her the helicopter so she can leave. What was I thinking? The woman doesn't want me in New York. Why would she change her mind in the middle of the Pacific Ocean?

For a moment there, we had a connection during

dinner, but no matter what harmony we find, it never lasts.

If she doesn't want to be with me, I can't force her. That's it. I'm going to tell her now, she can leave. It's not like I'm able to sleep, anyway.

I pad to my door and open it quietly. As much as I want to have the conversation out of the way, I don't think waking her up would improve the tone of that conversation. But then I doubt she can sleep.

A soft moan reaches me as I turn the corner.

And fuck me.

The dragon seems to have finally relaxed. I can only see the shorter side of the sofa by the window beside the patio door, currently draped with Paris's hair.

The moon illuminates her skin in the soft light that makes her look ethereal. A vision.

She didn't even bother to change out of her dress. Her shoulders strain as she arches her back. Her skirt is around her waist, exposing her silky legs, but it's her hand between them that roots me to the floor.

She moans again, working her fingers in and out. God, I wish I was on the other side to see her exposed pussy. But being here is somewhat more arousing. The mystery of it.

My hand itches to fist my painfully hard cock, but I

resist. The view is too delicious to disturb. And I don't want her to hear me.

I should do the right thing and turn around. Let her find release.

She arches again, and her other hand finds her breast, then squeezes it hard, massaging. Her breath is more labored now. She arches her neck and I step behind the corner. Shit.

I don't want to move because something tells me she wouldn't appreciate my voyeurism, so I stay with my back to the wall. Her moans grow and I give up. I wish I was a better man. Oh, who am I kidding...

I fist my cock, and to the melody of Paris's whimpers, I come in my shorts like a teenager. She lets out a satisfying sigh, and it takes all my willpower not to barge in there and fuck some sense into her.

Instead, I tiptoe to my room and get in the shower. And like the horny bastard I am, I come again, imagining the sinful body of the woman who wants nothing to do with me, and yet is tied to me forever.

The water beats down on my muscles as I stifle a groan, painting the tiles with ropes of white. I lower my head to the cold wall.

I haven't been with anyone since Paris. Has it been six or seven weeks? Fuck. I haven't been faithful to my hand for that long like... ever.

To my hand or...?

Holy shit. I have been faithful to Paris. I want the stubborn woman. I want her to be mine.

The realization doesn't make me feel any better.

* * *

The phone's ring penetrates the darkness. I groan and pat around the nightstand. Did I forget to turn off the alarm?

I rise to my elbows and check the screen. Fuck me.

"Pa?"

"Did you fucking sneak the renovations item onto the agenda of the next board meeting?"

This wakes me up completely and I sit up in bed. Fucking Cal. I guess he blindsided both of us. At least he could have waited to put it there last minute.

The digits on the clock on the nightstand are just shy of one o'clock in the morning. I run my hand down my face.

"Pa—"

"Don't you 'Pa' me. You wanted to embarrass me. You can't aggravate the board before the vote."

"Maybe the board would hear my proposal." I guess my hope never dies when it comes to him.

He grunts. "They can listen to you when I'm gone. Until then, I'm still in charge. When will I meet your fiancée?"

"Working on it," I answer on autopilot, stifling a yawn.

"Did I wake you?" He sounds appalled.

"I took a week off, remember? I'm on vacation."

"Wonderful. This is the best time to take time off. As if we don't have enough work. I reviewed the last quarter's numbers, and I'm disappointed with you and Cal."

And what's new? "Pa, can we talk about this when I return?"

"Sorry I'm inconveniencing you," he huffs. "What about the child?"

I flinch. "What about it?"

"Demand a paternity test. Don't let someone extort money from you. I did that every time some hussy claimed to be pregnant with me. Dodged a few bullets there." He snorts.

"The child is mine," I snap.

"Don't be naïve. It's not a van den Linden quality. And talk to Cal. I don't want to have another conversation about the renovations. The time is not right." He hangs up.

I sigh and hit my head against the headboard repeatedly. *It sounds like you're not appreciated, so why stay?*

Maybe Paris is right. Maybe I've been holding on to the idea of a family legacy for no good reason. It's

not like my contribution is wanted, let alone appreciated. And the competition has been knocking on my
door for a while.

I pick up the phone and call Cal.

"I didn't expect to hear from you." He pants, probably on his morning run.

"Did you sneak the renos into the board meeting
agenda?"

"I wanted to tell you—"

"Well, Cal, it's one thing to sneak up on Pa, but
you blindsided me, and I don't appreciate being
ambushed in the middle of the night by him."

"Sorry, but what the fuck am I supposed to do,
watching how the hotel becomes a ruin? I was going to
tell you, but I know you have other things to take care
of right now."

"Don't fucking make excuses. This could have
worked if we sneaked it in at the last moment. If you're
trying to go behind Pa's back, do it smartly, you moron.
Or did you just want to piss him off?"

"I wanted him to realize how serious I am about the
changes."

"Well, you certainly made him aware of the level of
idiocy he has to deal with. And you ruined my
vacation."

Well, more of us are responsible for that, but I'm
happy to share the feeling.

He groans. "Sorry, bro. I'm just desperate."

"You and me both, Cal, you and me both." I slide down on to my back and cover my eyes with my arm.

"I take it Paris is still fighting the idea of being tied to you for eternity?"

"Fuck you."

"Can I help?"

"You can help by keeping your nose in your own affairs and out of Pa's antics."

"Hm..."

"What the fuck did you do, Cal?"

"In my defense, Mom can be very persistent."

I sigh, not even sure where this is going, but certain that my day—or rather night—won't get better after I hear what he has to say.

"Spill it," I snap.

"I told her about Paris." He sighs and I exhale a long breath. "After she overheard us and you refused to budge, she was on my case constantly."

"Better on yours than on Paris's."

My chances with Paris are minimal as it stands, but if my mother interferes they will dwindle away completely.

"Sorry, Finn, but maybe it's for the better. Paris is rich and from a good family, her resume is right up Mother's alley. Maybe it's good."

"How? How is it good? She'll scare her away."

"But at least she won't be pushing Samantha on you anymore. Maybe she'll just let you do your thing."

"My thing is not going all that well. Paris is pissed about the getaway."

"Oh, she doesn't like to be blindsided?" He throws my earlier words at me. And the fucker is right. Damn it.

"Watch it, Cal."

He chuckles. "That's what you get for taking advice from your PA."

"Finish your run, and if possible, run into the oncoming traffic." I hang up and chuck the phone across the bed. It slides over the silky sheets and blinks at me, mocking me.

I throw away the blanket and walk to the glass wall that overlooks this side of the island. I slide the screen open and step onto the soft white sand.

The moon glitters in the sea, the waves hum in the air as the light breeze hits my skin. This place is breathtaking, but I can't even think about it.

Pa won't move an inch, and by the time he'll be willing to step down it might be too late for the company. Does he even want me to take over?

Demand a paternity test? That's his idea of starting a family?

Suddenly I'm pissed. At him. At Mother. At Cal.

At Paris. But mostly at myself. I crave his approval so much.

From the man who is too proud to step aside when his time comes.

From the man who never took us for ice cream because he was too busy making money or fucking other women.

From the man who has this fucking island only to do whatever he wants.

No regards for anyone but himself.

And yet, the need for his approval has been driving me for years. Fuck that.

I push both wings of the glass sliding doors open and march into the room. I yank the sheets from the bed, my phone tumbling down with a thud.

I don't even know what I plan to achieve, but acting on the sheer frustration and disappointment, mad at myself, I push the bed outside and drag it through the sand.

When I'm at a safe distance from the house, I leave it there and march to the garden shed, hoping to find what I need.

Chapter 16

Paris

I turn and groan. The freaking moon is so bright. I can't sleep here. I should have taken the bed when he offered.

Why am I so stubborn around him?

Because if I let him win even on the smallest insignificant matter, he would consume me.

Because I still dream of a perfect fairytale.

My palm finds my lower belly.

My fairytale.

A very different version from what I ever planned. I want this baby. So why am I hanging on to the idea of how it was "supposed" to happen? The how already happened.

It's not fair to me. But it's not fair to Finn either. The man stirs so much in me. And not all of it is bad. Can I give him a chance?

I'm frozen in this state of indecision and it's exhausting. Every time I chance a glance of a man I can see myself letting in eventually, he does something to destroy the tentative image.

Huffing, I flip on to my back and open my eyes. The light dancing on the ceiling is too warm for the moon. I sit up and look outside.

What the hell? A bonfire?

I scramble to my feet and scurry through the room toward the bedroom. "Finn?"

I knock on the door. "Finn, are you there?"

Silence.

Sighing, I crack the door open. The flickering lights are dancing on the floor, walls and ceiling here. I push the door open and freeze. The space where the bed stood yawns empty.

"Finn?" I croak, even though it's evident he isn't here.

The glass side of the room is wide open, and I finally spot him sitting on a large round daybed just outside the bedroom. Hunched over, he rests his elbows on his knees, staring at the fire in the distance.

I look at the empty floor where the outline of the bed is marked by the different coloring on the wooden floor planks, then back at the bonfire.

He burned the bed.

He burned the bed.

He burned the fucking bed.

I don't know what to make of it. Either I'm trapped on this island with a crazy person, or this was just the most ridiculous attempt at a romantic gesture.

He turns his head, and our eyes meet. There is so much resignation in his face. I can't reconcile it with the bully who carries himself like the world owes him something.

Several beats of time pass, perhaps an eternity, as we stare at each other amid the flickering flames. I almost turn to leave because it feels like I'm intruding on some personal crisis here, but my legs refuse to move.

I think he wants me to stay.

Or it's me who wants him to want me to stay.

Finn sighs, maybe, and looks away, boring his gaze back into the flames.

Slowly, like the flames were licking the floor here, I cross to him. Of course, my legs—having just refused to walk away—don't have any problems moving toward him. It's my head that protests quietly.

He practically kidnapped me. He doesn't deserve my... My what? I don't even understand what I'm walking into.

Finn doesn't acknowledge me, but shifts to the side, offering me a seat.

I take it and collapse beside him. For a moment, we

just sit and watch the fire. I've never been around a campfire, but I can see the appeal.

It's calming, but also intimate. And under the spell of the playful flames, I lean into that intimacy.

"What happened?"

He chuckles, but there is no mirth in it. "You were right. I shouldn't have brought you here. I shouldn't have tricked you. I'm sorry."

He looks at me and his gaze burns stronger than the blazing fire in front of us.

This is not what I expected him to say, but I know he means it.

If there ever was a moment of honesty between us, this is it. And it's like we need to absolve each other, let the flames eat our preconceptions, fears, hesitations, disappointment.

It can all burn, along with his father's filthy bed.

"I'm sorry I lied to you," I whisper in the way of accepting his apology. Because I was the one who started this, after all.

His shoulders relax a bit, and he nods slightly before returning his attention to the flames.

We sit there in silence, and for the first time since this whole thing exploded in our faces, I feel like we're sharing something real.

Maybe not the practical words we need to utter.

Maybe not commitments or arrangements that will have to happen at some point.

But something else. A silent bond. Or perhaps the beginning of truce and understanding.

"No one accepts me."

I wince at his words.

There is so much hurt in that short sentence, I almost tell him that I do. I accept him. But I'm not sure that's true yet.

On some level I do, with abandon. On another I do because of the necessity of our situation. But there is still a part of me that can't leap into this.

And yet, no one deserves to feel like this. I turn to face him. He moves his hand to touch mine. Just gently placing his pinkie on top of mine.

It's a feather-like touch, but it screams loudly. The raw need of wanting to be seen. Heard. Understood.

His profile glistens in the shimmering light.

He's beautiful, but that perfect face is marred with a fight he's been waging probably since he was just a little boy.

I can't tell him I accept him. But perhaps I can show him. For a few moments, I can accept him. Wholly. Honestly. Unconditionally.

I stand up, step in front of him and hesitate. Maybe I shouldn't. *Should and would are your biggest enemies.*

I don't know who am I right now.

Am I the woman who is too nice to everyone? Is that what I'm doing?

Or the woman who is tired of this back and forth between us and who'd rather surrender than continue waging the war?

Or is it that stupid hormone-induced lust that has been my companion lately?

Perhaps all of it.

Or something else completely.

Because a part of me just wants to make him feel better. In the world where he believes no one accepts him, I want to make him forget. I wish I knew why.

Taking another half step, I block the fire completely and my legs brush against his thighs. Finn's hooded eyes lock with mine as I gather my long skirt and straddle him.

He leans back onto his elbows, never disconnecting our gazes. I lower myself down and the slight friction against his shorts... Jesus. I'm so ready it's embarrassing.

Finn is impassive. So different from our first time. Like he's waiting to see how far I take it. Or perhaps he doesn't need to fuck at this moment.

Though judging by the steel in his shorts that nestled itself between my folds effortlessly, I don't think his body is on board with whatever hesitation his brain wages.

I circle my hips, stifling a moan. I want to lead, to help him find his release, but I'm falling apart before we even started.

My earlier orgasm only primed me up for this. I swallow, trying to figure out what I see in his face.

It's like he doesn't want to care. The fire heats my back, but it's the cool indifference in his face that breaks a sweat on my skin. Was this a mistake? Is he going to reject me?

I want to close my eyes, but his gaze holds me prisoner.

I circle my hips again, and this time he shuts his eyes briefly and shakes his head, like he's trying to shed an unwanted thought. Then he groans and reaches for my hips.

"No touching."

Finn's eyes snap open, and I realize it was me speaking. Where did that come from? The delicious darkness that crosses his face almost pushes me over the edge. Jesus, I'm a ball of sensitive nerves.

His gaze burns my skin, incinerating all rational thought. *Okay, Paris, you started this, so you'd better go all in.*

I let my eyes roam down his glistening torso and then reach to run my nails around the planes of his muscles. Finn falls onto his back, sucking in air. His hands jerk up, but he stops himself, balling them into fists.

Seeing the effect I have on him boosts me and I lean forward, darting my tongue out. And before I lower my head and trace his skin with it, I glimpse the arousal on his face.

I taste him. Tease him. Tempt him.

All while I grind myself against his erection. I don't even mind the layer of fabric between us.

His hand moves again, and I straighten up, gripping his wrists. He can overpower me easily, but he doesn't, and God it makes me feel powerful.

I continue dry humping him, moaning and whimpering, watching the subtle reactions on his face. The way he admires the view. The way his jaw is ticking with effort. The way he hums.

"Fuck, Paris, you should see yourself now. Such a beautiful girl."

His words break me, I arch my back, let go of one of his hands and find my clit to help me get there. And I do. I almost fall back as I fall apart, but Finn grabs my hips, holding me in place.

"Fuck," he cries, and takes over.

In one swift move, he shoves me to the side, turns me and props me on my knees, pushing me between my shoulder blades and hiking my hips up.

I'm still dazed from my orgasm when he drives into me, taking my breath away. I cry out and he stills.

A beat passes when I try to adjust to his size, but I'm crazed with arousal just from the feel of him inside me.

"Finn, for fuck's sake, move." I push my hips against him.

He chuckles and finally starts moving, and oh my God, I started this to help him find release, but I may need this more than him.

There is no finesse or gentleness as he pounds me like a piston. At least this daybed is on the sand or we would be flying around the tiles.

Finn leans over me, gripping the backrest with his hand as he rides me like a man possessed.

"Those sounds, Paris. All your mews are killing me. Let go, my good little kitten."

My brain doesn't even process his words before I scream his name and fall apart for the second—well, third time—tonight.

My elbows collapse and I fall face down, screaming into the fabric of the mattress, wonderfully spent.

But Finn wastes no time. He flops on his back next to me and maneuvers me around like a rag doll, flipping me around and on top of him.

I straddle him again, but this time I'm facing the bonfire and a very impressive cock.

"Scoot up, kitten." He drags my hips up his torso to his face and then gently pushes my back. He lowers my hips down, almost violently, and I'm afraid I might smother him.

"Finn, this won't—" My words die as his tongue dives into me. I almost fall face down onto his cock, completely losing any control of my body.

He eats me like I'm the most delicious meal, with a fervor and dedication that wipe all thoughts from my mind.

When I fist his cock he hums against me, and I almost come from that slight vibration.

I want to take him into my mouth, but I don't think I can control my jaw while he's driving me insane like this. I try to move my hand, but I'm completely spent, so I lower myself and lick his dripping tip.

God, he tastes good. I moan as he does something with his tongue that hits the right bundle of nerves, and then he lifts my hips and I whimper at the loss of the connection.

"Be a good girl and take my cock down your throat, kitten."

I don't know if he realizes that speaking so close to my pussy sends divine shivers everywhere.

"I've never done this before. I don't think I can

control it. I don't want to snap my jaw involuntarily—"
I moan as he breathes at my entrance.

"Don't worry, kitten, I'll happily lose my cock in your gorgeous mouth." He hikes up his hips before he dives back to eating me.

I relax my jaw and take him as far as I can. I need to support myself with one hand, but I wrap the other one around his base. Jesus. This would be so much easier if he wasn't doing such a good job, making me lose my mind.

But he tastes so good, and then I realize how his ministrations change the rhythm to match my efforts. He pauses to deal with the influx of sensation now and then, and I love the harmony.

It's not just him driving me crazy. It's the other way around too, and suddenly the game adds to the thrill, and I finally let go of my worries and enjoy him while chasing my own high.

"Fuck, Paris." He utters a guttural groan, holding my hips just above his face as he comes into my mouth. I swallow all I can before I take a real breath, but there is no reprieve.

The man is crazy. He dives back in, feasting on me like I'm the only source of protein for his stamina. It doesn't take long before I see the stars, writhing and shaking, completely out of control.

He flips me around, flat on my back, and covers me

with his body. He possesses what feels like inhuman strength.

I don't know when he lost his shorts, but I'm still in my dress, though I'm pretty sure the skirt is ripped.

Finn stares into my eyes for a beat, our hearts hammering against each other and suddenly I feel self-conscious.

I initiated this, and now we've crossed another bridge, but I'm not sure where it's led us. Or rather misled us.

As if he senses my hesitation—or perhaps learned how to read my mind while I rode his face—Finn shakes his head. "Don't."

That's all he says before he captures my lips in a gentle but urgent, kiss. It's in such a contrast to the fucking we've just done, I don't quite know how to handle it.

But I know I don't want him to stop. It's way more intimate than what we've just done. A kiss that flutters in my stomach, speeds up my already hammering heart and plants a seed of hope.

He cups my face, sucking, teasing, biting ever so gently. And I reciprocate, because our story might not be a straightforward one, but it deserves an honest attempt.

Maybe not forever. But at least for now.

Chapter 17

Finn

The sound of the ocean echoes like white noise as we both lie in silence, but neither of us is succumbing to sleep.

It's like we finally jumped through the invisible barrier and moved our relationship forward. But we don't want to fall asleep, fearing things will feel different again during the daylight.

We can't avoid reality for much longer because the dawn is already greeting the darkness, but I want to enjoy this new forged connection between us. Okay, it's just physical, but it counts for something.

Fuck, I almost lost it when she straddled me earlier. That bold move mixed with the hesitation I felt from her was the sexiest thing ever. But I'm painfully aware she couldn't get off this island soon enough earlier.

Paris is snuggled against me, and I'm pretty sure

this is the first time I've ever cuddled with a woman. And the weird part is, I don't mind it.

Understatement.

I'm enjoying it. She fits nicely under my shoulder, her head resting in the hollow under my neck. In the madness of my life, this kind of stillness would normally drive me crazy, but here with her, it calms me.

Something has shifted between us. She looked like she was retreating right after sex, but she welcomed my kiss and then we settled into this silence. I'm just not sure what its significance is.

She smells of my soap, and now of me. Like she is mine.

Maybe because she saw me at my most vulnerable earlier and we've woven this unexpected bond.

Idiot, she's having your child, for fuck's sake. That doesn't change the fact she wanted nothing to do with me just a couple of hours ago.

"So, was this a pity fuck?" I ask.

She chuckles and shifts. Resting her chin on her hand, she looks at me. This just-fucked look on her will be the death of me. She's the most beautiful woman— person—I've ever seen.

"It might have started as one. You seemed like you needed the release. But I was after my own as well.

This baby makes me horny." She buries her face into my chest, groaning.

I snort. "I've seen." Shit. Did I just admit my voyeur moment?

She snaps her eyes back to me. "You've seen?"

"I happened to almost interrupt you earlier." I nod in the house's direction. "Next time come and find me. Well, and then come." I wink, and she gasps.

Rolling on to her back, she covers her face with both hands. I laugh and flip around. Bracketing her face with my elbows, I rest my leg between hers. I pry her arms away and above her head, but she closes her eyes.

"Look at me," I order, and she shakes her head. "Look at me, Paris," I warn, and she opens one eye. Quirking my eyebrow up, I wait, and she sighs and opens both eyes, glaring at me.

I swipe loose strands of hair from her face. "It was the hottest thing I've ever seen."

She groans and lifts her head, banging her forehead against my shoulder. I laugh and take her with me, rolling onto my back.

We stay silent for a moment, but there is no way I can sleep, so I decide to potentially spoil the night and unearth another item.

"Would you have found me?"

"What do you mean?" Her breath is warm on my

chest. She draws mindless circles on my shoulder and it feels so right.

I want to freeze this moment. Minus the topic, because if I'm honest with myself, I fear the answer.

"Did you plan on finding me and telling me about the baby?"

"Yes." She doesn't hesitate and it makes me unreasonably pleased. "But first I was working up the courage to ask London for your full name." She pushes up to a sitting position and I don't like the loss of her warmth, but I guess this isn't the time to be selfish.

She pulls her knees to her chin and rearranges the skirt around her. Fuck. How am I only now realizing she's not naked? I got so lost in her, I... Okay, let's file this analysis for later.

"What do you mean courage?"

I push up as well, with my back against the rattan backrest. She plays with the hem of her dress, thinking. Or avoiding the conversation, I'm not sure.

"Growing up, Lo has always been the queen in every situation. She takes what she wants, and I used to try to be the nice one and remain in her shadow. It's not her fault. I love my sister, but her personality is so powerful that I've always been London's twin. Nobody cared about me, Paris, much.

"She's always been adventurous, and I was... I don't know, just drawing in my room. When you mistook me for her, I felt liberated and I went with it. When we were growing up, we took each other's places all the time. But confessing to Lo I pretended to be her now, I..."

"I get it." And I do.

While there has never been rivalry between me and my siblings, I've tried, all my life, to get out of the shadows so my father sees me. No good has come out of it. Until the burned bed today.

She looks at me with a sad smile. "I'm sorry."

I take her hand and kiss her knuckles. "Me too."

She cocks her head in question.

"About many things, but about you feeling that you needed to pretend to be someone else. For what it's worth, I think I met the better twin."

A sound escapes her that grabs my cock's attention and she lunges at me, seizing my lips. Her kiss is electrifying and redeeming. "Thank you for saying that."

"It's true."

She smiles and settles on her haunches. We stare at each other, an unexpected harmony coursing between us. We're good at this wordless communication. Hopefully we can find the same synchronicity in words.

I tap my leg and she nestles herself in my lap, the stupid skirt in her way.

"You ripped my skirt," she huffs, laying her head on my chest.

"Not enough, if you ask me."

She laughs and pushes off me, back on to her haunches.

My cock stirs from all the fidgeting and friction, and then hardens completely when Paris pulls her dress slowly up her thighs, her long fingers trailing up her silky skin.

Without breaking eye contact, she drags the fabric up, caressing her thighs.

Fuck, it's almost like our first night. Her sensual undressing is out of this world. Strip clubs could take lessons from her. It's wanton and graceful at the same time. A fucking turn-on.

She shimmies off the dress and drops it to the ground in one elegant motion.

"Better?" She moves her torso in a fluid dance move, and I lose my mind completely.

I jump up and take her over my shoulder, enjoying her squeals. "What are you doing?" She beats her fists against my ass and I laugh as I run toward the ocean.

The waves are at my knees when I slide her down my body. "Let's clean you up, you dirty little kitten."

"Technically, you got me more dirty," Paris sighs as we lie wet and naked on the daybed again.

She's on her belly and perched on her elbows, the water droplets sliding into her cleavage.

"Are you complaining?" I swat at her ass and prop myself sideways, wrapping my leg over hers.

"About the orgasm, no, but the manhandling beforehand... hmm..." She purses her lips, pretending to think about it. "Not so much either."

She giggles and turns on to her back, stretching her arms above her head and sighing contentedly, just shy of purring.

Kitten.

I lean down and kiss her belly. "Maybe I should treat you with more care, though."

My heart jumps to my throat as I try to swallow around it. Fuck. What if I hurt the baby? I wasn't even thinking about it. I pounded her like an animal and then threw her around and over my shoulder.

I look at her, panic rising, but I'm met with a blissed expression.

She reaches out and rakes her fingers through my hair, a smile lingering. "Relax, caveman, I haven't gotten too far in the pregnancy book yet, but I know I should just treat my body the same way as before. I checked to make sure I can dance, do yoga and Pilates."

I eye her for a moment, the panic just barely at bay. With my hand on her flat stomach, I vow to study up and treat her more gently.

"Stop worrying and kiss me." She pulls at my hair.

And I crawl up her body, planting kisses on my way, loving her reactions and the feel of her. This is too good to be true, and I make another vow to myself.

I can't fuck this up.

I finally reach her mouth and seal that vow with a punishing kiss. Letting her know she has no choice in this anymore. This is happening. Not that she knows what's going on in my head.

The sun is above the horizon and we still lie there, unable to move anymore, but unwilling to sleep.

Just staring into the slowly dying fire and touching, like we want to make sure the other person is still there.

"Do you want to tell me about this?" Paris points to the ashes of my father's bed.

I wish I could explain my actions with words. But I acted on pure anger and frustration. So I tell her what I know before I can consider her judgment. "My father pissed me off."

She stays silent for two or a thousand beats while I question most of my life choices. "Do you go around burning things when you're pissed off?"

I snort, not expecting her to take that direction.

She turns her head, looking at me. "I think it's something I should know."

"This is my first act of arson. Or an attempt at a campfire." I stall and squeeze her hand. "I've been desperate. My father insists I need to marry before he hands me the company."

She flinches and closes her eyes. "Is that why you insist on marriage?"

"No," I say way too quickly. Frankly, I can't know. Both needs rose at the same time. "That's why am I going about it all wrong."

"But you proposed to get your company?" She sits up now, moving away from me.

"Paris, I-I don't think so." I sit up as well and run the hand down my face. "I really enjoyed our first night, and I texted you after and London... well, it felt like you ghosted me. Not something I've ever experienced, so I was mad at you. Disappointed. When I saw you on the fucking catwalk at that charity fashion show, I-I couldn't see through the dejection and anger at your little charade, but a part of me... a big, big part of me was relieved. That I found you again."

She relaxes slightly, sighing.

"And then I found out you were pregnant, and it all got too complicated. Yes, marrying you is an easy solution to get my company, but it's not the only reason. I want to be around you and yes, I know, we don't know each other, but we're tied together whether we like it or not. I want to dive deeper." I look away, scratching my neck.

I sense her moving, but before I can freak out that

she's leaving, her warm breath on my back calms me again. While it's somewhat comforting, fuck, I can't deal with another rejection from her. Not right after we just rekindled something.

"I think this pregnancy is forcing us into something and we'll never know what our motivations are, or if there are any others. But Lo showed me the text you sent the morning after the one-night stand, so I believe you wanted to explore more of us."

She puts her hand on my shoulder and I chance a look at her. "I told you that night it wasn't a one-night stand for me. It might have started like one..."

She smiles. "It wouldn't have been for me either, but—"

I turn away. I'm too tired to deal with another but.

She sighs. "Remember my bucket list?"

"I remember you stealing my coffee," I tease, not really feeling lightness in this conversation, though.

"Donating it," she huffs and leans her head on my shoulder. We watch the last sparks of the former bonfire as she continues.

"Another item on my bucket list was a one-night stand. But that was pushing my boundaries too far, and when an attractive, hot god of vengeance thought I was someone else, I saw it as an opportunity."

I pull her into my lap again and bury my nose in

the crook of her neck. I'm not sure how I feel about her confession.

I'm just a failed one-night stand for her.

Or maybe I'm too tired to interpret what all of this means.

"So, you think I'm hot?" Let's move away from the loaded questions.

She throws her head back, laughing. "That's what you focus on?"

"Focusing on the important." I shrug, grinning.

"Maybe I need to list everything that annoys me about you, so your head deflates enough to enter the house again." She giggles, but it turns into a yawn.

"You need to rest." I lean back and pull her with me, adjusting her on top of me. Where she belongs.

"I can't sleep like this."

"Hush, kitten."

Chapter 18

Paris

I moan, my limbs sore from all the gymnastics last night, but at least I'm rested. I think.

Opening my eyes, I smile at the most beautiful, peaceful view of crystal clear water and white sand.

The only thing missing is Finn. I stretch. I don't know when he left, but the daybed's roof is pulled up, shading my naked skin from the sun that is already high.

It might not be morning anymore, but my morning sickness lingers anyway. I should try to eat something.

I make my way to the house, strangely aware of my nakedness, but kind of enjoying that it's just the two of us, and that there is no need for modesty.

The scent of Finn's soap and the sound of water lead me to the bathroom, and I stop in the doorway.

He stands under the pellets of hot water, surrounded by steam. With his hands on the tiles, his back stretches into a perfect V.

Ripped shoulders, tanned skin, a perfect ass. I take it all in, admiring my view.

Finn shifts and our eyes meet. I'm still sore from last night, but somehow his one look primes me for more already. Jesus.

"Good morning, kitten. Hop in."

I swallow. The man is too sexy for his own good. Or I'm too hormonal. I take one step toward him when my eyes land on his impressive erection.

"Already missing me." I don't even bother to lift my gaze, ogling him. Delicious.

"Get in now." His order carries a note of impatience.

I lean against the vanity, trying to look sexy and not think about my irritable stomach. "I think you owe me a show."

Something crosses his face, and he goes still for a moment. Then he licks his lips and my breath hitches.

There is a glass wall and some distance between us, but I swear I can taste him in my mouth.

He fists his cock and I'm so mesmerized by the sight of it that I can't look away. The veins of his forearm, the size of him, the glistening tip. It all pools in my core as I try to remain upright watching him.

He plasters one hand on the glass wall and I'm drawn to it like a moth to a flame. I reach up and place my palm against his, the coolness of the glass such a contrast with the heat flowing through me.

Finn's eyes roam down my body, offered to him but unreachable through the barrier between us. He can't touch me, but it feels like he is. My senses heighten and I might come just from looking at him. Having him look at me.

He lets out a groan and strokes himself almost violently. All his muscles are taut and beautiful, but I keep most of my attention on his hand.

"Fuck, kitten," Finn grunts, and I snap my eyes to him as the ropes and ropes of white paint the glass between us.

My knees buckle under the intensity of his hooded eyes on me. If I ever felt adored in my life, this moment rivals it tenfold. Jesus.

We stare at each other, our hands still touching without contact, and I realize my own arousal drips between my legs.

I guess there is a remedy for morning sickness, or at least a therapy to make you forget about it.

Finn slides to the side and grabs me, dragging me with him under the stream of water while seizing my lips.

His kiss is urgent, ravishing, worshiping, hungry.

Like I'm his oxygen and his lifeline. Like he can't get enough of me.

And God, I could get used to that.

I only hope we can draw on that same need and energy when we get back to the real world.

* * *

"No, Barry, it's because I believe you're the best for the job. I'm emailing you my suggestions right now, and when I'm back you can present me the top-line concepts."

I didn't expect putting Barry in charge would feel this right. He's thrilled and I'm relieved. I'm truly relieved I don't have to be the only one carrying this responsibility.

"I appreciate your trust." Does he sound emotional?

"I'm sure I made the right decision." I smile, the breeze playing with my hair as I watch Finn through the screen door, whisking something in a bowl.

His hair keeps falling into his eyes and he keeps tossing his head, but even that ridiculous move he manages with sexiness. Jesus, I'm completely high on Finn van den Linden.

Well, this relaxed, playful, caring version of him.

Not the angry, nervous, choleric explosiveness he usually spreads around.

"Thank you, Paris. Though—"

Oh boy, what now? "Yes, Barry?"

"Come back as soon as possible. Preferably before I kill the Rodriguezes."

I chuckle. "I'll call them and make sure they behave. Or maybe I'll just fire them." That would feel good.

"Really?" Barry's voice carries too much hope for my comfort. Has everyone been waiting for me to get rid of them?

Why did I even say that to him? "I'll call them to keep them off your back. Goodbye, Barry."

I hang up and sigh, closing my eyes.

"Is everything okay?" Finn slides the screen door open and pulls me up.

He kisses me and holds me close, and I immediately feel better. This man's scent—cologne, his natural musk, whatever it is—is my Xanax.

"Yeah." I sigh. "Barry is thrilled about his new responsibility, and I'm relieved. Thank you for your advice."

"But?"

How is he so attuned to my thoughts already?

"Well, there is this couple, the Rodriguezes, who have been renovating their house for months now.

They drive us crazy with all the changes, but they pay the bills..." I don't even know how to explain the situation.

Finn rubs my arms. "Paris, are you having financial troubles? Do you need money?"

I flinch and step back. "What? Of course not. I don't want your money."

"It's not like I'd miss it." He throws his arms up. "Don't act so offended all the time." He grinds his jaw.

And his signature annoyance is back.

"Then stop offending me. I have a very healthy trust fund portfolio and my company is thriving, if you need to know."

"Okay, kitten." He levels his tone and reaches his hand out. Somehow that plus the pet name placate me enough to step back into his embrace. "When you say they pay the bills, it sounds like your bottom line depends on this one client."

The statement shocks me. When he puts it like that—the truth glaring me in the face—I feel like an idiot.

"But we've done so much work for them already, and it would be nice to see the project completed," I say to his chest, because I can do without his scrutiny.

"But not at any cost." He nudges my chin up with his finger. "I know close to nothing about creative jobs like yours, but I always imagined they bring joy. Why put up with assholes?" He kisses my forehead.

He's not patronizing, just helpful. And that is almost worse. I don't know how to reconcile that. How to accept his help. Especially since he has no idea how hesitant I am to pursue my true creative calling.

I smile at him. "It would feel good to fire them."

He grins. "You see. People who don't appreciate you shouldn't pollute your environment."

"And yet—" I can't help but point out his situation. Partially to take the attention off me.

"That's different." He sighs and takes us both down to the seat. The lounge chair squeaks in protest as we descend, but Finn seems too far away in his mind to realize.

I wrap my hands around his neck. "I don't see how it's different, aside from me building my own firm and you being born to own yours," I challenge.

"Yeah, I was born into it, but it might be foolish to wait my turn. By the time my opportunity comes, the company might be gone." He plants small kisses on my shoulder, my clavicle, my neck.

It's not a heated need, but rather a gentle connection. I can give him that. Whatever he needs to draw from me to be the man he could be without his father constantly upping his stress level.

We have a long road to travel before this becomes

something real outside of the most pressing necessity, but I want to try.

To stand by him.

To share with him.

To not be alone anymore.

"Why don't you spend your time building something that's yours, then? You want the family legacy because there was never another option presented to you. But you can build your own legacy."

"Yeah, but I practically grew up in that flagship hotel in Manhattan. I really want it."

"Then fight for it. But not with your father. With the board. You need to choose, the legacy or your father's approval. They are connected, but they are not the same."

The torment in his eyes is real, and I cup his face and kiss him.

"Now I'm getting pity kisses?" He chuckles but pulls me tighter, diving into the kiss deeper.

When we come up for air, I whisper in his ear, "This one was compassionate. A step up from the frustration we used to share, if I may say so."

At that, my stomach growls.

"I better feed you, kitten, before you get hangry again."

* * *

"That is so good. Don't stop. Don't stop," I moan, as Finn's fingers dig into my soles.

We're back at the daybed, mostly because the couch was too small and there is no other bed. We ate and took another nap and now we're just lounging lazily, pretending we have no worries in the world.

And I'm enjoying an amazing foot massage. Finn sits at the edge of the bed with my feet in his lap. His hair and skin are wet from the swim he took while I was napping, and I can't say I mind the view.

"I don't think you showed this level of appreciation last night." He leans down and bites my toe.

"Hey." I pull my foot away, but he yanks my ankles, dragging me closer. "Well, maybe there is a reason for that," I tease.

His eyes snap to me, mischief and something dark on his gorgeous face. "Excuse me?"

"I'm just saying..." I feign coyness. "Last night seems so long ago, no wonder this massage is top of my mind."

"Long ago?" He pivots, jerking me to him, my pelvis hitting his cock. "Do you need your memory refreshed, kitten?"

"I might allow that later, once you prove yourself as a masseur."

He laughs. "I think your mewing is proof enough.

Talking about later, do you want me to call you the helicopter?"

He's looking at me, but his face is unreadable.

Expectant?

Pleading?

Or done and ready to leave?

Just like that, he's casually throwing around my departure. What's going on?

"Has the weather cleared?" We haven't even resolved our next steps. I'm not ready to leave. Almost as much as I wasn't ready to stay yesterday. Jesus. Was it only yesterday?

"Yes," he croaks and shifts to the side, avoiding my eyes. "I have to tell you something." A beat of silence passes before he looks at me. In that short moment, my heart rate skyrockets. "Because I want to be honest with you. The weather has never been a problem." Carefully, he watches my reaction.

I slide to sit beside him, our shoulders almost touching. "You lied to keep me here?"

If we didn't spend the night together and didn't talk about his father and so many other things...

If I hadn't seen the man who was raised with a golden spoon but learned to cook for his sister...

The man who desires his family business. Not because it's his rightful inheritance, but because he sees the opportunities to grow it.

The man who showed me bliss seven ways to Sunday and back. Who is a generous lover. Who makes me laugh and reads my body like it's his favorite book.

If the past twenty-four hours hadn't happened, I would have been pissed, but I know he meant well. And yes, he shouldn't have lied, but God, I'm happy I stayed.

"It's not worse than tricking you into coming." He cocks his head.

Oh, that boyish grin. I'm defenseless.

"Maybe I can overlook your proclivity to lies since this entire thing started with me lying. I guess we're even now." I smile.

The relief is visible in his shoulders. "No more lies." He nods.

I scoot to him and cup the back of his neck. "No more lies."

He seizes my lips and kisses me until I'm breath-less. Weightless. Doubtless.

This man is a part of my life now. Whether we are used to it or not. We'd better try to make it work.

But it's not the necessity that ties me to him anymore.

We deserve a chance. Not because I have to give it to us, but because I want to.

"Can we pretend for one more night that the weather conditions are bad?"

The suggestion gets me a dark smirk. "There is a hurricane out there. We better stay." He fists my hair and lowers his forehead to mine.

"We better. It's safer."

"Safety first."

"What should we do?" I muse.

"I have a few ideas." He flips us both around and covers me with his beautiful body.

* * *

"It looks like a three-year-old planned this." I peel away the plastic sheet and peek behind it. Half of the space is already finished with new tiles.

Finn, sprawled on the sofa behind me answering his emails, laughs. "Wait till you see my parents' house. Tacky meets old-fashioned at its best."

See his parents' house? That would mean meeting them. I'm not sure how I feel about that.

"It's an ironic coincidence that you tricked me into coming here to redesign the place without knowing the renovations had started already."

Let's not talk about meeting parents just yet. This train is rolling fast enough as it is. Missing stops and all.

"Yeah, I'm going to fire Reilly for that."

I chuckle. "I might need a signed affidavit from your assistant to confirm you didn't know about this."

"I admitted to all my lies already." He pats the spot beside him, throwing his phone on the coffee table.

I take the seat and he kisses my temple. "I was thinking maybe we can start from the beginning."

Taking his hand, I put it on my belly. "I don't think we can rewind this."

His palm is warm through my beach dress and goosebumps sprout all over my skin.

"That we can't, but I have a proposal."

"Not this again," I huff.

He wraps his arms around me, not allowing any distance between us.

"Hear me out." He kisses my temple again and lingers there, his words warm on my skin. "When we get back home, let's date. Let's give us a real shot."

For the first time since this whole thing sneaked up on us, we're truly on the same page. But there is so much at stake for him.

"What about your father's ultimatum? You need to marry. Not only to get your business. To save it."

He cups my face. "I appreciate your concern, but I don't want to marry anyone else."

Chapter 19

Paris

"You better run, kitten. You only have to the count of five."

The threat is deliciously dark, but it's the want in his eyes that reverberates in every single fiber in my body.

"One," Finn says with goosebump-inducing confidence.

I stand up, staring at him, still not believing this is happening, while shaking with anticipation. Holy hotness.

Finn has been pushing my boundaries for the last couple of days. Way more than my bucket list.

We talked about my business and his advice is spot on, but he also encourages me to take steps I've never considered or ones I've feared before.

And when it comes to us... Well, I don't think I've ever felt this free.

We've stayed longer than we should have. But at the same time, we crashed the getting to know each other part and can hopefully venture into an everyday reality stronger and more connected.

"Two." He raises his eyebrow with a perfect poker face.

I'm wearing a white bikini and I'm pretty sure he can see what his game is doing to me. Soaked between my thighs, and my nipples are practically pushing through the fabric.

"Three," he rasps. "You don't want me to catch you, kitten."

Yes, I do. I do. But I want the game too. I turn around and dash away, his dark chuckle too close behind me.

My feet stumble in the soft sand, but I don't look back as I round the house. I have no chance—he is on my heels in no time.

I steal a glance over my shoulder and meet his mischievous grin. I switch direction and almost trip, but I find my balance. Zig-zagging between the palm trees, I try to escape him while I desperately want him to catch me.

The hunt is exhilarating and the anticipation

builds inside me. Funnily enough, this whole thing started when he hunted me after the coffee shop fiasco.

I slip, the sand sliding under my feet, but before I fall, strong hands catch me in midair.

"You're mine now, kitten. Mine to do whatever I want with."

The threat is so deliciously dark and full of temptation, I don't even try to protest or fight him.

Finn flops me into the hammock suspended between two palm trunks. My legs are dangling as my ass sinks into the fabric.

I'm completely at his mercy in this position, and by his hungry look he's incredibly pleased with this scenario.

"Are you mine?" He scoops up my knees and pulls me closer to him, slinging my legs up to his shoulders.

I'm practically upside down, unable to move, his erection perfectly aligned with my center. And so ready. I want to grind myself against him, but even as I try to swing closer, Finn is in control.

"Answer me, Paris," he demands.

My mouth goes dry.

Am I willing to push my own boundaries in this direction?

I think my body is ready, but my mind is conflicted. I'm not sure what to expect. Shouldn't we talk about it first? What does 'to do whatever I want with you' really mean?

But then if we talk about it, we would lose this crazy anticipation. *Christ, Paris, make up your mind.*

Besides, his question feels like so much more than a simple need for consent. Am I his?

Finn strokes my legs gently and I shiver. He kisses my ankle. "I'll take good care of you, kitten. Do you trust me?"

I'm trapped, at his mercy, yet I have the control. That thought empowers me, and I push away my hesitation and really ask myself what I want.

I want this man.

I want to further explore my boundaries with him.

I want freedom.

"I trust you," I croak, and he thrusts his hips, giving me a bit of that friction I so desperately need. "I'm yours."

If there was hunger in his eyes before, the satisfaction and adoration there now splits my chest open. This is so much more than fucking. How did that happen so quickly?

But all thoughts leave my mind when he says, "Tell me when it's too much."

He unties my bikini. The flimsy triangle falls to the side, exposing me.

The slap between my legs comes so unexpectedly

that I cry out, but the initial burn and shock are immediately replaced with an intense heat that has me bucking my hips without thought.

"Aren't you a greedy little kitten?"

"Greedy? Not at all. As you may remember, I can take care of myself." Who is this wanton woman? I raise my eyebrows in challenge. "I don't need you."

Whatever shadow has just passed across his face, I want to feel it all. "I guess I'll have to punish you until you remember how much you do need me," he warns.

The next five slaps come in a quick succession, lighting me on fire. I'm moaning, writhing, begging. Finn teases my core with his fingers, not really hitting the spot, and I groan in frustration.

A sinister chuckle escapes him, and I realize that not giving me what I want is part of the game.

"Finn," I whimper.

"What is it, kitten? Still not greedy?"

The bastard. "I'm greedy." I try to move, but the stupid sling has me trapped. "I'm greedy. I want it all. I want you. Goddammit, Finn."

He shoves two, maybe three fingers into me. "This greedy little pussy is the most beautiful thing in the world. So tight. So ready for me." He pumps me to the brink of orgasm and then withdraws.

"What the fuck?" I snarl and he laughs.

"Beautiful and greedy." He sinks to his knees and dives in with his tongue.

Again, I'm so close I scream at the influx of sensation. But as I clench, practically at the precipice of my release, Finn pulls away.

I scream my frustration. "I swear to god, Finn, you stop this right now."

He raises his arms in surrender. "But of course. You're in charge. If you want me to stop, I won't continue." The smirk on his face makes me murderous.

"That's not what I meant." I try to hoist myself out of this stupid trap.

"Then be specific. Tell me what you meant." He traces his fingers around my core, almost touching me where I need him, but not really.

"I want you to fuck me. I want you to make me come."

"I thought you didn't need me."

"Finn," I warn, and he laughs, but finally he plunges into me.

Lesson learned. Sometimes the reward is worth the wait.

* * *

"Are you going to your brother's?" Finn asks as he opens the door of his town car on the tarmac.

"No, I'll go home." He raises his hand to protect my head as I get inside and rounds the car to sit beside me. He gives the driver my address and hands me a bottle of water.

I frown and take it.

"Have you drunk enough today?" He pulls his phone out.

What? "Yes."

He flips through his phone. "Drink more. You need to stay hydrated."

Is he for real? I'm not five years old. I twist the bottle cap open. "Yes, daddy."

He snaps his eyes to me, and I realize the mistake of my choice of words. "Keep that name for the bedroom, sweetheart." He winks. "And drink please."

"Can I drink when I'm thirsty?" I close the bottle and slide it into the door.

We have just landed, and I'm already annoyed with him.

"Do you fight me on everything out of principle?" He slips his phone into his pocket and turns to face me, his jaw ticking.

And here we are, barely the first few breaths of Manhattan air, and we're back to cat and dog.

"I know when I need to drink," I snap, and of course in that moment I realize I didn't drink enough on the plane, if at all.

I yank the bottle out of the door and down it in one gulp.

Finn captures my lips, biting, teasing, kissing me with a possessiveness that strips me of my thoughts. But I'm still annoyed he pushed the water on me. Even though I needed it.

His idea of caring for me is infuriating.

We arrive at my place and he helps me bring my luggage in, walking inside like he's been here before.

"Where is your closet?"

"I thought you'd head straight for the bedroom," I quip.

"You need to rest."

I sigh. There is no point arguing with him. Mostly because I'm exhausted, and he's right. He puts my luggage in the closet.

"This place is great. You're very talented." He kisses my forehead and marches downstairs.

His compliment comes on the heels of invading my space and annoying me with his helpful suggestions, and I almost rebut on autopilot before I realize what he just said.

"Thank you."

The lower part of my townhouse is a large open concept, not the typical layout. Finn looks around and marches to the kitchen, where he opens the fridge.

"What are you doing? Are you hungry?"

"I'm making sure you have enough food. Do you have a housekeeper?"

I'm so conflicted right now. I'm too tired to fight him and strangely pleased about his care, but not so sold on the delivery.

His dominance might be hot in the bedroom, but I've survived for thirty-three years without him, and I don't need him to parent me.

"My housekeeper comes twice a week. And I do my own shopping."

He blinks a few times and looks at me expectantly, as if waiting for a punchline. I fold my arms across my chest and stare back.

We stay like this for longer than is reasonable, but he can't just take over my life completely.

Finn's jaw is ticking like it did many times before our getaway. Maybe it's an infliction that appears once he enters the city.

"I'll get my housekeeper to stock your fridge tonight." He starts toward the front door.

"I'm not hungry, and I can do my shopping tomorrow."

"I don't want you wandering around supermarkets."

I raise my brows. "Ever heard of Instacart?"

He sighs like I'm the biggest pain in the ass. "Okay, but call me if you need anything."

"Get out of here before I kill you." I swat at him playfully.

He grabs my wrist in mid-air and pulls me to him. Colliding with his firm body is my new favorite thing. The sense of safety and belonging is comforting.

I can't deny the growing heat in my chest about his caring—if somewhat overbearing—concerns.

He lowers his forehead to mine. "It will be strange to sleep without you tonight."

That we can agree on, and I almost invite him to live with me. *You meet a guy and immediately plan the wedding.* London's words ring an alarm in my head.

We agreed to date. Let's focus on that. "We both have an early morning, but maybe you can stay over this weekend." Everything with us has been a sped-up version of a relationship.

"I like that. Get some rest."

"Why didn't I think about that?" Barry slaps his thigh. "You're a genius, Paris." He gathers his notes from our meeting while whistling.

"You've done great. I just polished your concept."

"You're too kind, boss, but we now have a great foundation to deliver the best proposal. Let me get the team to roll with it." He pushes the glass door of the boardroom with his hip and almost skips in excitement on the way to his desk.

Finn

Were you able to eat your breakfast? I missed you last night.

I read the text and roll my eyes.

"Barry seems over the moon." Shayna enters with her notebook.

I've been holding meetings since I arrived this morning. I didn't even get a chance to eat anything yet. Shit. Finn and his clairvoyant questions.

"You did well to put him in charge," she continues. "So how was your getaway? And don't skimp on details."

I shake my head. "What's on the agenda, Shayna?"

She pouts. "You have a meeting with Gina Acardi at four."

"Oh, is it today? Great."

I promised my sister-in-law I'd look at the space she's turning into a new restaurant. I didn't commit yet because it's a commercial project, but with the Quaintique pitch well underway I might just dive into this one.

Only if I like the space. *I thought creative jobs bring joy.*

Which reminds me… "Get me the Rodriguezes on the line. Is there anything else?"

"Besides you dishing on your clandestine getaway that didn't turn into business?"

"Get the Rodriguezes on the phone now, Shayna."

She huffs. "You're no fun."

"I want privacy for the call, so I'll take it here." I doodle on my notepad, slightly nervous but also energized about the call.

"Privacy? Are you? Is this—"

"Shayna, get them on the phone now." I try to sound strict. And I don't fail.

My assistant pivots and runs to actually do her job for once.

The call with Mrs. Rodriguez goes better than I expected, mostly because she's so stunned by my resolute manner that she doesn't speak. She sniffles theatrically as if I killed her cat, but eventually accepts my decision.

Relieved, I lean back in my chair, feeling accomplished. For years I've been shying away from confrontations or from challenging, risky business decisions. And now that I'm leaning into all these changes, it feels good.

Maybe it's a variation of nesting. Cleaning the house before the baby comes. My hands immediately go to my belly.

My life has transformed. And I wouldn't trade it.

Shayna knocks on the glass. I look up, dropping my hands as if she caught me doing something illegal.

"What's that smile about?" She eyes me with raised eyebrows.

"What do you need?"

"There is someone asking for you at reception. They didn't want to tell me anything."

I grab my phone before I leave the boardroom.

"Did you fire them?" Shayna chirps by my side.

I nod and she says something else about a celebration, but I stop listening when my eyes meet a young man in jeans and a leather jacket. He doesn't look like a potential client.

"Ms. Paris Lowe?"

"That's me." He hands me an envelope. "What is this?"

"You've been served, ma'am. Have a nice day."

Chapter 20

Finn

"I won't admit you were right, Reilly. You can stop staring." I type, ignoring my gloating assistant.

"You can deny all you want, but the getaway worked." He continues to neglect the phone buzzing at his desk. And all of his other duties.

"Do your fucking job for once, Ry."

He mumbles something but saunters to his desk, leaving my door open. What does one have to do to get any work done here?

Though after my last few days with Paris, the work feels duller than ever. And that's something given the general state of things here.

You need to choose, the legacy or your father's approval.

Maybe she's right. And yet, getting my company

and going about it behind Pa's back feels wrong. At the same time, it might be the only way to save it at this point.

We need to talk.

CAL

Have you bought the ring yet?

Out of all people, at least he could support me.

I'm not buying a ring. That's what we need to talk about.

CAL

You suck. I'm updating my resume.

You don't have the moves for the Chippendales.

CAL

Fuck you.

I snort. Though updating our resumes might be more realistic than ever before.

"Of course, send her up." Reilly's voice carries over to me.

That makes me look up from the boring projections that don't look encouraging no matter how long I glare at them.

"Ms. Lowe is on her way to see you. You can no longer deny the island did its magic."

I stand up, unreasonably pleased that Paris is dropping by but trying to look nonchalant about it because this idiot will never stop.

"Go to your desk now, Reilly, if you want to see your Christmas bonus," I threaten, and he ambles away, craning his neck down the corridor.

The minute I catch a glimpse of her striding toward me, I know this is not an unplanned surprise visit. And definitely not a pleasant one.

She looks ready to spit fire, marching down the corridor like a warrior princess. I'd be turned on if I wasn't concerned.

Okay, I *am* turned on.

And worried.

She stops in front of me, her nostrils flaring. She kicks the door closed, takes a frustrated breath that I think should help her cope... with what? And then she jerks her head. Shocked?

"Is this your office?" she asks, surprised.

Okay, not what I expected.

"Would you like a tour? So nice you dropped by." I'm pretty sure what's coming is nowhere in the vicinity of nice.

She inhales sharply and swats at my chest with a legal-size envelope. "You think I'm a liar?"

Okay, what the fuck is going on? "Well, you claimed to be—"

"That's not what I'm talking about and you know

it. I was all in, giving you a chance." She continues whipping the envelope at me. "Giving us a chance."

Enough. I grip her wrist and pull her to me. "What the fuck are you talking about, woman?"

She snaps her eyes to me and glares. Whatever war is waging behind her eyes, it's a fucking turn-on, but by the feel of it, that's definitely not the direction my mind should be taking now.

"I'm talking about this." She yanks her hand from me and plasters the envelope against my chest. "A court-ordered paternity test? Really?"

"What?" I snatch the documents and tug them out. Scanning them, I swear. "This is not my doing, Paris. I swear." My hand shakes as I try to rein in my anger.

"That's the best you can come up with? Is that your signature on the petition? Is that your lawyer?" She pokes the paperwork with her nail.

I grab her hand and twirl her, pushing her against the door and caging her with my hips.

"That is my family's lawyer petitioning the court, and I'm going to assume the signature is a crafty forgery from my father. Welcome to the inner circle of Charles van den Linden, sweetheart."

Her eyes widen and she gasps. And the asshole that I am, I thrust my hips against her so she can see what she does to me.

So she knows she's fucking mine and I won't let anyone fuck it up.

I'm vaguely aware a lot of that anger should not be directed at her, but fuck. "Thank you very much for all the benefit of doubt you're extending my way."

Her breath hitches and I lose it completely. Fisting her hair, I seize her lips. She groans against me, but then she grabs my lapel and pulls me closer.

Our tongues and lips dance in a mad choreography, taking and giving and punishing. Channeling all the frustration and meeting in understanding. Apologizing and fighting for control. Bruising our egos and licking them better.

Everything is in that kiss.

My need to hurt her for blaming me.

My need to apologize that she's been attacked by my father like that.

My need to connect with her beyond the constant doubt.

My need to kiss some sense into her so we can start building something.

My need to own her. To claim her as mine.

But it all turns desperate pretty quickly. As the paperwork floats to the floor, I lift her skirt and hike her up. Paris wraps her legs around me and I find the last remains of decency and lock my door.

* * *

"Is this your office?" Paris asks again, popping a piece of cucumber sushi into her mouth.

We're sitting on the brown leather sofa in the corner, eating the lunch that a smirking Reilly brought us.

She tried to fix her appearance, but her just-fucked face glows. And I'm guessing Reilly probably heard something. Or knowing him, he used a cup against the door to amplify the experience.

For some reason, it makes me feel like a king.

Not that staking my claim on this woman—the mother of my child—in the middle of a work day in my office should make me feel this satisfied. It feels wrong. And yet it doesn't.

I lean in and kiss her. "Yes, why?"

"It looks like a ninety-year-old retiree has just moved out of here and you haven't had a chance to redesign or add any personal touches."

She takes another bite, looking around, clearly thinking.

I let out a long breath through my cheeks and put my food down on the coffee table, sinking deeper into the seat. "And that's the state of the entire company." I sigh.

Paris drops the empty sushi box into the takeout

bag, folds her legs under herself and scoots over to me. She runs her hands through my hair. Never have I let someone touch my hair, but I don't mind her fingers grazing my scalp at all.

"You can't tell me your father would forbid you from buying new furniture, or placing a picture frame on a shelf. You wouldn't even have to use your company's money."

I kiss the inside of her forearm as her fingers still playfully rake through my hair.

"I guess I never felt at home here. It's like I've been waiting all my life, and since getting here Pa's cronies haven't taken me seriously, so I... I've never really settled. It doesn't feel mine."

"Yet you feel the company *is* yours."

She kisses my temple mindlessly. It's such a simple gesture. And then I realize I'm running my hand down her thigh passively and the whole tender connection splits something inside my chest.

The stillness. The rightness. The serenity of the bond.

"Maybe I just never thought longer and deeper about it all." I run my hand down my face. "Not very masculine to admit that."

She smiles, and it fires up something inside me. "There is strength in vulnerability, Finn. You'll figure it out."

I cup the back of her neck and kiss her. Since I started working at headquarters I've been feeling stuck, and I accepted it as part of the price to pay to get to the top. But maybe that was just an easy, lazy excuse.

"I have a meeting, but feel free to wait for me. That desk needs some X-rated experience before I throw it out."

"You, Finn van den Linden, are insatiable. I have a meeting as well."

We stand up. "Can I come over tonight?"

"I have the photography class."

I groan. "I forgot you're a serial hobbyist."

"We can have a quickie before that." She winks, grinning.

"Send me the location of your meeting. I'll pick you up."

* * *

"Finn," my father's PA drawls when she sees me. "You look dashing today."

"Thank you, Suzanne." I nod curtly. "Is he in?"

"Call me Suzie, Finn."

Over my dead body. I scowl, but she's unperturbed, rounding her desk in her outrageously work-inappropriate dress and putting her hand on my lapel.

"Your Pa is busy right now." She purses her lips, looking at me through her fake lashes.

This woman could be a porn star. It would suit her much better than embarrassing this company in front of its CEO's door. Suzanne probably got this job in a nasty breakup with my father. Probably still fucks him on the side.

These things never used to bother me, but I can see them through Paris's eyes now, and obsolete doesn't come close to describing the culture and values of this company. The legacy I'm so desperately waiting for.

Fuck. I remove Suzanne's hand from my chest and fight the urge to wash my hand. "Is he in by himself?" I ask harshly and her face reddens.

She touches her throat like I've just offended her. "He's busy, Finn. Do you want me to make an appointment?"

"Fuck it." I storm past her and barge into Pa's office.

Feet apart, he's wiggling his shoulders, finding the position for his club as he focuses on a ball on his mini putting mat. Busy my ass. He swings just as I bang the door closed behind me.

"You made me miss," he snarls as he turns. "Ever heard of knocking? What the fuck is Suzie doing out there?"

"What is this?" I throw Paris's summons on his

desk. He leans into his club and cranes his neck, unimpressed.

"I'm assuming you know what it is, so what's the point of your question, son?"

I grind my teeth so hard it hurts and breathe to clear the cloud of anger and deception, but I'm failing miserably. "What were you thinking? How dare you meddle in my affairs?"

"How dare I? Someone claims pregnancy and you don't even bother to check it out?"

"That someone has a name, and I know the child is mine." I fist my hands. Fuck, I have never been this mad at him.

"Okay, okay, Finn, for Christ's sake, don't get all worked up about it. I did it for your own good. Your mother found out it's Paris Lowe you knocked up. Not the worst match. It's a mystery where their money came from, but it's a decent name to match with ours. I just wanted to make sure the child is really yours before I give you my blessing."

I snort. "I'm not asking for your blessing. I'll marry who I want, when I want." I pace. Probably the worst move, showing him my control is slipping.

"*When* you want? I'm offering you this company on a platter." He steps closer and cups the back of my neck, squeezing. "And you can't even seal the deal with some lucky chick to take what's yours." He pats my cheek.

"I'm not marrying because you set a ridiculous ultimatum, Pa."

He steps back as if affronted. "If you don't marry—"

"Then what? You're going to sit in this chair forever?"

"Watch it, boy," he warns, but something strange passes through his face. If I didn't know him, I'd say it's almost respect. Has he been trying to provoke me all this time?

"Call off the lawyers and stay away from Paris. I think I deserve your seat on merits that have nothing to do with my relationship status. And you know it."

"Oh, is that so? You think the board wants an illegal racer and playboy with no shred of responsibility to his name to lead this company?"

I jerk my head before I can hide my surprise.

"Yeah, you think I don't know about that? Your behavior could destroy this name, Finn, so you better think twice about how you're going to answer my *ultimatum*. Bring Paris Lowe to meet us, and marry her. A bastard child won't score you points on your rep card."

He turns to his golfing mat. "Close the door on your way out."

Chapter 21

Paris

"So what do you think?" Cormac Quinn asks.

Leaning against the naked brick wall in his bespoke three-piece suit, he looks like he owns the place. Well, he owns the beautiful cavernous space by the Hudson, but he might as well own the world. Or so he believes.

I'm not sure if I like him, but I definitely like this place. I love it, in fact. The minute I stepped inside, my creative heart rejoiced. It's large, it's empty, it's full of potential. Like a blank canvas I can paint.

Am I ready to leap into the commercial business?

Didn't I decide that when I agreed to pitch the Quaintique redesign? This can be like a warm-up round.

I take my time walking around, my stilettos echoing on the cement floor. My imagination has already sketched several potential concepts, and I'm not sure which one excites me more.

My sister-in-law Gina, who's in charge of developing the restaurant's concept and setting it all up, watches me with a smile. Like she already knows I'm too far gone to refuse. I bite my lip and walk over to stand beside the owner.

"I think this place has a lot of potential. Do you have a vision for it?" I try to sound as aloof as possible while awaiting his answer with a queasy stomach.

If he has a vision and it's too stuffy, too tacky or too ordinary, my excitement will deflate faster than it built. And it built the minute I set foot inside this place.

"My vision for this place is simple: make me a shit ton of money and become the talk of the town within a year." He smiles at Gina. "My apologies."

Everything in him screams that he doesn't give a shit that my brother's restaurant is the current talk of the town. His apology is as genuine as a politician's promise. But his answer is a dream.

Gina already told me the budget is practically unlimited. And now he's suggesting we can create the best without his micro-managing. A dream client.

"Let me sketch a few ideas for you—" My eyes catch a figure marching down the empty space in front of the glass wall that fronts the future restaurant.

When I sent Finn the address, I didn't expect him

to come early, and by the looks of it, planning to invade my meeting. What the hell?

He yanks the glass door open and Cormac Quinn raises his eyebrows and bristles. It's just a split second, but both men look like they might pounce.

"What are you doing here?" I ask at the same time as Finn snaps, "What the fuck is going on here?"

I glance at Cormac, mortification spreading heat across my face. He glares at Finn.

"Finn, please wait for me outside. My meeting hasn't finished yet." My voice shakes and so does my body. Who does he think he is?

He shoots daggers at Quinn and then his eyes land on me. "You can't work with him."

"Excuse me?" My voice echoes throughout the empty space.

"Who are you?" Gina's voice registers with me, but I continue glaring at Finn. Is he for real?

"You're on my property, van den Linden, invading my meeting. Get the fuck out of here," Cormac says, with such contempt it's jarring even for an entitled prick like him.

My eyes dart between the two men. "You know each other?"

"I wish we didn't." Cormac shrugs, looking unimpressed.

The vein on Finn's temple is about to pop as he fists his hands. "Something we can agree on, Quinn."

Quinn quirks up his lips and looks at me, a picture of nonchalance. "Ms. Lowe, put your hound on the leash and let's finish here." He smirks. "We'll wait."

Finn is about to open his stupid mouth, but I push him in the chest, walking him out. At the contact he refocuses on me, slightly confused but at least he doesn't protest, and exits.

I march a few feet away from the entrance. The large glass wall I admired just a minute ago is now laughing at me. It's quite obvious the two people inside are in the front row for this spectacle.

Aware of the witnesses, I take a few breaths before I face the lunatic. His expression is startling, his energy completely unreasonable.

"What the hell, Finn?" I ask softly, and my tone finally snaps him from the rage into, well, I don't know what, but at least his neck vein is safe. For now.

"You can't work with him." He runs his hand down his face.

"Oh, we're back to you telling me what to do?" I scoff. "Making sure I have a safer car, drink enough water and have enough food might be adorable. Slightly deranged, but kind of romantic. But you will not control who I work with."

He sighs, a heavy exhalation that makes no sense to

me, but suggests there is something more going on. Something I may not understand, but it doesn't give him the right to humiliate me in front of a potential client and behave like a madman.

He lowers his head, breathing heavily. I'm not sure if he's trying to calm himself down or just regrouping before his next attack.

"You can't work with him," he repeats, this time more of a plea and less of a demand, but still... He has no right.

"Like hell I can't." I have never condoned violence, but I want to punch him so badly right now. "Have you seen the space? It's a dream to design."

He throws his arms up in exasperation. "This is personal. I don't want you around that asshole."

"Are you kidding me right now?" I cry out. Fuck the witnesses. This whole thing can't get any worse.

We glare at each other. Me upset, mortified, humiliated, and once I pass those emotions, also confused.

And really hoping there is an explanation. A justifiable reason for this unreasonable behavior. I really hope so, because my child has half his DNA from this god of vengeance.

Finn sighs heavily. "What would it take for you to drop him?"

Wait. What? "You can't do that!" I push him away. Screw the non-violence. This is excessive.

He pants. Something is very wrong, because I endured his moods before but never have I seen him this feral. "Watch me," he snaps, and before I can react, he marches back inside.

I follow on his heels, but I can't stop the tornado anymore.

"You, lady." Finn points at Gina. "Find another designer. And you." Finn turns to Cormac. "So much as breathe in her vicinity and I'm going to end you."

* * *

"Get in the fucking car, Paris." Finn tries to take my arm, but I yank it away and start walking. "Please."

His plea shouldn't stop me, but it does. There is regret in the simple, yet powerful, word. Well, too late for that. But I stay rooted, with my back to him, tears threatening to spill freely.

We're in the parking lot, not far from the crime scene. After a very awkward apology, I left with Finn. More to get him away from there than to comply with his demands. But there is no way I'll let him bully me more.

Fuck it. I whip around. "How dare you? How dare you humiliate me like that?"

"I'm sorry." He shakes his head. "I-I saw you standing there with that excuse for a man, and I lost it."

"Obviously," I huff.

"Paris, believe me, you're better off nowhere near that man." He steps closer, but I retreat from him. I don't need his touch or his scent to fog my senses.

"Well, you made your opinion abundantly clear. In the worst possible way."

He sighs and lowers his head, resigned. And it angers me even more, because all my instincts scream to console him. But I won't be the good girl here. This man will walk all over me with his explosive personality if I don't draw the line.

"Finn, I'm going home now."

He looks up, all the fight gone from him. "Of course." He extends his hand to lead me to his car.

"I'm calling an Uber."

He looks like I slapped him. "Paris," he sighs, with so much hurt.

"Don't, Finn. I need some time alone. To collect my thoughts. To somehow accept what has just happened." I swallow around the lump in my throat. "Hopefully."

I pull out my phone and call the cab.

"I'll wait with you."

I want to send him away, but I don't have any strength left for another confrontation, so I say nothing, and Finn stands beside me. In silence, fidgeting, but leaving me my space.

I stare at the app, as if I could move the small black car avatar faster, trying to ignore how his presence impacts me.

I should demand an explanation, but I need to sort this out myself first before I give him a chance to manipulate me into deeming his behavior acceptable.

The car finally arrives, and Finn opens the door for me. "Can I come by later?"

"I'll call you." I slip into the car.

Finn lowers himself to look at me. "Will you?"

The regret on his face is heartbreaking. But so was his previous behavior. I can't deal with this shit.

I close my eyes and rest my head on the backrest. "Goodbye, Finn."

* * *

I lie on my sofa, staring at the ceiling. I've been like this for I don't know how long, but I don't have the motivation to move.

I'm exhausted. Disappointed. Upset. Frustrated. And so confused.

I turned off my phone because the messages from Finn were ceaseless. I have read none of them.

In the best-case scenario, he wanted to warn me against Cormac Quinn. But even if Quinn was a serial killer, that wasn't the way to go about it. Okay, if he was a killer maybe the reaction was warranted.

The doorbell rings and I groan. I wish my phone was on, so I could check my door cam app, but without that option, I stand up and shuffle to the window and sigh.

I open the door and Gina marches in. "You weren't answering, and it looked like you might need company."

"Hey, sis." London winks and pushes past me.

"London, out of all people, said no alcohol." Mila shrugs and dangles two large bags of chips as she comes in.

Sydney just hugs me and holds me long enough for me to start crying.

"I'm pregnant," I bawl.

"Oh," Gina and Mila utter in unison.

"Okay, let's move this party." London takes over and ushers us to the sofa.

I plop down with Gina and Mila on each side of me and Lo at the other end. Sydney takes the armchair across from us.

"Is the handsome idiot the father?" Gina puts her feet on the coffee table.

I chuckle humorlessly. "Yes, to both. Idiot and father."

Mila rips open the bag of chips and we all reach in. London retreats. "You go first, Paris, it's your party."

"This is hardly a reason to celebrate." I grab a handful of the salty snack and almost moan when they reach my tongue.

"Okay, give us a bit of background," Mila says with her mouth full.

"A one-night stand with lifetime consequences. Such a fucking cliche." I sigh.

"Well, there are worse ways to get pregnant. Are you excited about the baby?" Gina asks.

I smile for the first time since the earlier disaster. "Yes. And I kind of like the father, too. But then he goes and behaves like—"

"An idiot," we all say at the same time, and I giggle. It feels good.

"Don't hate me, but it was kind of hot." Gina looks at me, shrugging in apology.

"What exactly happened?" Lo asks.

I groan and cover my face with a throw pillow, probably leaving greasy fingerprints on the silky fabric.

Gina summarizes what went down at Quinn's place. Only her version is entertaining, and not at all as mortifying as the live take was. The girls ooh and ah and giggle.

"Are you seriously finding his behavior attractive?" I drop the pillow and take another handful of chips.

"Of course not." London stands up and goes to get something in the kitchen. "How dare he interrupt your meeting and demand you drop your client? That's appalling. But it begs the question, what made him do it?"

All four pairs of eyes turn to me. I scrunch my face. "I don't know. I was so upset I didn't let him explain. I needed space more than his words." I lean forward, dropping my head.

"It felt personal." Gina rubs my back.

"Okay." Lo returns to us with a tray of glasses with sparkling water. "As someone in a very happy relationship—and who would have guessed that a year ago—the key is communication."

The other women nod.

"I know, but everything has been so wrong... Unexpected. I didn't plan on getting pregnant. And then he wants to be involved. And he has been really caring and... It wasn't supposed to happen like this."

"But it happened," Mila says. "Look at me and Gio. We were engaged and he hated me... That's also not a story I would want to tell my kids."

"These things rarely happen the way we plan or dream," Gina says. She married my brother when they were nineteen, and it would have been a fairytale if it hadn't taken them seventeen years apart to finally find each other again.

"Look, Paris, you want the baby, don't you?" Sydney speaks for the first time.

I nod.

"And it looks like he does as well," she continues. "Jesus, what's his name?"

London snorts. "Finn van den Linden, the idiot."

We all giggle.

"So," Sydney says. "You're stuck with Finn van den Linden the idiot for the rest of your life. You can either let him fully in or keep him at bay, but—"

"For all intents and purposes," London interrupts, "you're like a married couple. So you better communicate. You listen to his reasons, give him shit for the poor, really messed up execution, and you make up." Her instructions are casually pragmatic, just like her.

"That easy?" I snort. "I can't just let him walk all over me like that. His behavior was unacceptable."

My doorbell rings again.

"Let me get it." Gina rushes to the door and we all watch.

Instacart?

"Did you order groceries?" she asks but signs for it anyway. "Come and help me."

I watch as the four of them carry three large boxes to my kitchen and start unloading them.

"Wow, are you planning a party? That's a lot of food." Mila pulls out organic milk.

"I suspect Finn ordered it."

Lo snorts and the three other women stop in their tracks.

"That is romantic," Sydney sighs.

"Or annoying," I mumble, and blink away the tears.

If only I wasn't so conflicted about the whole situation. But one thing is true—I'm stuck with Finn. I'm having his baby.

My family might not have started the way I envisioned, but it's up to me to design how it will look. And designing is my gig. But how do I build it around a man who can't control his temper?

Chapter 22

Finn

"Checkmate." Cal moves his queen and leans back in his chair.

Taking a sip of my whiskey, I knock my king down with my finger.

The city down below our penthouse glimmers with lights. Another longest day in history coming to an end. Not fast enough. Not fucking fast enough.

"Did you just let me win?" Cal leans on his elbows and studies me. "You know, I can't believe I'm going to say this, but maybe you should take your Porsche for a spin, because I want my brother back."

I snort. "Yeah, I'm about to become a father. I'm not racing, you moron."

"Very responsible of you. But that baby might need immediate therapy if it sees this face every day." He circles his finger in front of me. "Let's go clubbing or get drunk. Or, I don't know, talk to me for fuck's sake." He takes a sip of his margarita. "Though I'd prefer the first two options."

"I'm not going out." I stand and trudge toward my room.

It's been two days since I pried Paris from the hands of Cormac fucking Quinn.

Two days, ten hours and forty-five minutes to be exact since she left in the fucking Uber, not subjecting herself to my company for a second longer than needed.

Two sleepless nights, and still my bed looks like the best place to stay, because nothing else has any appeal. Just darkness.

An unexpected force tackles me to the floor. "What the fuck, Cal?"

He grips my neck in a headlock, straddling me. I kick at him, but the element of surprise gave him the advantage.

"Listen, bro, you talk to me right now. What the fuck is going on?"

"Let go of me first. What is this, high school?"

I elbow him, but the fucker squeezes tighter, his girly drink breath on my skin.

"But you'll spill the beans or I'll beat the shit out of you." He loosens his grip.

"Suit yourself, dickhead." I push him off me, but I don't hurry to stand up. "I really screwed up."

"What's new?" He sits up, leaning against the sofa.

I flip him off and sit beside him, panting. "I marched into Paris's meeting and dragged her out, demanding she drop the client."

Cal whistles but says nothing.

"The client is Cormac Quinn."

Cal tenses beside me. "That explains the behavior, but I doubt she saw it that way in the moment. She must get it though. Not that I condone the behavior."

"She didn't let me explain. She said she needed space and that she'd call me."

"And I take it she hasn't yet."

I nod, and with my elbows on my knees, I bury my face in my hands.

"Maybe it's one of those situations when a woman says she needs space, but what she really means is for you to grovel?" Cal offers.

I turn to him. "Again, not high school. We're having a child, for fuck's sake. She has to let me explain. First, she takes her sweet time telling me she's pregnant, then she takes her time even letting me in, and now this. By the time we finally get together for real, the kid will be eighteen." Frustration takes hold and crawls up my spine. "Anyway, I didn't think it would take her this long."

The bastard chuckles. "Or rather, you didn't think. Period. The punishment should fit the crime. A normal person with a functional family background would have waited for the meeting to finish and then explained what his problem was."

"And you would know that how? With our family, neither of us is normal." But I know he's right. "Unless you have a time machine, your analysis is pointless. As hard as it is for me to admit, I know I ruined things."

"But as you pointed out, you're having a little van den Linden together, so you need to explain and get past this. Don't wait for her to call. She wanted space, and she got about two days judging by your pathetic stubble. Let's move on."

I stare at him, scratching the two-day shadow on my chin. I've been suspended in limbo. I messed up and I want to explain. But I want to respect her wishes at the same time. All the while dealing with this hollow space in my chest. Or the tight knot in my stomach. Both became chronic symptoms of Paris's absence.

"Don't overthink it. Just talk to her. If she is half as miserable as you, she'll give you a chance."

"And what if she isn't? What if she's happy to be rid of me?" I regret admitting my fear immediately. We don't normally do that, but I'm desperate again. To his credit, Cal doesn't jump on the opportunity to mock me, and instead pats my shoulder.

"Well, then you'll know. Either way, talking to her is the only way to move forward. And selfishly, as your roommate, I really need you to finally take a shower."

I flip him off and leave to shower. Little brother has a point. Maybe more than one.

* * *

The following day, I pace in front of Paris's house. A hundred bouquets of red roses are practically blocking the entrance to her townhouse. She should be here by now. How long does the woman work?

I should have called her assistant. Or ambushed her at work. What if she has one of her classes or workshops?

Nervous anticipation cruises through me. Fuck. When was the last time I was this worked up? When was the last time I wanted something this bad? For her to understand at least, because I'm not optimistic enough to hope that she'll forgive me.

My phone buzzes and I consider ignoring it, but maybe a distraction will help me release some of this pent-up tension.

"Where are you?" Cal sounds worked up.

"Waiting for Paris. What's up?" I stop my pacing. Something is off.

"Has Pa called you?"

"That's the last thing I need right now." I put my hand into my pocket, because at this point I want to pull my hair out.

"Old Christenson called an emergency board meeting." Cal lets out a long puff of breath.

"Shit."

"Or maybe not. You should call him. Talk to him. If Pa hasn't called you, that means someone probably blindsided him."

"Or he's behind it. His way to take control of the narrative around the sinking quarterly results." I shrug. I don't really care.

Wait? What? I don't care?

As I turn and look at the sea of roses—I might have gone a bit overboard with the arrangements—I realize I truly don't give a shit about the board meeting.

"In that case, that's even more reason to get the scoop. Perhaps this is an opportunity to present our ideas to the board."

I turn around and stop in my tracks. Fuck.

I almost didn't recognize her. Paris's long locks frame her face, this time raven black, and holy shit she is ravishing.

She's wearing huge dark sunglasses and high-heeled boots that run up her knees. Her white woolen coat hugs her waist, and its fur collar gives her an air of royalty. I want to bow in front of her.

"Cal, I gotta go." I disconnect the call while he protests then immediately calls me back. Without breaking eye contact with her, I turn off my phone and slide it into my pocket.

Paris stares at me motionless. Or I assume her eyes are on me, but the sunglasses cover half of her face.

Could she have gotten more beautiful in two days?

An untouchable aura surrounds her, as if she built an invisible wall around herself. Okay, fucker, stop stalling.

In our brief relationship, we've stood like this so many times already. Always at odds, with too many regrets, lost dreams and unspoken promises. But each time we've reinforced the bridge between us.

Unlike before, the blame is completely on my side, and she has the upper hand. She'll decide which side of the bridge I remain on.

I hate how much power she has over me, over this. But I got us here.

What's crawled its way into my chest though, is the realization that I'd do anything for her to choose us.

"I like your hair," I rasp, rooted to the spot. And that's what I lead with? Fuck me.

She licks her lips. The red of them is the only color in her monochromatic outfit. It's distracting.

"Thank you."

Okay, that's better than fuck off. "Can we talk?"

She sighs. "You blocked my entrance."

"Do you like it?" One can hope.

"Nothing with you is subtle, is it?" She takes a step, carefully maneuvering around the baskets, pots and vases.

The meaning of her jab is not lost on me. I take a step gingerly. She didn't invite me in, but she didn't send me away.

Not that I would leave.

Paris stops at the landing and unlocks the door, then turns to me. The whole ascent took a fraction of time, but I feel like I've just reached a summit in the Himalayas. Never in my life have I felt this insecure. Or eager.

I grew up believing I had to fight hard for my father's approval. Fuck. That whole paradigm was a walk in the park. Or perhaps I never really needed his approval. I just wanted it. With Paris, I not only want her, I need her.

And when did that happen?

"What am I going to do with this many flowers? Such a waste, Finn." She plucks one rose from a bunch by her door. "But it's romantic." She might smile shyly, but I can't be sure because she covers it with the flower, inhaling the scent before she opens the door.

Without looking back, she waltzes into her living

room. She doesn't close the front door, so I take it as an invitation.

Shedding her coat, she turns to me, still holding the rose. It contrasts with her tight black dress.

Perfect. Beautiful. So worth fighting for.

"I want to apologize for acting... like—"

"Like an idiot? That's the word you're looking for." She doesn't move, and her stillness is fucking scary. So much restraint is almost inhuman.

"Yes. A complete idiot. When I saw you near that asshole, something snapped. Cormac Quinn bullied my sister and she..." I fist my hands. "It almost ended up in tragedy."

She gasps and pulls her sunglasses up into her hair. Her eyes are puffy, rimmed with red. Fuck. I hate myself for hurting her.

I itch to reach out for her, but I realize I have no right. That's a hard pill to swallow.

"I'm sorry Saar had such a horrible experience."

"So do you understand now—"

"Finn, I understand you hate Quinn. But that still doesn't mean you can humiliate me in front of him, barging into my meeting. It doesn't even give you the right to demand I don't work with him."

I take a breath, grinding my teeth. "I overstepped. My action is inexcusable, and I'm really sorry. Is there any way we can get past this?"

"Look, I've been racking my brain for almost three days now, and I don't know which way to move. I don't want this baby not to have a father, but I don't want to be locked in with someone I don't know."

I'd be annoyed by the we-don't-know-each-other spiel again, but given my fucked-up behavior, I can't argue her on that point.

"This is all new to me, Paris. I've never been in a relationship. I've never had to compromise in my life. I'll fuck up. But I want to try. I believe we can be good together. Maybe you can trust that I'll try. I trust that you won't lie to me."

She flinches at that. Maybe reminding her of her mistakes in this weird relationship isn't the best tactic, but I'm desperate here.

"Everything in this relationship is backward." She sighs.

"But maybe backward is what we both needed. You enjoyed the freedom the initial lie gave you, you enjoyed letting go and spending the days with me on the island. You can't deny that. There is a connection—"

"A physical connection is not enough to build a lasting relationship."

"So let's give ourselves a chance to discover what else connects us." It takes fierce effort not to shake her right now.

"Okay." She sighs. "But I think we should refrain from sex. It confuses everything."

Come again? I blink a few times. "Okay."

If anyone told me I'd agree to celibacy at any point in my life, I'd have him committed to a psych ward.

She jerks her head ever so slightly, as if surprised by my quick agreement. Then she nods and comes closer, reaching for my hand. The gentle touch sends a current of something potent through me, and I squeeze her fingers.

We stare at each other, the silence between us peaceful. Perhaps not harmonious yet, but something that will continue pulling us closer.

"I have an ultrasound appointment if you want to come with me."

I pull her to me and wrap my arms around her. "I'd love that."

She snakes her arms around my waist and melts in my arms, but we don't move, just enjoy the closeness.

"I won't work with Quinn."

Her words send my heart racing. Fuck. I adore her. "Thank you." I nudge her chin up. "Is kissing also off the table?"

She chuckles, cups my nape and pulls me to her.

A kiss has never felt so redeeming. Unfortunately, I have to break it too quickly. This no sex rule is going to be the death of me.

* * *

"Okay, Gina is disappointed, but she understands." Paris sits down next to me in a luxurious waiting room.

"Thank you." I kiss her temple.

"Look, you support my bid for Quaintique and they are your direct competitor, so the least I can do is to sit this one out. It was such an amazing place." She sighs. "But I don't want to work with a bully. It's enough that I have you in my life." She looks at me sideways, her lips curving up.

"I'd take you over my knee for that, kitten, but rules are rules." I shrug and enjoy the excitement that flicks through her eyes.

Let's see who breaks the rule first.

She crosses one leg over another and takes a magazine from the table beside her, and I bite the inside of my cheek to stifle a chuckle.

"This hair suits you well. Maybe you should keep it like this longer." I take a shiny black strand between my fingers and lean in to smell it.

Her shudder jolts me with satisfaction. I might not always act like the civilized person she deserves, but I affect her. She can fight that all she wants, but I affect her as much as she triggers me.

"I enjoy being different all the time." She returns to her magazine.

I take it from her. "To hide the real you?"

She looks away. "Maybe I shouldn't have let you in again," she mumbles.

What will it take to let her shine on her own? But I don't push anymore right now, because I just got back into her good graces. I won't push my luck.

We sit in silence for a moment. I scan the diplomas on the wall by the reception area. "So do we know this doctor?"

"We'll meet him in about five minutes."

"Yes, but who recommended him? Is he the best we can get?" I shift to look at her.

"Finn, chill, he's the best we can get." She cups my face. "He's the doctor I want."

Her words relax me a little. "I'll check him out."

"You do that." She chuckles, and before I can respond, her name is called.

We enter the examination room and Paris gets into the gown, which shouldn't give my cock ideas. Especially not now when we're in purgatory.

But all ideas about the sex ban evaporate when the technician comes in and starts the ultrasound.

As soon as the chaotic, fast heartbeat fills the room, I grab Paris's hand and we both stare in awe at the grainy picture that shows nothing.

But the sound is so potent. So alive. So real.

She looks at me with misty eyes, and in that look

something weaves between us. A connection that eluded us until now.

Because we fought reality.

We fought the path that brought us here.

But right now, in this moment, the heartbeat of our child finally unites us.

Chapter 23

Paris

I stare at the heap of bronze and papier mâché in front of me, trying to come up with something nice to say, but I'm coming up empty-handed.

Chrysal, the artist who created it, is playing with a chopstick, flipping it between his two fingers. Why he carries around chopsticks is beyond me.

The silence stretches as I walk around the thing. It has four legs, each of them different. One is shorter with carved biblical motifs. One of them is smooth bronze with an almost blinding shine. The other two have dents and holes in them, damaged on purpose, I guess.

"Is this a table?" I try to sound uninterested, because that's the only way I can remain polite enough about this monstrosity.

"Yes, or it can be a desk." He leans back in his chair and puts his booted feet up on a wooden bench.

"Or a desk..." I echo his words because, oh my God, how does one eat or work on a wavy surface of papier mâché, printed with a wild mosaic of colorful geometrical shapes? How does one concentrate? "So, Chrysal, do you work with other interior designers?"

"Not yet, I wanted to offer you exclusivity."

"Are all your ideas focused on creative use of materials..." Okay, that was sort of a compliment. "Or are any of them functional?"

He stops flipping the chopstick and looks at me, studying me with hooded eyes. Either he's high as a kite or his eyes are pure black. "What do you mean functional?"

"My clients like pretty, luxurious items that are pieces of art, but they need to serve them as well. I don't know, like being able to eat at a table. Or write on a desk." I trace my fingers over the porous surface of the thing in front of me.

"They can put this in their foyer, and everyone will see my piece as soon as they enter their home."

"So it's a sculpture?" This man is either delusional or he's fucking with me.

"It's a table."

"Look, Chrysal, I don't see an opportunity for

collaboration, but I'll keep you in mind on a one-on-one basis if I have a client with this kind of eccentric taste."

"Whatever," he huffs, and I rush outside.

Was I too harsh? The people pleaser in me is trembling with regret, but the artist in me, the professional businesswoman, and the future mother, for that matter, all rejoice in my ability to tell someone off gently but firmly.

And he didn't seem crushed.

This is why I don't want people to see my lamps. I wouldn't be able to deal with the scrutiny. And not everyone would be as nice about letting me down as I was here.

Thank God I haven't shown them to anyone. As I walk down the street to my car, though, a nagging feeling crawls up my spine.

Why does someone so completely clueless about functional design have the guts to share their work with the world? And me? Knowing my sense of space only allows for quality home accessories, but I still can't take the leap.

I take the elevator to Finn's floor with the hired crew following on my heels. We get off and march down the corridor toward his office. I know he's not there, and we have a window of about two hours to get things done.

"Hello, Reilly." I smile, and his assistant almost chokes on his drink. "We haven't met officially. Good job of luring me to the island. If you know the owners of the house in the pictures you sent me, I'd love to *actually* remodel their property."

He swallows and jumps from his desk. "Ms. Lowe, I didn't know you were coming... Finn is not here."

"The guys downstairs let me up since I've been hired to redesign Finn's office."

"Hired?" He frowns.

"Well, that might have been a little white lie. You know those... like the island property." I shrug.

He looks over my shoulder at the bulky movers and his face turns crimson. He licks his lips.

"But Finn didn't tell me about it."

"That's probably because he doesn't know. We better get started now. I'll take this furniture to my storage facility unless you can arrange for something else. Is there a freight elevator we can use?"

Reilly stares at me and then shakes his head like a wet dog. "Who signed off on this?"

"Reilly, it's a surprise gift from me to Finn. I signed off on it."

"But—"

"We're wasting time. When will he be back?"

"Two hours, maybe sooner."

"Then let's get going."

Ninety minutes later I thank the moving crew and sit down on a new beige leather sofa in Finn's office.

"What do you think, Reilly?"

He looks around at the modern, soft beige decor accented with navy blue. "It's very Finn. And it doesn't fit here at all."

I smile. "I couldn't have him buried in that stuffy décor. No wonder he's always so... hostile."

Reilly chuckles. "I'm afraid that's a birth defect."

We both laugh. "In any case, he spends so much time here that it should lift his spirits."

"It's amazing. You did well. It's almost like you know the man." Reilly wiggles his shoulders as he pirouettes, admiring the new office.

"What's going on here?" A voice bellows from the door.

Reilly squeals and I stand up. "Mr. Van den Linden, we haven't officially met. I'm Paris Lowe." I offer my hand, but he ignores it.

"I haven't signed off on this," he snaps, appearing like he's going to throw up just from looking at the new furniture.

"It's a gift."

He frowns. "You're trying really hard to get my boy. What's in it for you?"

Reilly lets out a strangled breath. "I-I... the phone. I better answer it." He rushes out of the room to answer a phone that has been silent.

What's in it for me? I don't even know what that means. Before I collect my thoughts and try to figure out how to deal with this level of venom, he speaks again.

"There is a reason you refused the paternity test," he accuses.

Heat burns my face. Is that what he thinks? "Are you suggesting I'm lying about the father of my child?"

"It's interesting timing, isn't it? My son is about to take over the company and you show up, conveniently tying him to you for the rest of your life." He folds his arms across his chest, glaring at me.

"Mr. van den Linden, you don't know me, and I doubt you know much about my relationship with Finn. I have a feeling you don't trust me by default, but I don't owe you anything. I don't need to explain myself to you."

Somehow I talk with a level voice, but I'm shaking inwardly. I ball my hands into fists. I hate confrontations.

"You don't need to explain yourself to me. There's a reason my son hasn't put a ring on your finger yet. But I see you don't give up easily." He looks around with contempt. "A gift." He snorts and leaves.

I stare into space long after he's gone. The arrogance of that man. Living with him must be like standing under constant gunfire.

While the chance encounter leaves me with a bitter aftertaste, I'm happy to have experienced the man first-hand. It explains so much about Finn.

No wonder he has all this pent-up anger bubbling under the surface all the time. What kind of a person do you become when you're exposed to this level of disrespect, egotism and plain vile?

It's like being bullied all your life by the one person you seek acceptance from. When your every idea is dismissed. When you don't get a chance to show what you're capable of.

I might hide my art and shy away from more lucrative—and hence public—engagements for the fear of being seen. But I'm fighting against my own block. Finn comes to work every day and fights with the world, with the board, with his own father.

"What a pleasant surprise."

I refocus and my eyes meet the dazzling smile. Overwhelmed by the previous meeting and all my thoughts, I dash across the room.

Wrapping my arms around his neck, I pull him down for a kiss.

A guttural hum reverberates through both of us as our lips fuse.

"My day has just gotten even better." He keeps his forehead on mine. "You look beautiful."

"What about the office?"

He steps back and walks around. "My computer is disconnected." He frowns at me.

What? He hates it. Oh my God. Heat burns my face beyond my ears. "Sorry, we didn't get a chance... we were rushing. I thought you..."

Finn turns and jerks me to him, laughing. "You need to be more confident in your own work, kitten. I love it."

I melt into him. "You do?"

"Though it might severely impact my productivity."

I quirk up my eyebrow.

"Well, I'll probably be hard all day long thinking about the talented designer who created my work environment."

I laugh. "How was your meeting?"

"Not as good as the surprise waiting for me here." He leans against his new desk, pulling me between his legs.

"Do you want to talk about it?"

"Kurt Christenson is an old friend of my father who owns a good chunk of our shares. He warned me that if father doesn't step up his game, they will vote to replace him."

"Isn't that what you wanted?"

"He didn't say that my name is being considered. He made it sound like they were disappointed that not even the young van den Linden blood has created the positive change here to improve the bottom line. Pretty much they hoped that me and Cal would turn the company around, but since that hasn't happened..." He shrugs.

"So it was a warning."

"Yeah, but the warning was delivered to me. Not to his friend, my father. The message between the lines was clear. Step up."

"But that's great. It's your chance."

He sighs, playing with my hair. "Yeah, but my efforts... My father blocks or sidetracks them."

"I guess there isn't an easy way to show that to the shareholders."

"Not if I don't want to scheme against him and go behind his back."

He pulls me closer, embracing me. It's not sensual, but still intimate. It's like he draws energy from me. Or just seeks support.

Warmth spreads through me, because suddenly we feel like a couple.

"I feel like I'm stuck between choosing my work or family. Like a decent person would choose the family, but if I don't choose the company, the family will be destroyed. And if I go behind father's back to fix things around here, he would never forgive me."

"I just met your father."

Finn scrunches his face, worried. "Sorry."

I chuckle. "He's a proud man, and I don't think he'd ever admit his mistakes. But maybe it's not a choice between the family and the firm. This firm is a part of your family. It's van den Linden legacy. Your father might come around once he sees all the improvements. He'll recognize it."

"Somehow I doubt that, kitten, but I appreciate your support."

"I think this is one of those cases when it'd be easier to ask for forgiveness rather than seek permission."

"Maybe you're right. I need to talk to Cal and see where he stands." He kisses my forehead, deep in thought. "I really hope I'll be a more supportive father."

His wish—or an attempt at commitment—is laced with vulnerability.

I kiss him. "For what it's worth, you've had plenty of experience in what not to do." I try to lighten the mood, really wishing I could take some of the load from his shoulders.

"Thank you." He lowers his lips to mine, and this time the kiss is reverent. As if in our connection he'll find all the answers... or at least solace. And I give gladly, contentment pooling in my stomach.

"I'm glad you like your new office." I grin at him when we come up for air.

"I might not enjoy it for much longer, but I appreciate all the effort. You're fantastic at this."

I grin at him. "And I'm sure you're good at your job."

"Yeah, but my passion gets squashed every single time." He sighs.

Passion.

I think of Chrysal, a man who has no qualms about realizing his passion no matter what the result is. About Finn, who is so passionate and caring about his family business and has no choice but to watch it deteriorate.

And then there is me. Passionate about my work, but very hesitant about going all in. How fortunate I am that I don't have a large ego to stop me from seeing the reason ,or someone impeding my efforts all the time.

I'm my own blocking power.

I'm not even sure what to do with that realization.

At the end of the day, the bucket list *has* pushed my boundaries.

Chapter 24

Paris

I've never been this well fed in my life.

Or this horny.

What was I thinking when I suggested no sex?

It's been two weeks.

Two weeks too long. My vibrators haven't gotten this much action in... ever.

Finn slices tomatoes, moving around my kitchen like he's always lived here.

Watching him is addictive.

I sit at the raised breakfast bar as he glides around. He's elegant and confident. So hot. Probably the hottest man alive, my ovaries and horny hormones scream.

Having him around is addictive. His scent permeates the air here. His ties get thrown on my dresser.

Somehow, his toothbrush appeared beside mine. His protein powder is in my cupboard.

We don't do sleepovers—because the stupid rule is hard to uphold as it is—and yet he's present everywhere in my space.

And I love it.

He looks up and winks at me. I clench and stifle a groan. With his large hands, he tosses the tomatoes into a salad bowl. It's simple food preparation, but it feels like watching porn.

Loose hair falls into his face and he blows the strands away. I want to rake my fingers through them. I need to do it.

He would fist my hair and hike up my skirt and...

"Are you okay?" His concern brings me back to reality. Did I moan out loud?

Finn glares at me with that annoying tell-me-right-now-and-don't-lie look. I guess he misinterpreted my moan.

"I'm okay. Just tired, and the work has been a lot lately." *This stupid abstinence has been a lot.*

"I have something to cheer you up."

Your cock can cheer me up. Or I'll do with your tongue or your hand.

"What is it?" I ask, because I'm a lady and I can control my dirty mind, my smutty needs. Can't I?

And when my logical brain reappears from the fog

of lust, I'll admit that the last two weeks have helped us grow as a couple. I guess in order not to have sex, we stuffed our days with activities.

Dinners in discreet restaurants, movie theater outings, couples massages and a few other outings where we could remain anonymous. Finn has always frequented the gossip pages, and I'm not ready for that exposure.

He took me for a ride in one of his sports cars a few times, which unexpectedly was a lot of fun. Just driving aimlessly on a freeway. And we even went apple picking upstate.

I'm exhausted, but I also had the opportunity to appreciate the man Finn is. When he told me about his reason for hating Quinn, I came to understand one thing. It clicked together with all the other times he's acted like a steaming ogre.

Finn cares.

But his family situation, his father's lack of respect in his personal and professional life, the constant pressure, has pushed him to express his care in a very irritable, angry fashion. I guess the years of not being heard would encourage you to scream and fuss louder.

So in the last two weeks, I've simply let him care for me. Okay, sometimes I roll my eyes, because he can get quite ridiculous.

My fridge would feed half of my street. And the

fucking gifts can get annoying—case in point, the pair of sensible boots I got today. Heels are not dangerous in pregnancy!

But it's nice to be cared for. It really, truly is nice.

Finn puts a pan with chanterelles to the side and turns down the heat. He rounds the island, kisses my temple and goes to the briefcase he left at the dining table.

I watch his ass. His perfect ass that I wish I could dig my heels in... *Stop it, Paris.*

He slides a folder across the counter.

"That doesn't look like a gift. Is it a prenup?"

A beat passes. I snap my eyes at him at my poor joke. Because who knows how far his care would go?

Something flashes across his face. It's excitement or mischief. I don't know, but suddenly I'm dreading the folder, darting my eyes between it and Finn.

He chuckles. "Open it, kitten."

I flip through the paperwork and pictures, understanding what I'm seeing, but not comprehending the actual meaning. "We had such a good run for two weeks that you wanted to piss me off and taunt me with photos of Quinn's property? What the hell, Finn?"

"Read the deed, woman." He casually returns to the stove and continues his culinary wizardry.

I refocus on the documents in front of me.

"What?" I stare at him.

He shrugs, smiling like a Cheshire cat.

"You bought that building? Why?"

"You liked it. Now you can design it." He turns to the fridge, focused on his task.

I don't blink for a moment, speechless, and Finn faces me with a wink. "'Thank you' are the words you're looking for, sweetheart."

"What exactly am I designing there? How on earth did your arch-nemesis agree to sell it? To you?"

"What can I tell you: money talks."

"I can't believe he sold it." I'm stunned by this gift. "It must have cost a fortune."

He winks. "Priceless. As a gift for you, it was priceless."

My smile is ridiculously wide. "I still can't believe it. And Quinn selling to you—"

"He might not exactly know who the buyer is. Or he finally grew a conscience for what he did to my sister—who is here, by the way, and would love to meet you." He starts preparing our plates. "You can design whatever you want there. Come up with the ideas and present me the budget, and we will choose the best option to resell it later or keep it."

He takes the plates to the table, throwing around the options casually like we're discussing where we should go on vacation next. "And who is *we* in this?"

He looks at me like I just landed from another planet. "You and me, of course."

I blink a few times. "This is either the most outrageous or the most thoughtful gift I've ever heard of."

He smirks and comes to take my hand. "At least you didn't go with the annoying 'oh my God, Finn, I can't accept this.'" He kisses me and leads me to the dining table.

"Oh, I'm accepting this." I practically purr at the idea as I sit down. "It's going to be so much fun." I can already see several concepts. "But what if we come up with something really cool and viable? Will we have to sell it? And what's the budget?" I shove the food in my mouth, thinking out loud. "Maybe I should invest my money as well. If we go with the original idea of a restaurant, we should consult with Gina. Maybe it can be more than a restaurant."

"Kitten—"

"Yes?" I say through my stuffed mouth.

"Keep overthinking, but please slow down with your food."

I stop the fork halfway to my mouth and assess my nearly empty plate. When did I gobble that down?

A little frazzled, I look back at Finn.

His playful smirk brings me back to the present moment. Me, who always gets stuck planning ahead.

And him, pulling me out of that spiral, back to the here and now.

Peace descends on me.

Between us.

And in that moment, I know I love this man.

I stretch my back, groaning with pain. I've been hunched over for—I glance at my phone—hours. Jesus.

Stepping away from the workbench, I admire my work.

This lamp is challenging with all the little details. My chest fills with accomplishment. I really like its current state. Maybe I can give it to my parents for Christmas.

Maybe I can be seen.

I tuck my raven hair behind my ear. I've kept it this way. *To hide the real you?* Finn asked, and probably didn't realize he unearthed something within me. Like he sees something in me I don't want to hide anymore.

Maybe I don't have to hide.

My phone pings, and I notice several missed calls from Finn and Shayna.

SHAYNA

Finn's been waiting here for half an hour.

Geez, I really lost track of time. I put down the wire cutters and pick up my phone.

Send him upstairs

SHAYNA

Really?

Now

Nobody has ever been here aside from the cleaning lady and Shayna.

Maybe I can be seen slowly. With people I trust.

As soon as the idea pops in, anxiety takes root. What was I thinking? Showing him my little workshop. He'll think it's a waste of time. Another pastime of a professional hobbyist. Maybe I can still run and meet him downstairs.

But then the elevator dings and Finn steps out. He's wearing a navy suit that hugs his muscles in all the right places. His hair is mussed to perfection. My heart somersaults.

This is unreal. The hold the man has over me. He's just stepped out of the elevator, a scowl on his face, and I swoon.

"Did you forget about our plans?" he starts, but then stops, looking around. "What is this place?"

"My workshop," I whisper. "Sorry, I lost track of time." I reach to untie my apron.

"Don't!" He raises his hand. "I like the goggles and the smock."

His eyes full of hunger, he strides toward me like he's going to devour me instead of his dinner. He cups my face and kisses me breathless, moving the goggles into my hair at one point.

"You're so fucking hot, kitten," he breathes.

My nervous system goes haywire at his words, his presence, his kiss. Him. He's making me feel all the feels. It scares and completes me at the same time.

"You're not too bad yourself, Mr. van den Linden."

He cups my ass, his forehead on mine, and we grin at each other. We've been doing that a lot. Like we don't need words, just gazes and smiles to know who we are to each other. For each other. With each other.

"I'm sorry I kept you waiting. I got lost in work."

"I got something for you, but care to show me first what kept you?" He steps back and starts looking around.

"It's just... a hobby, I guess."

He raises his eyebrows. "You made all of these?" He points to the shelves lining the wall.

Hiding is so much easier. Safer.

My palms are damp, and I don't quite know where to look. "Yes." The word barely passes through the gravel lodged in my throat.

He turns to me, and instead of mockery, there is

something in his expression that is close to… That can't be. Awe?

"Holy fuck, Paris, if you're this good at all your hobbies, no wonder you pursue them with such dedication."

I look away, my cheeks burning. I start undoing the smock, just to do something with my hands. Of course, the string gets tangled.

"Kitten—"

"Yes?"

"Keep the fucking smock on I said," he growls, the demand charged with all the pent-up sexual energy we've been harboring in the name of getting to know each other. "These are amazing. Simple and beautiful. Are they functional?"

I chance a look at him. Still no mockery. "Yes, they work."

"Can I have one?"

"What?"

"Can I have one?" He turns to the shelves. "This one, if it's for sale." He points at a large reading lamp with a gold and black pattern. It's one of the more extravagant designs, but I love its boldness.

"You want it?"

"Yes. How much is it?" He takes out his wallet.

"Stop it. I don't sell them."

"What? Why not? These have no owners?"

"It's just a hobby." I pull the goggles from my hair. "Shayna will wrap it for you tomorrow and have it delivered. I'm glad you like it."

"I think I know what we can do in our space," he says. I like how he calls the building by the Hudson River our space even though he bought it. "A store. An exclusive store for these one-of-a-kind, designer lamps."

I snort. "No."

"What do you mean no?" And the grumpy bully is back.

"I'm not showing them to anyone."

"Why?" He puts his hands on his hips.

I'm pleased he likes them, but one step at a time. "Didn't you say you have a gift for me?"

"Oh, no, no, no, kitten, don't try to change the topic. What's happening right now?"

I sigh. "I'd rather see that gift, and we'll be late for dinner."

"Fuck dinner. Do you love making these?"

I glare at him. "Yes."

"Well then, you'll share your passion with others. What's the point otherwise?"

When he puts it like that, I really can't argue.

"Paris, you have a gift. Please don't hide it."

"Let's see how many people laugh at your new lamp, and then we'll decide."

He rolls his eyes. "Stupid woman." He puts his

briefcase on the workbench, clicks it open and pulls out a black box. "This discussion is not over, but here is your gift."

I smile. "What is it?"

"Open it."

The box is sleek, black, and luxurious. I notice the logo and heat rises to my cheeks. Shit. I look at Finn. "You got me a toy?"

"I see you're familiar with the brand." He smirks.

"This is not fair."

"What are you talking about?"

"We said no sex."

"And that's why I'm giving you this. If I can't take care of you..."

I whimper. The box is small for a vibrator and my curiosity gets the best of me. I put it on the workbench and unwrap it. The toy inside is pink and gold with a small suction cup.

"It's for your clit." Finn steps behind me and whispers into my neck.

"Obviously." I swallow. Damn him. I don't want to use it alone.

"I'd enjoy it with you, but I'm respectful of the ban." His breath on my skin makes me shudder. Oh, he's playing dirty.

"I know what you're doing."

"I don't know what you're talking about."

"You're tempting me, so I'll lift the ban."

"With a toy for your personal use?" He pretends I'm being ridiculous. "But you should make sure it works."

My underwear is drenched already. "To make sure you don't have to return it," I breathe.

"Yes, exactly."

He cages me between the workbench and him, with his hands on each side of me. Without thinking, I press my hips against him. He's as hard as I am shaking from desire.

I whip around. "But we have a dinner reservation."

"Fuck that, kitten. You said it yourself—the pregnancy makes you horny. We need to take care of you."

"We? Did you come here to seduce me?"

He kisses me, his lips soft on mine. "I'd never do that. No sex means no sex."

"So you didn't buy this..." I turn on the toy and the buzzing fills the space between us. "To have sex with me?"

"I bought it to watch." And with some magical moves, he pulls down my underwear, hikes up my skirt and smock and hoists me onto the workbench. "Be a good girl and spread your legs."

I scoot farther back on the table and lift my heels to its edge, obeying while I'm trembling with a need so strong I might just orgasm from the thought itself.

Finn steps back, his eyes wild with want. "Look at you, kitten. Fuck, I miss this pussy. The prettiest pussy in the world."

Oh God, this man. What his words do to me. He parks his gaze between my thighs, his Adam's apple bobbing. Without a thought about disinfecting the toy, I press it against my swollen bud. The moan that leaves me doesn't even sound like me.

I think I might come in seconds. "Touch yourself," I order. My voice is raspy, but the effect my request has on Finn boosts my confidence.

I squeeze my breast through the fabric of my frumpy smock with one hand and arch my hips to meet the toy.

Finn unzips and pulls his cock out. Seeing him fisting himself in front of me is an aphrodisiac.

He steps closer and cups my nape, pulling me in for a kiss while jerking off. His lips on me are urgent and demanding.

The kiss, him, the toy, it all makes me dizzy and I almost collapse on to my back, but he's got me.

We stay close to each other, panting into each other's shoulders, while drawing pleasure and chasing release.

"I'm coming," I cry out.

"Wait for me, kitten," he grunts, and the movement of his hand turns violent.

"Finn—" I contract and barely hold the toy as I come.

"Fuck—" Finn spills himself all over my apron as I grasp his shoulder, shaking.

The toy drops from my hand, and Finn wraps his arms around me and kisses me savagely.

He continues nibbling on my jaw and then whispers into my ear. "I told you to wear the smock. We didn't ruin your dress."

"The way you're holding me against you, we've just ruined your suit."

"Fuck the suit." He bites my earlobe.

"Finn," I whisper, the three words on my tongue, but my heart hammers in my temple suddenly.

"Yes, kitten?" He nuzzles my neck.

I fear the L word would change things between us, so instead I say, "Please fuck me."

Chapter 25

Finn

"Fuck, kitten, you take me so well."

I pound into her with all the build-up of the past few weeks, gripping her hips in the vice of my fingers. Paris is bent over the workbench, moaning and writhing, meeting my thrusts with wanton desire.

As soon as she green-lighted sex, we were both naked, hungry for each other. I knew the toy was an excellent gift.

"Harder," she growls.

I fist her hair and pull her to me. "The kitten turned into a tigress." I bite her ear and her moan almost sends me over the edge.

This woman is everything I never knew I missed in my life. I'm almost grateful—almost—for the sex ban, because we spent time together alongside our normal routines, and it's been so much better than the forced stay on the island.

Just normal. I really like this woman.

I won't deny that her punishing little ban has been hard, but shit, the reward right now...

"I'm coming," she pants.

"Not yet, kitten."

She whimpers as I pull out. I pick her up and turn her, hoisting her legs around my waist. I walk us to the glass wall of windows.

"Are you crazy?" she protests, but her words turn into a groan when I impale her again, pinning her to the cold glass.

"I'm crazy about you, kitten. I want the world to see who you belong to. And I want to see your face when you come."

"You're insane." But her words don't match her actions as she bucks her hips and digs her heels deeper into my quads.

I grip her chin. "Eyes on me."

She snaps her hooded gaze up to meet mine.

"Who do you belong to?"

She whimpers again. "You. I'm yours."

Never have I heard sweeter words. They flow through me like smooth whiskey, making my legs weak while spreading heat in my chest.

We both reach climax, staring into each other eyes.

The intimacy would normally scare me, but it doesn't. I don't want to look away.

I want to drown in her.

To protect her.

To care for her.

She's mine.

We stare at each other, spent and happy. Well, I know I am.

Still inside her, I turn us around, because suddenly I hate the idea of anyone seeing her like this. This is just for me.

And if she lets me, it'll be only me forever.

"Are you okay?"

She hums, nodding and smiling.

"Where is the bathroom?"

She moves to lower herself, but I grip her tighter.

"Show me." I kiss her forehead.

"You really don't have to carry me." She points to the door across the room.

"Shut up."

I take us to a small bathroom where we barely fit together, and I'm forced to put her down. "Are you sure you're okay? I kind of lost it at one point."

She leans against the door frame with the most adorable just-fucked expression. "Yeah, you lost it completely, displaying my ass for everyone to see."

I groan. What the fuck was I thinking? "I might

need to kill everyone now, or rinse their eyes with bleach."

"It's the fifth floor. Nobody looks up here."

I wet a hand towel and drop to my knees. Hooking her leg over my forearm, I open her and press the warm towel against her center.

"What are you doing?"

I look up at her. "What does it look like I'm doing?"

"You've never done that before." She sighs and sags, and I stand up to steady her.

"I should have." I kiss her and throw the towel to the sink, then carry her back to where our clothes lie on the floor.

Sitting her on the workbench, I find her panties and help her put them on. Next, I pick up her bra and hook the straps over her shoulders. She is still, gazing at me.

"What?" I fasten her bra and lean down for her sweater.

"Never did I imagine that Finn van den Linden would be dressing me instead of undressing me."

I put my briefs on. "I did both, kitten."

"And it's not nearly as weird as I'd have thought." She smiles at me, still dazed with a post-orgasmic glow. And so fucking beautiful that my eyes hurt.

"By now you should be used to it. I care for you."

"Well, yes, but usually by growling and bullying

me into something that may or may not be good for me."

"I don't know what you're talking about." Though she might be right. A little.

Her stomach growls and she covers her face. "This baby is making me hungry."

"And horny, thank God. Lucky for you, I can take care of both your needs."

We grin at each other for a long moment and then I finish dressing so we can leave and feed her.

"My parents would like to meet you," I say once my car drives us to her house.

"Are you sure your father doesn't want to kidnap me and take me to a clinic for a paternity test?" She looks at me, skeptical. I hate how my family dims her glow before she's even met them.

"Don't worry, I'll be there to protect you. Besides, you'll meet Cal and Saar and they'll be on your side too. We'll be on a power play." I pull her close and kiss her temple.

"What about your father's ultimatum? Is he expecting you to marry still? Won't the pressure increase once they know we're dating?"

I lift her onto my lap and cup her face. "We are doing this on our own schedule. They can pressure me all they want. I'm waiting for you."

She blinks a few times and then crashes her lips to mine.

* * *

"I'm really nervous." Paris keeps adjusting her skirt as I lead her to the front door of my childhood home.

"You should be." I smirk.

"Finn!" Her eyes widen.

I kiss her quickly. "Kitten, you've met my father. Don't expect my mother to be any more sympathetic. They're stuck in their own ivory tower. Towers. Separate ones." I chuckle, but she doesn't appreciate my attempt at lightening the mood.

I kiss her again and she melts in my arms.

"Look, sweetheart, you don't need to impress them. I've been trying to do that all my life and I'm still falling behind on that particular goal. If you hate them, this is the first and the last visit until they learn to appreciate you." I tuck a strand of her hair behind her ear and kiss her forehead gently.

"I know, but still... The people pleaser in me is having a major meltdown."

"We can leave at any time. Storming from family functions is well established in our circle. Focus on Cal and Saar and just survive my parents."

I tug her toward the entrance, so she can't over-think it any longer.

We step into the museum of excess that is my parents' house and Paris gasps. Her wide eyes dart around the ostentatious foyer, and I can practically hear her screaming inwardly as she takes in the gilded decor, including the thirty-arm chandelier above our head.

"I wish I could hear your inner commentary right now." I snort and she goes rigid, glaring at me.

"Mr. Finn." Our housekeeper comes running. "I'm sorry I didn't hear the bell. Come, your siblings are in the drawing room."

"Hello," Paris says shyly.

"Miss." The housekeeper nods, probably perplexed that our guest acknowledged her.

"This is Paris Lowe, my girlfriend." I startle the housekeeper even more, because I've never bothered to introduce her to any of my visitors.

Come to think of it, I've never brought anyone to my parents' house. Even growing up, I preferred to hang out at my friends'.

We enter the sitting room and Paris squeezes my hand while her eyes flit over the tacky and opulent details, including the portraits of stern-faced people who are not even our ancestors. Her cringe makes me chuckle. Her baffled reaction is endearing and entertaining.

She's so authentic. It's a shame my folks won't recognize her unique charm and sense of style.

"Finn." Saar jumps from the heavy brocade sofa and throws her arms around me. "Oh, I missed you so much."

"Hey, Bambi. I missed you too." I kiss her forehead.

"Jesus, Finn, drop the nickname. I'm not five anymore," she mumbles, but immediately redirects her attention to Paris.

"This is my girlfriend, Paris." I put my hand on the small of Paris's back. "This is Saar, my little sister."

"So nice to meet you. Just know we're here for moral support. They can be scary, but they don't bite." She hugs Paris, who goes rigid for a moment.

"Are you sure about that?" Cal joins us, a tall glass of what is probably a gin and tonic in his hand. "I'm Caleb. Nice to finally meet you."

"And you." Paris smiles and finds my hand, squeezing.

We don't get to warm up the conversation with the friendly side of my family, because the housekeeper returns. "Dinner is served."

We make our way down the long hallway. I've never realized how dark it is in here. Or maybe this is normal and I'm the lucky bastard who gets the brightness of Paris Lowe, and now everything else feels dim.

"Here you are." Mother practically floats across the room, the sleeves of her silky dress flailing behind her. "Paris, darling, you look lovely. Finn, did you know we sit together on the board of the Creative Arts Foundation?"

"I didn't know that." I glance at Paris, who looks like she wants to disappear, but she offers a stunning—if not a little fake—smile.

"Let's go. You know how Pa hates waiting." Mother kisses Cal and Saar and floats in front of us toward the dining room.

"You didn't tell me you know Mother," I whisper, holding Paris close around her waist. Something tells me she might flee.

"The board meets once a year. I forgot." She stops. "Actually, don't take it the wrong way, but your mother is someone you rather try to forget." She scrunches her face.

I laugh. "I wasn't that lucky. She's pretentious, but she isn't unkind."

"Finn," Mother's voice slices through the air.

"You're who matters here tonight." I kiss Paris's forehead and drag her into the lion's den.

* * *

"Samantha has been asking about you. You promised to take her out the other day," my mother says as the staff finishes serving our dishes.

"I doubt she's asking about me. She knows I'm in a relationship." I put down my spoon and lean back. I didn't have an appetite to begin with, but this is too much. "I don't appreciate you bringing this up while my girlfriend is here."

"I don't think Paris minds you seeing other women, since you're not marrying her." Mother slurps her soup, smiling at Paris while throwing daggers.

"Mother," I warn.

"Melody, it might come as a shock to you, but even without the ring on my finger we're still in a committed relationship." Paris smiles. "Your home is lovely."

She swallows around that lie, but I'm grateful she tries to remain civil and divert the conversation.

"Paris, have you designed any celebrity houses?" Saar jumps in. Thank God for reasonable siblings.

"Yes, some, but I can't divulge that information. I'm hoping to expand into commercial projects."

"Like offices?" Cal asks.

"I'm actually pitching for Quaint—" The words die on her lips.

"Paris also designs and makes lamps." I try to save it, but Pa's glower is pronounced as he drops his spoon and waves at the staff to clear the first course.

"Oh, have you seen the beautiful lamp Finn and Cal gave me for my birthday? You should have a look, my friends were amazed, raving about it. I promised I'll get them the designer's contact information." She looks expectantly at me, and I exhale.

I didn't mention it to Paris, because Mother looked at the gift like I had pulled it from the garbage. Clearly it's her friend's taste that moved the lamp into a different light.

"It's beautiful because the designer and creator is talented, Mother." I bring Paris's hand to my mouth and kiss her knuckles. She gives me a shy smile.

The staff brings out the main dish while Saar tells us about her work in Italy, and Cal updates Pa on some business at the hotel.

"So you're sure the child is Finn's, Paris?" Pa drops the bomb halfway through the main course.

The whole evening has been digestible only because Saar and Cal are going out of their way to keep the conversation flowing at the lightest possible level.

"Pa," I growl, and squeeze Paris's thigh under the table.

She drops her fork.

Takes the napkin and pats the corners of her mouth.

She folds it and puts it next to her plate.

The silence in the room is so loud I can hear Saar's

every breath, and she sits on the other side of the large table.

Paris squeezes my hand and moves it to my thigh. She doesn't let go, but I'm not sure if she is about to stand and leave or kill my father.

It feels like all her moves take hours while my heart thuds and I grind my molars, considering my father's murder before she has the chance.

She finally turns to my father and her smile would melt a fucking diamond. It startles my father. I don't think anyone ever smiles at him.

"Mr. van den Linden, I'm pregnant with your son's child, and in the interest of our future interactions or your ability to ever meet your grandchild, I'd appreciate if you'd stop questioning my morals and my motivations. Let me remind you I refused your son's marriage proposal. I have nothing to gain from this situation, and your lack of respect is frankly ridiculous. Let alone offensive and in very poor style."

She takes a sip of water while my father gapes at her. Then she turns to my mother. "Melody, don't you ever mention another woman in relation to your son in front of me. I'm sorry you're disappointed he is with me, but that doesn't give you the right to scheme. Not even behind my back, let alone to my face. My family might not be old money like yours, but we mind our manners."

Mother gasps. "You're a guest here. How dare you?"

"Silence," Pa bellows. "Young lady, the child will be a bastard because you won't wed my son. If you think you can attack us while under my roof with your clearly loose ideas about belonging to this family, you're mistaken. I question your motivations because any decent woman would have married my son by now."

I stand up so quickly that my chair tumbles to the floor, the thud echoing around the cavernous room.

I've never been this disgusted by him. His ego. His chauvinism. His lack of morals and heaps of pretense.

"Watch how you talk to the mother of my child. Don't you dare talk about her at all. I've never been this embarrassed by you. You attack the woman I love without even trying to get to know her. Without showing any interest in her, missing out on the wonderful human she is, because you're stuck in the last century and care more about appearances than honesty."

"Son." My father scolds.

"Oh, fuck it." I grab Paris's hand. "We're leaving."

I drag her behind me, her heels echoing in the museum of a house.

I swear again as soon as the evening air hits my lungs.

"I'm so sorry." I rake my hair and face her, and almost stumble when I meet her expression.

She's grinning at me, her eyes glowing. Fuck, her whole being is glowing. "You love me?"

Fuck. I laugh and pull her to me, kissing the hell out of her. "Yes, sorry the first time I said it was to my folks and not to you."

"We can add it to all the other backward things this relationship is built on." She plays with the hair at my nape. "I love you too."

"That's good. Really, really good."

We grin at each other for a moment, and then I seize her lips again.

And I vow to make the phone call I should have made a long time ago.

Chapter 26

Paris

"You'll be late for work—" The words die on my lips as Finn cups my mound. This is his new morning routine. Invading my shower. Not that I mind.

My orgasm comes so quickly it should be embarrassing.

"I love it when you scream my name, kitten. Can't get enough of it." Finn murmurs into my ear as he continues ravishing my body like he has nothing else to do. "I love you."

"I love you too, but I need to get out of here now. I don't want to be late. Today is—"

His mouth fuses with mine for a heated kiss, but he lets me go. "You're going to be wonderful."

"I better be, since I'll be the breadwinner soon." I chuckle and he swats at my ass.

I sound way more confident than I am. I hate presenting. I mean, I don't mind pitching my ideas to people, but presenting in front of a panel or a committee judging your every word? I shiver.

I wrap a towel around me and distract myself by admiring his ripped body under the stream of water for a moment, before I snap into the reality of my busy morning.

It's been two weeks since the dinner with Finn's parents. He's leaving the company, and I think the situation with his father will only escalate.

But we've been happy in our little bubble, mostly catching up on all the sex we missed during the ban. What was I thinking there?

"I'm attending a movie premiere tonight. Will you be my plus one, Ms. Lowe?" He turns off the water and steps out, shaking his head and spraying me.

"No." I step to the side and grab my hairbrush.

These moments of domesticity between us infiltrated my life without me noticing or overthinking, and I love them.

I love waking up beside this man.

I love having him cook for me.

I love talking to him.

I love him.

I almost wish he'd ask me again to marry him. I might need to do it this time around. But I'm not yet ready to face the scrutiny of marrying a van den Linden.

"Come on, Paris. At some point, we need to make this official."

"And at some point we will, but if I can delay the media frenzy, I will. Maybe we can start with dinner at a popular restaurant, not a movie premiere full of cameras."

I don't tell him I'm mostly avoiding being one of the harem of women who he has discarded before. "Besides, it's Thursday and I have my dance class."

I've been keeping the particulars of this class from him because I have a feeling he might not understand. Though he's been supporting me on all other fronts, so I should trust him with this.

"You never told me what kind of dance it is."

Shit. It's not like I could continue for much longer. My hand goes to my still flat stomach, and when I look up in the mirror, I catch Finn's eyes on my palms, his gaze soft with emotion.

He steps closer and wraps his arms around me, placing his large hands over mine while kissing my neck. "Everything okay?"

He cares so much, and right now he misinterpreted my hesitation and I'm grateful for that. I will tell him tonight what my Thursday hobby is.

His breath on my skin is an aphrodisiac, but the moment is tender and peaceful as he caresses my belly.

In our private bubble, we talk little about the future, just basking in the bliss of the present, but I guess the awareness lingers, regardless.

Sighing, I lean into him. Of course he's hard. "You're a sex addict."

"I'm a you addict, kitten."

My stomach growls and he laughs. My bodily functions have been spoiling a lot of moments lately. Another side effect of pregnancy I could live without.

"Let's feed you. Eggs, or toast with jam?"

"Just toast. I'll dry my hair and be right down." I open the drawer, pull out my hair dryer and almost close it with my fingers still in.

Finn takes the dryer from my hand and kisses my knuckles. "Are you sure I can leave you alone?"

"I'm just nervous. The presentation—"

"You'll be fabulous. From what you've told me about the project, I'm confident you'll dazzle the Quaintique executives."

He says it with a conviction that bolsters me with equal confidence. "Thank you."

Kissing my temple, he saunters out. Naked and so hot. How did I get so lucky?

I style my hair and get dressed, rehearsing the Quaintique presentation in my head. My stomach growls again and I rush downstairs, regretting that I only asked for a piece of toast.

The smell of bacon and eggs hits my nose. Damn it. He made himself something better. My mouth waters.

Finn looks up and his eyes widen, full of hunger and adoration. "How do you get more beautiful every day? No wonder I'm hard all the time."

"And here I thought you keep watching porn."

"That's only for inspiration." He shrugs.

"And thank God for that." I climb behind the breakfast counter and look at my perfectly crisp toast, and then at the pan where Finn's eggs and bacon sizzle.

"Every fucking morning." He guffaws and scrapes his breakfast onto my plate.

"Thank you. I love you."

"Yeah, you better," he grumbles, and turns to the fridge as I dig into his former feast.

"My family has a table at London's gala tomorrow night," he says. "We should figure out the seating."

I groan.

"It won't be that bad. Pa will schmooze, and I'll make sure Saar sits on your other side."

"You can't blame me for my lack of excitement at spending a night being judged."

"They've judged me all my life and look at me."

I snort. "Exactly," I tease.

"Hey..." he protests half-heartedly. "I'm happy to sit with your family." He starts making his eggs.

"If we sit together, there goes our little bubble and we'll be official."

"Sweetheart, after tomorrow's gala, we're official. And I'm putting the ring on your finger. If you think I'll let you dance with anyone else, or that I'll keep my hands off you all night, you better think again."

I blink a few times and then I jump down, round the island and pounce. Finn stumbles but steadies us quickly. Our mouths collide together.

"Finally, my proposal got the response I was hoping for."

"Officially, you haven't proposed yet." I grin and glimpse the clock on the oven. "Shit, I have to go."

He kisses me again. "Good luck. Not that you need it."

Well, if the day continues this way, by the end of it I'll have everything I ever wanted.

I should have known it was too good to be true.

I roll down my black fishnet stockings, smiling. I have been smiling all day.

The presentation at Quaintique went really well. Though we left disappointed because they informed us of personnel changes that may lead to another presentation.

But it was still the biggest, most concrete step in this new direction. I told Barry he'll lead the project, and I swear the man grew a few inches.

I want to focus on the baby and on the lamps and the building Finn bought. After speaking to Barry, I realized how much I need to move away from daily execution and stay in just a creative role.

"I can't believe this is your last class. You're such a natural." Celeste leans against the wall beside me in the dance studio's changing rooms.

I've been taking private burlesque classes for several months. It started with my bucket list, but as with the coffee snatching, it grew from there.

Here, with Celeste, I can discover my sexuality while enjoying dancing and movement. Burlesque helped me unleash my inner goddess, and I feel better in my body.

Thinking of it now, I don't even know why I felt I couldn't tell Finn about it. It's not like he hasn't reaped the benefits. But London poked fun at this, calling it a stripper class, and people misjudge burlesque so often.

"I'm going to miss the class. Maybe I can still continue for a while."

"Talk to that man of yours, or bring him over. I'm

sure he'll enjoy the show." Celeste purses her lips and shimmies her hips.

"I'll tell him. You're right. He'll love it."

"And demand private shows," she says with her heavy accent. Celeste came from France ten years ago, but never lost the purring intonation completely. It adds to her grace and elegance.

She is curvy and soft, and I've never met a woman who is more comfortable in her own skin.

Celeste's phone pings with a message. "*Merde.* I'll be right back."

She dials and murmurs into the phone. Something is wrong. I turn away to keep from intruding on her conversation and change from the corset into my clothes.

Celeste returns, tapping her phone in her hand.

"Is everything okay?"

"No, one of my dancers got sick and canceled on me. Tonight we're performing at this small club that was going to give me a long-term contract. I can't lose the opportunity. Things are tight as they are already."

"I'm sorry. Can I help somehow?"

She shakes her head but then thinks better of it. "Yes, yes, you can, *mon amie.*"

I frown, startled by her sudden enthusiasm. "Okay. How?" I mean, I can write her a check, I guess.

"You step in."

I laugh.

"I'm serious, Paris, you're great. You know the choreography. You can totally do it."

"Are you insane? I can't perform in front of people."

"But of course you can. You're a natural. Please, please, please. I really need tonight to go well."

"You're crazy, Celeste."

Is she? Can I try it? If I was still pushing my own boundaries, then this would be the perfect opportunity. But do I need to push my boundaries further? Do I need to be seen like this?

Celeste bounces on her heels as she waits for my answer, her puppy eyes chipping away at my self-doubt. Or maybe I'm just boosted by the presentation's success earlier today.

"You know what? Let's do it. But it's a one time thing." As soon as I say it, my stomach squeezes, anxiety cruising through me.

"Yes, yes, yes." Celeste hugs me, kissing my cheeks. "You're the best. You're literally saving my ham."

I laugh. "Bacon. The expression is saving my bacon."

"Whatever, it's pork, anyway." She beams. "Let's find you a boa, and something to wear so you'll be comfortable. This is a classy joint and your choreography is perfect for it."

"It's not a strip club, I hope."

Her mouth shapes a perfect O and she looks truly offended. "Of course not, darling. I'm a performer, not a hussy."

She finds me clothes and we take an Uber to get to the club. It's a small underground place in Chelsea with a Thirties aura. I love it immediately, but the nerves are still present.

In the tiny backstage space, Celeste introduces me to the other three dancers who greet me with relief.

One of them, Celia, starts helping me with makeup while everyone chats and giggles. This is surreal. I can't believe I'm doing it, but I'm excited to try something this different.

My fashion show experience was tainted, so this would be like a proper goodbye to my bucket list.

One girl paces around and keeps running to check the audience through the heavy red theater curtain.

"I'm glad I'm not the only one stressed out."

Celia curls the iron around a strand of my hair and scoffs. "She has some new sugar daddy and is hoping he comes to watch her." She unrolls the iron. "Perfect. You're ready."

I turn to the mirror and almost don't recognize myself. My hair is curled around with two large feathers sticking out, and my makeup is... well... beautiful, but too much. I smile at myself. Okay, this is just a riot.

My nerves only get worse as the performances start, and by the time my number approaches I'm ready to burst out through the fire exit and buy Celeste's dance school to compensate her.

I'm last before the break, and I walk on to the small stage like a newborn lamb. My number starts with my back to the audience. I close my eyes. With the first beats of the sultry music, I decide to pretend this is just the class.

I've danced to this score many times before and my body recognizes it immediately, letting me unleash my freedom and fully immerse myself in my burlesque persona. I start moving and hear a first smattering of applause even before I turn to face the small crowd.

But I tune everything out and dive into the experience. It's the first and last time I'm doing it, so I might as well go all in.

And I do. Halfway through the performance, I lean into the femme fatale I can be for these few minutes, and I even start improvising, enjoying the reactions of the audience.

I end my dance straddling a chair, the applause boosting the adrenaline and endorphins coursing through me.

I blow a kiss to the audience and stumble backstage on a high.

"You were amazing." Celeste embraces me and the girls cheer.

"It was scary and amazing, and oh my God, how can you do this every night? But thank you. I loved it."

Celeste hugs me and then tenses. "You can't be here."

I turn to see the fuming man. Finn's father.

I check my phone yet again and dial Finn's number, but it goes to his voice mail. I sit in the middle of my living room in the darkness like I have been for the past two hours.

Please don't let his father get to him before me. Finn would laugh at this if I get to tell him the story, but not if his father poisons him first.

And the entire experience was for nothing, because Celeste lost the contract amidst the hell that Charles van den Linden caused at the club.

My phone rings and I almost jump. Finally. But my excitement dies when I see London's number.

"What the fuck, Paris?" Lo growls at me. "Great timing. The night before my biggest event? I could have done without a major publicity crisis."

My heart thuds in my temple. "What are you talking about?"

"Jesus fucking Christ, you don't even know. Check your phone."

Several photos come through and I go completely still. "Oh my God."

"You've been dancing at a club? Stripping?"

"For the umpteenth time, it's not stripping. It's burlesque and I took off a boa, for God's sake. How did those pics get out? Why would he do that?"

"Who?"

"Finn's father."

"What?"

"He was there." I hiccup through my tears as I tell her what happened. *I will destroy you and enjoy every minute of it.* His words echo in my mind. I didn't expect him to destroy me publicly.

"Fuck. What is Finn saying?"

"I don't know." I sob. "He has been at some movie premiere and hasn't answered yet."

"Do you want me to come over? Do you want my PR firm to get involved? Or let's get Gio and Mila on it."

"I need to call Dad and Bianca."

"They are sleeping. You do that tomorrow. Try to reach Finn and I'll call Mila. We'll get this fixed." She stops and sighs, confirming how unfixable this is. "We get this mitigated."

"Thank you, Lo."

The front door opens and the man I love stands there. I can't see his face in the darkness of the room, but by his stance and the way he freezes in the entrance I know he knows.

"Finn just came in. I'll talk to you later."

I hang up and don't move, because the space between us feels like a minefield.

He flips the light switch and frowns, looking me up and down.

"So it's true." He shakes his head.

I check my reflection in the window. Shit. I should have changed.

"Finn—"

"This is what you have been doing on Thursdays?" The contempt in his voice cuts through me like a sharp knife.

He keeps fisting his hands, his jaw rigid.

"I have never—"

"Don't lie to me. Don't you fucking lie to me again." He steps toward me, but then shakes his head and turns sideways.

"Finn, I've been taking burlesque classes. I've never been to that club before. A friend needed help because one dancer got sick."

"And of course my father is there that *one* night." He mocks me. "So much for keeping this in our own bubble. Is this the reason you wanted to keep us secret, so it doesn't get out that you're a stripper?"

"Stop it right now. I'm not a stripper. I dance burlesque because it helps me feel better in my body. Maybe I shouldn't have danced in public tonight, but your father happily grabbed at the opportunity for a smear campaign."

"And do you think I enjoyed defending you to him after I was completely blindsided? You lied to me. You fucking lied to me again."

The hurt, the disappointment, the resentment in his features will haunt me forever. No matter how and when we fix this, I'll never forget his angst.

"I didn't lie." I try to keep my voice level. "I didn't tell you about burlesque because it was something very private and intimate, and I feared you'd react like..." I swallow, my heart breaking into a million pieces. "Like this."

He shakes his head, looking at me like I shattered his dreams, puked all over them and then went to high five his father.

We glare at each other in silence, me pleading for him to step out of the fog of anger, him... I don't know, deciding our future?

I must look horrible with the smeared, teary

makeup in my sexy get-up, but I hope he can see the real me.

"Finn, say something please."

He shakes his head. "I need time to process all of this. I need space."

"Finn—" I know I owe him the space and time to process, but I fear once he steps over that threshold, we won't find the way back anymore. "Finn—"

He opens the door and stops. "You didn't want to share something because it was private and intimate. How can we have a chance, then, keeping things from each other?" He doesn't turn to me, and his voice is full of anger. "Loving you isn't enough for you to trust me. I have always been just a bucket list item for you. A failed one-night stand."

Chapter 27

Paris

A buzzing tone wakes me up. I scrunch my face, a startling pain shooting down my leg from my hip. Jesus, I fell asleep on the floor. After Finn left, I cried while calling him repeatedly. No response. I sent him several messages, but they remained unread. I shouldn't have let him leave. We should have dealt with this together. And we will. He'll be back.

I sniffle, surprised to have any tears left. I scramble to my knees, finally realizing the sound is coming from my phone.

I flip the phone over and deflate when I see it's not him.

"Hey, Mila." I sound like I sang all night.

"Paris, are you okay? Did I wake you?"

"I dozed off. What time is it?"

"One in the morning. Listen, Gio's gotten some photos taken down. He's also talking to Art Mathison, who can wipe them all out, hopefully. He's some cyber genius. I don't know him, but his wife is Violet, the gallery owner?"

"Mila, focus," Gio says in the background.

"Sorry, anyway, we agreed it would be best if you left for a few days. Until things die down. Is Finn with you?"

She hurls the words at me. Jesus, people have been working an all-nighter to save my reputation while I slept on the floor. "No."

"Why the fuck isn't he with you?" Gio says impatiently. "Get him. I have my plane on standby to take you wherever you want. Spend a weekend in Europe or something. This will die down quickly, but just in case the media vultures camp in front of your house, it's better you leave. Whoever leaked this, they're connected."

"It was Finn's father." I don't know why I choose to unveil that tasteful tidbit right now. Perhaps to share the blame. To not feel all alone in the mess that I've caused. And here I thought I couldn't sink any lower.

"Fuck. What was he thinking?"

"I guess I'm not good enough for his son, so he used

the opportunity." I'm bitter, tired, hurt, desperate. "And now his son thinks that, too."

It seems that bitterness tops the pile of sour feelings swallowing me. In their turbulent relationship, the two van den Lindens finally found some common ground. Hating me.

Loving you isn't enough for you to trust me.

I stifle a sob.

"What do you want to do, Paris?" Gio urges.

"I'll come over and help you pack," Mila says, her tone soothing. "Go to Europe for the weekend, or to California, and we'll take care of things here. I'm sure Finn will come around."

Will he? "You don't have to come. I'll manage. I'll go to England to stay with Brook."

"Are you sure?" Gio sounds perplexed. The Cassinetti boys never visit my little sister, so I understand his surprise.

"Yes, I'm sure. Just please clean the mess up quickly."

"Sure, sis. My car will pick you up in half an hour."

"Thank you. For everything."

I'm jetlagged. Pregnant. Exhausted. Nauseous.

Heartbroken.

And the loud music coming from Brook's living room is not making things better. Not in the least.

I should have stayed closer. I should have stayed home. Finn went off the grid, but perhaps his PR team gave him the same advice as me. Though that's just wishful thinking because he's been kept out of the coverage. And it's not like we've ever been officially linked to each other.

Why doesn't he answer my calls? He was pissed, but he's never shied away from a fight.

It's been the longest two days of my life. I wonder if my heart will ever recover. Mila texted me earlier that some scandal erupted with a dairy family heiress and she's positive my thing is under control now.

I need to return and talk to Finn. Find him and force him to listen. To lean into love, not hatred. *I want love, not hate.* My words come back, haunting me. I hope that's what he wants still.

The irony isn't lost on me. I fought so hard to keep us away from the public eye, and I ended up surpassing his media game several times over.

Still, in this fucked up crisis, I needed him to stand by me, but I see his point of view. Out of all the things I might have thrown at him, I blindsided him in a situation that involved his father.

Fuck.

"Hey, sleepyhead." Brook enters, dressed to the nines. "I thought we could hit the town and celebrate your visit. You look like someone who needs cheering up."

"You went out last night. When do you sleep?" I scoot my knees closer to me and she plops on the bed, lying on her back.

In her sparkling black pumps and equally shimmery red halter top, she looks like a supermodel. She's the only Lowe sister with blond hair, which she hated when she was little.

It was just another thing that made her different from us, starting with her name. Brooklyn just wasn't metropolitan enough, like our names.

"Sleep is overrated. I'll sleep when I'm dead. We always hit the town when you visit."

"I'm pregnant, Brook."

She sits up, staring at me. "Oh, fuck, are you running away from the father? Do you know who the father is?"

I roll my eyes. "Jesus, your imagination is wild. I'm not running away from him." I sigh, my eyes welling up again. "He doesn't want to see me at the moment."

"Asshole. I hate him already." She scoots closer and sits beside me, snaking her arm around my shoulders.

"He is an idiot. You'll be the best baby mama ever. How dare he—"

"It's complicated."

And I tell her the story of Finn and Paris that started with my little lie. And hopefully didn't end up with another fuck-up of mine.

"Shit." It's all she says once I finish.

I'm proud I got through it without completely breaking down.

"He seems like a cool dude, though. I mean you lied, ghosted him, sent him away and avoided him for so long, it doesn't make sense that he would draw the line at wiggling boobs in a corset. He didn't care what his family thought about you and defended you. I don't get it."

"That's what is puzzling. I understand he stormed out, but that he hasn't cooled down yet is just plain weird."

"Maybe he lost his phone." She shrugs.

I chuckle, but there is no humor in it. "That's your thing, Brook."

"Well, it gives me the opportunity to always own the latest iPhone." She pokes my ribs. "Come on, let's go out. It will cheer you up. I've missed you so much."

"Why don't you ever come to visit, then?" I turn to her and she flinches. "Dad isn't doing all that well,

Brook. You'll regret it if you don't spend some time with him now."

She looks away, biting on her thumb's cuticle. "Has Baldo been home?"

"God knows where he is." Why would she ask about him? "I think he calls Bianca once a year, but that's about it. But there are six other siblings, your stepmom and your father. You haven't met Massi's children yet, or Sydney's little girl. Hell, London and Gio are in committed relationships and you practically don't know half of the extended family. Whatever keeps you here, Brook, I never understood. You can party in New York as well, by the way."

"My life is here."

"Is it though? Your secret career you never want to talk about and your shopping sprees and partying? It's not like anything is holding you here."

I don't even know why I'm going on about this. I guess it's an easy distraction from my own shitty situation.

"If you came here to judge me, I might as well go out and enjoy my life."

I have an apology on my tongue when a loud banging on the door startles us.

Brook lives in a swanky condominium building in Notting Hill with a doorman, so whoever is trying to break down the door right now should have been announced.

"Fuck." She jumps out of bed.

"What's going on?" I shuffle behind her, but I stop when she doesn't open the door.

"Go away, Dylan," she yells at the top of her lungs.

"Brook, baby, open up. I know you're mad, but let me apologize," the Dylan dude yells back, still banging on the door between his words.

"Go away." She leans her back against the rattling door, fisting her hands, shaking.

"Should we call the police?" I whisper.

"Bloody hell, Brook, open the fucking door right now or I'll break it." The banging gets louder.

We both jump as my phone shrieks. I set it on the highest volume for fear I'd doze off and miss Finn's call.

Now the high-pitched sound adds to the overall mayhem around us, but I remain rooted, unable to move. The man on the other side of the door is about to kill us.

I wished so much for Finn to finally call, and now I'm hoping it's not him. I don't want to miss his call.

More invectives and banging continue outside. Missing Finn's call is definitely low on the disasters list right now, and yet I find myself torn between the two sounds, paralyzed by indecision.

"I'll take care of it." Brook, who looks scared, but

unlike me is not useless, rushes to get her phone, while my heart rate skyrockets with every new bang. My phone quiets.

Brook returns and I catch the end of her phone conversation. "Thank you, Collin."

The idiot outside is going to kick through the door. "Who is Collin? You didn't call the cops?" I snap in a low voice.

My phone rings again. I cover my ears, my nerves reverberating through my body. Calm down. Calm the fuck down, Paris. This can't be good for the baby.

Now I'm even more upset at myself for performing, at Finn's father for using the opportunity to sabotage my relationship, at Finn for siding with him.

He sided with his family.

That thought takes root in my head, blocking all the other sounds. I keep my hands on my stomach, hoping against all reason that this is just a long, exhausting nightmare.

"Okay, you twat, what did I tell you about coming back here?" a voice thunders on the other side of the door, snapping me back to high alert.

I have no idea what's happening, but by now I'm shaking as badly as Brook is.

"Brook, you fucking called your dog on me again. Are you fucking her, big guy?" Dylan's voice comes out all cocky and Brook closes her eyes.

"What are you doing? I'm going to sue you, dick-head," Dylan continues shouting.

"You do that." The stranger chuckles.

After a few moments of squabbling, the sounds retreat.

My breaths are coming in short bursts, not filling my lungs enough. "Who was that?"

"Dylan is my ex. Collin is my neighbor, former Special Forces." Brook bites her cuticle again, this time drawing blood.

"Brook," I sigh and step closer, but she jerks away.

"It's okay. Collin's got it. I'm good." She sounds about as good as a shelter dog, but I don't get a chance to react because someone knocks.

It's not even a normal knock, more like some sort of a code.

Brook dashes to the door, and without looking through the peephole, she opens it. A bulky—like super huge—man enters.

"He's gone. I had a quick word with the guard downstairs. The ass-hat must have slipped in while they were distracted."

The man notices me and frowns. "Hey, I'm Collin. We live two floors up with the missus."

"Oh, sorry, this is my sister, Paris," Brooks says awkwardly, fidgeting with nervous energy.

"I won't keep you, but you either talk to the cops or hire a bodyguard, Brook. What if I weren't home?"

I need so many answers right now, but more than that I need to hear Finn's voice. I dash to the bedroom, and I groan when I realize all the calls were from London.

Sighing, I dial her number.

"Finally. Jesus, where have you been?"

Her voice isn't annoyed or teasing, it's not even the angry aloofness she bestows on people. The tone is closer to concern.

In the scale of all the emotions of the past minutes, hours and days, her question hits me with eerie finality.

"Is Dad okay?" My voice is loud, startling me.

Brook and Collin go silent in the other room.

"It's Finn. He's in the hospital," Lo says, and I go still.

So still I forget to breathe.

"I went with Dad for some tests, and I ran into his brother. Apparently he went racing and had an accident. He's been in an induced coma since Friday."

Since the night he left my house.

"Racing?" My brain is not offering helpful thoughts.

"I don't have any details. Caleb said he didn't have your number. I think the van den Lindens kept this out of the media. I'm assuming it was illegal racing."

Still no coherent thought, just pain spreading through my chest, stabbing my battered heart again and again.

I drop my phone and collapse to my knees, howling.

This can't be happening? He was racing? He's in a coma? I can't lose him. I can't do this alone. Oh my God, what have I done to us?

By the time I'm able to render an intelligible word, Brook and Collin are staring at me shocked.

Brook squats down next to me. "Come on, honey. Lo told me what happened."

"I have to go home."

"I know," Brook's voice is soft. "I'm coming with you."

* * *

My legs shake as I step out of the car in front of Mount Sinai Hospital. Brook hooks her arm through mine as we rush inside.

It takes us a good half hour to finally get to the private wing where Finn hopefully lies. Why don't I have Cal's or Saar's number? Goddammit. I tried to call Finn's office, but of course Reilly isn't working.

"You're not on the visitor's list, Miss. I can't let you see him," a nurse says gently, but firmly.

"Look, she's his fiancée." Brook jumps in. "Isn't his family here to vouch for her?"

God, at least one of us has a functional brain. We spent the flight in complete silence while she force-fed me and made sure I drank enough water. Her care reminded me of Finn and made me cry harder.

The nurse sighs, her lips thin. "Okay, I'll talk to them."

I breathe my first sigh of relief since I finished the stupid performance on Friday night. Brook strokes my back and I try not to shake, but it's useless. I need to calm the fuck down. For the baby. For Finn.

The nurse's rubber soles slap back toward us, and the sound fills me with unwarranted hope. That hope dies as soon as I see who is coming with her.

"You're not welcome here." Finn's father looks down his nose at me. "This is all your fault."

My lip shakes as I try to find words to plea with him.

"Hey. She didn't send him racing," Brook argues.

He jerks his head. "Who are you? Keep your voice down."

"Mr. van den Linden, is Finn okay?" I need to know.

That's the first step. I need to know.

"No, he's not okay. Your immoral antics drew him

to that track. He might never walk out of here, and that's on you. You broke this family."

A loud sob escapes me.

"Don't talk to her like that." Brook raises her voice again. "Finn has the right to see her."

Charles van den Linden looks at us with contempt. "Yes, and he also has the right to never see her again."

My heart breaks into a million small pieces, and that's before he adds, "Which are exactly his wishes."

His words barely register as my vision blurs, and everything goes dark.

Chapter 28

Finn

"Call Paris," I tell Mother and close my eyes. Fuck, I need to stay awake, but it doesn't work. The darkness claims me.

When I wake up again, my hospital room hasn't changed much. Full of grim-looking faces. Okay, not full, because Cal and Saar aren't here right now. And neither is Paris.

"Have you called her?" Why is talking such an effort?

"Finn, you're up." Mother's voice must be coming through a loudspeaker. "Let me get the doctor." She rushes out of the room.

Her swift action makes my head spin. Why can't she move slowly so I can ask her again about Paris?

My eyes land on my father, who is looking at me with the same contempt as ever. "Where is Paris?"

He looks out of the window and adjusts his sleeves. "She didn't want to come."

I think I understand all those words individually, but they make no sense. My head isn't right. They said the swelling got better while I was sleeping for three days, but the fog remains thick.

Thinking hurts.

Talking hurts.

Being hurts.

When I say nothing, Pa continues.

"It's for the best, Finn. That woman was no good for our family. She tricked you, and now she's gone. I'm sure your resignation was her doing as well. She broke the family, so as far as I'm concerned, good riddance."

Oh, yeah, I resigned on Thursday. Jesus, was that just three days ago? Or a week? Pa didn't take it the way I expected. There was no yelling, no accusations. He simply took my letter of resignation and said *I see.*

It was anti-climactic to say the least, but I was happy there was no drama. And oddly deflated. Not that I expected him to beg me to stay, but I was hoping he'd have reacted somehow.

Not sure why after all these years I'm still hoping to get a reaction from him. Other than disapproval and disappointment.

The concerning part is this time I didn't get either of those.

"She didn't want to come?" I ignore the rest of his attack because I have no energy to argue. "What did you tell her?"

"Me? Nothing. We asked her to come, and she said she doesn't want to see you. Let it be, boy. You need to focus on yourself right now. Thank God I haven't officially accepted your resignation. We'll fix it all. Just rest."

I want to tell him I'm not coming back to work for him, but first I need a phone to call her myself. This makes no sense. But before I get a chance, Mother returns with a short Asian man.

He introduces himself as Dr. Lee. He flips through my chart, looking just as comfortable in his ironed white scrubs as he does in his gloomy expression.

He straightens and looks down at me, his face screaming he believes he can cure cancer. I guess his degrees are worth every penny we pay here.

When he returns to studying the chart for what feels like half a day, I clear my throat. Fuck, it feels like a gargantuan effort while I'm lying here immobile. "Alright, Doc, give it to me. I'm on a tight schedule of self-pity here."

He looks at me finally. "How are you feeling, Finn?"

"Seriously? I guess that's pretty obvious. I can't

move and my life has just been uprooted on so many levels. How do you think I am?"

Fuck this shit.

Nobody tells me anything.

Why isn't she here? I need to talk to her. To see her. To tell her.

"I understand you're upset. Can you tell me how your pain is on a scale from one to ten?"

"Twenty," I snarl.

"Finn," Mother breathes and sniffles, tapping a white handkerchief at the corner of her eyes.

With a sigh, I answer several questions about my vital functions.

"Finn," Dr. Lee says, and makes a dramatic pause. Just spill it finally. "You've got several injuries that are non-life-threatening. The head trauma is under control now, though you'll probably be experiencing headaches. Our primary concern is your fractured leg. We'll run a few scans, and once you're cleared to go under the anesthesia, we'll operate. Chances are that after the physiotherapy you'll be able to regain your leg's full function."

I raise an eyebrow, and even that hurts. "Marvelous. When can I get out of here?"

"Finn," my father barks now.

Lee ignores my snark and continues, "The surgery is crucial, but it carries some risks, including infection, nerve damage, or, worst case, chronic pain or partial paralysis."

All other thoughts evaporate, but the asshole in me continues with the sarcasm. "Chronic pain? Partial paralysis? Wonderful options."

Lee still seems unperturbed by my antics. "If successful, you could regain full function."

"If?" Pa snaps. "I'm not paying thousands and thousands of dollars to have an 'if' prognosis. You fix him and you fix him well. It's a fucking broken leg, not brain damage."

"Charles." Mother puts her hand on Pa's shoulder. It doesn't help his flaring nostrils, but at least he stops talking.

"You fractured your leg in seven different places. We'll do as many reconstructive surgeries as possible, but this can be a long process. And its success depends on your cooperation during the recovery."

I sigh. "Fantastic. Let's get started, Doc."

I blink a few times. Why does my mouth feel like a desert? I swallow, my throat filled with gravel. This is one shitty hangover. Wait? Where did I party?

The antiseptic smell, the distant hum and beeping finally orients me. Shit, I had the surgery. They should have warned me the waking up part isn't all that peachy.

I pry my eyes open, but that doesn't work either, and my lids snap shut. I'm not giving up though, and after a few attempts I flutter them open.

My gaze meets with a scowl. An owl? Am I hallucinating? What the fuck? I blink a few times and the blur clears.

Cal sleeps in a leather recliner beside me. I scan my surroundings. The room is still the same, more a bedroom than a hospital room if it wasn't for the hydraulic bed and all the machines.

They could invest in better art, though. The owl glaring at me from the painting across the room is weird.

"Cal," I rasp, and for a second I wonder if I even made the sound.

But he opens his eyes immediately and straightens up, staring at me like I've just landed from a different galaxy.

"What do I need to do—" I swallow and breathe a few times. "To get some whiskey around here?" Fuck, making jokes hurts.

He snorts and drags his hand down his face before he jumps up. "Fuck, you asshole, you scared the shit out of me."

He gets a glass with a straw and puts it to my lips. I

take a sip and close my eyes, panting. "That surgery took all my energy."

I remember Dr. Lee talking, and then after a scan deciding I was good to go.

I wanted to call Paris, but felt I'd better do it once I was out of the surgery. All that feels like two minutes ago.

"Or the stroke and the two weeks in a coma probably didn't make you feel virile." He sits down, shaking his head.

I want to respond to that, laugh at him or just send him to hell, but somehow the words roam in my brain and don't find purchase.

"Yeah, dickhead, you had a stroke during the surgery. They induced coma. Fuck, bro, I'm so happy you're up."

"What?" I ask with my eyes closed, because keeping them open is exhausting.

"Don't worry. We'll talk later. I'll get the doctor."

When I open my eyes again, it's dark. Cal is standing by the window, looking outside.

"Hey."

He turns. "Hey, sleepyhead. Feeling better? All

that beauty sleep will give you an unfair advantage with the ladies, fucker."

I curl my lips up, and then I remember what he'd said before. Stroke. Fucking stroke. I scrunch my face and Cal rushes to me.

"Are you in pain?"

I shake my head, but internally I high five myself. If he saw my grimace, then I can move my face. Is that how it works?

I wiggle my fingers and toes. I think they are moving. But isn't that the thing with paralysis—that you believe you're moving them even when you're not? Fuck.

"Am I okay?" I hear my question, and I immediately know I'm not okay because who asks that?

"Well, you're alive. That's something. Saar and Mom were here almost all afternoon, but I sent them home and took the night shift babysitting you. Pa was here this morning. We've been taking turns, but I'll call them if you want."

I shake my head. "What about Paris?"

"What about her? Just rest, we can talk later."

"I've slept for weeks, I'm good. Has she come to see me?"

"Why would she after you sent her away, and from what I heard made it quite clear you never wanted to see her again?"

I close my eyes. Did I? Why would I have done that? Do I have amnesia? I try to replay the events since I resigned. Pa called me later that day and told me Paris was a stripper, and then articles circulated, and we fought and I left.

I was upset and went to clear my head. Fuck. And woke up in the hospital. Pa told me she didn't want to see me.

"Cal, she didn't want to see me. She's upset because I stormed out after her pictures—" I can't finish, the idea of all those fuckers jerking off to those pictures makes me want to explode.

"Okay, well, maybe you don't remember it well. I ran into Gio at the Madison Club a few days ago, and he was pissed. He said you're an asshole, and if he ever sees you near Paris again, he will personally end you."

"She didn't want to come. Didn't want to see me." I keep repeating it, but none of it makes sense. Why would Gio threaten me? I screwed up, but for fuck's sake. She decided to break it—

"Cal, was it you talking to her? After the accident, did you call her?"

"No, but I ran into her sister and told her what happened."

I force my brain to connect the dots, but it's a useless effort because sleep is trying to claim me again.

"How did Pa know she doesn't want to see me? I

can't believe he would have called her. But then she isn't here, is she?"

"Pa can't stand her. Why would he know anything about it? It's not like they talk. He blames her for your resignation. He leaked those photos to discredit her, 'so you'll see reason,' as he put it."

I close my eyes. All the years I wished that my father would pay attention to me. Want me by his side. And here we are, he extends me attention only to manipulate situations to his own will.

"Where is my phone?" I wish I could speak with the urgency I'm feeling, but my words are coming out in slow motion.

He disappears from my line of vision, and I consider moving my head to follow him, but by the time I build up the stamina he's back with my phone.

"It's dead. Let me plug it in."

"Are you fucking kidding me? Charge it enough to get her number."

"Okay, chill, dude. It's midnight anyway."

"I don't fucking care."

He looks at me like I'm deranged and takes his time plugging in the phone.

The nurse bursts in. "Are you okay, Mr. van den Linden?"

"Call me Cal, Mr. van den Linden is my father," my idiot brother drawls.

"Hi, I'm Carly." She beams like a fucking lighthouse, but at least she doesn't forget her duties and walks over to me—while eye-fucking Cal—and puts her fingers on my wrist. "Your pulse is high. Are you in pain? Do you feel dizzy?"

All her questions seem addressed to Cal.

"I'm fine," I growl, and she startles and jerks her head toward me.

"Just your heart monitor showed—"

"It showed that I'm pissed and frustrated. Correct. Stop flirting with my brother and go print an AMA for me."

She gasps. "You can't leave. You've just woken—"

"Carly, I haven't asked for your opinion. Get a doctor to sign off on my release right now."

She stares at me, frozen.

"Move now, and I'll get you a date with him."

She looks at Cal as if that was the deciding factor here.

"Carly, sweetheart, don't listen to him," my traitor brother says. "I'll take you on a date, regardless. He's not in his right mind."

"Fuck you, Cal. Go and get the doctor, because I'm getting out of here anyway."

Cal raises his arms in exasperation. "And now we know the stroke damaged his brain."

"Find me clothes if you don't want me to have another one. I have to go see her."

* * *

"Can you go faster?" I growl as Cal navigates the wheelchair toward the elevators.

"Shut the fuck up. I'm doing my best. Fuck, if you have another stroke, or something happens to you—"

"Nothing will happen to me if I see her."

"This is so romantic," Carly chirps, her shoes squeaking against the linoleum as she tries to keep up.

After the longest negotiation of my life, the doctor made an exception and under the condition that nurse Carly travels with us with her medical kit and we take an ambulance, the doctor allowed me to leave the hospital for a few hours.

I still had to sign the AMA, pay for Carly's time and the ambulance, but never have I spent money with more determination.

By the time we pull up in front of Paris's house, it's almost four o'clock in the morning.

"I don't think she'll appreciate you waking her up," Cal says as the driver and the paramedic help me out of their vehicle and into the wheelchair.

"Cal, I swear to God—" I growl, as a throbbing pain sears my leg. I pant, sweat trickling down my temples.

Maybe having a shower and buying flowers first would have been a better idea.

"Are you okay?" Carly asks, and I look up.

Cal has his arm around her shoulder. And I'm fucking paying for this.

"I'm fine. Just help me up the stairs and take the stupid wheelchair away."

"No, you stay in the wheelchair." Carly steps away from my brother and puts her hands on her hips. "You're too weak. You won't get the girl if you crack your skull on the pavement." Her voice is so stern that it renders me speechless.

Cal smiles like a Cheshire cat. "And your leg is fucked up."

"Okay," I grumble.

The two paramedics carry me to the door and ring the bell.

"Thank you, but please get lost." I wave them away.

Fuck, I had a stroke, but I'm going to have a heart attack now. The imaginary clock ticks in my head, filling me with regret. I should have never stormed out of here that night.

"Do you want us to ring the bell again?" Cal asks from the street.

"I'm good." I move the wheelchair closer and knock. And knock, and then ball my hand into a fist and bang.

I almost collapse out of the chair when the door swings open.

"What the fuck? I'm calling the cops." The woman snarls and then jerks her head down, surprised by the handicapped intruder.

Her blond hair is in a messy bun, and she is wearing a black, silky camisole. And she isn't Paris.

"Who are you?" By now I'm pretty sure a heart attack is in my imminent future.

She raises her eyebrows and snorts. "Are you for real? You're disturbing us, not the other way around. Who the fuck are you?"

"Where is Paris?" Did she sell the house? Has she moved?

The woman puts her hands on her hips and leans forward, tilting her head. "I see it's not just your legs, but also your brain that is damaged," she says sweetly, speaking like I'm deranged.

I fist my hands. Cal snickers down behind me.

I bow my head and take a deep breath. "I'm Finn. Where is Paris?"

Color rises in her cheeks and she folds her arms across her chest now. "Get the fuck out of here. Is this some sick joke?"

"Do I look like I'm joking?"

"Finn?" The gasp from inside of the house pulls my attention.

The infuriating woman turns, and I finally see her.

Across the room, she feels so far, and yet finally close enough.

Still on the stairs coming from the upper level, Paris slides down, collapsing onto a step, her arms wrapped around her belly.

Something is very wrong.

Chapter 29

Paris

"You should have stayed in bed. You know what the doctor said." Brook crosses the room and squats by me. "I'll take care of this."

The door clicks closed and my eyes clash with Finn's.

Finn, thinner and pale.

Finn, with an expression full of pain.

Finn, in a wheelchair.

Jesus.

I thought the pain I've been nursing for the past weeks couldn't get worse, and yet here we are. How long can you test your heart before it gives up?

"Kitten," he whispers, rolling across the floor toward us.

Finn, his voice an instant balm on my soul.

"I didn't invite you in." Brook jumps up, holding her hands in front of her.

"Brook." My voice comes out broken.

"No, he doesn't get to destroy you again. After all the suffering he caused, he thinks he can just waltz—wheel—back in." Brook turns her back to me, blocking my view.

But I need to see him.

I need to know he's okay.

He doesn't look okay.

My heart hammers inside my temple, the deafening sound of impending heartbreak. But can my heart take more?

Why?

Why did he come?

Now, after two weeks of agony? When I've finally been feeling better?

Bullshit. I am nowhere close to feeling better. I persevere and push through, while slowly dying inside every day.

"Paris—" Finn's voice slices through the air like an arrow, piercing my chest. As if it punctured my lungs, the air whooshes out of me.

"Brook, let us talk," I push through the lump in my throat.

She whips around and stares at me for a moment. "Are you sure?" she asks softly.

After what she's been through with Dylan, I don't blame her for trying to protect me, but I know I'm safe with Finn.

Well, physically I'm safe. I don't think my heart can be saved anymore. But at least I might get some closure.

I nod, and Brook walks to the sofa and gets a warm blanket. She wraps it around me, and I move one step higher.

With four steps between us, I feel like I've reinforced my defenses. But as soon as I look at him—his haunted gaze, his hunched posture, his beautiful face—I know my attempt was naïve.

"I'll be upstairs. Just call if you need me." She kisses the crown of my head and turns to Finn. "She needs rest, and no anxiety or stress," she snarls.

He flinches at her words, but doesn't look away from me. The sound of Brook's footsteps wanes above us, but we continue staring at each other without words.

The air between us fills with regret, shattered expectations, misguided actions, and a lot of pain.

We don't even need to say all of that because we feel.

One thing that remains in the ruins of our relationship is the undeniable connection. Our painfully forged bond.

"Are you okay?" Finn starts, and then shakes his head.

"No." I almost smile at the conversation. "Are you?"

He wheels closer. Still too far. But that's good. "The baby..."

My hands go to my stomach. "Is okay. We had a scare, but we're okay."

The sigh shudders through him and he sobs once. "Thank God."

I slide one step down. "I collapsed when I came to see you in the hospital. I've been on bed rest since. Are you okay? Nobody wanted to tell me anything."

"I'm better now, knowing the two of you are... okay."

"You don't look good."

He chuckles humorlessly. "Well, head trauma, I fucked my leg up, and I had a stroke during surgery."

A sob rips through me. "Oh my God, Finn. What were you thinking?"

"I wasn't. I'd have come sooner, but I was in a coma."

I hide my face in my palms and try to deal with all the conflicting thoughts. A big part of me needs to hug him, feel him, make sure he's whole.

But we can't kiss this mess better. Can we?

I push up one step up again, clutching the blanket closer.

"What's the prognosis?" I wipe my nose with the back of my hand.

"I'll live." He dismisses my question. "I've been asking for you all the time when I'm conscious. I missed you, kitten."

Kitten.

"Your father told me you never want to see me again."

"Fuck." Finn hits the armrest of the wheelchair with his fist. "You were the only person I wanted to see."

I cover my mouth, trying to keep it together, but tears spill freely. It's like we're suspended in this horrible place where the entire world has colluded to keep us apart.

And it's lonely and painful and so cold here, but we can't sort through the rubble yet, because we caused some of the destruction in the first place. We triggered the collapse.

Finn shakes his head. "How did we get here?"

"I stole your coffee, pretended to be someone else, then you kidnapped me, humiliated me at a business meeting..." I dig my nails into the battered cuticles of my thumbs. "I didn't tell you about my hobby, and your father dragged me through the gossip columns for that, you stormed out of here and went racing from what I heard. I tried to get in touch with you non-stop, but you never returned my calls or messages, and when I wanted to see you, your father told me you never wanted to see me again."

I sum up the gory details of our relationship. Of our non-romantic love story. A story we drafted and it got us to here.

He sighs. "There were many wonderful moments in between. When we were happy. When I couldn't focus on anything until I saw your smile. When I was the luckiest man in the world to wake up beside you every morning—"

"When you made me feel seen and appreciated," I jump in. "You helped me see how I'm always hiding. I got the Quaintique business, by the way." Remembering the good eases some of the hurt.

Like we are removing one piece of the rubble at a time. The question is, how deep is our love buried under all the hurt?

"I always knew you would." He swallows, and our gazes fuse again, full of longing. "We also made the baby together. And spent an amazing week on the island."

"You burned the bed."

"At your suggestion."

I chuckle, and the sound and sentiment feel so strange and yet so peaceful.

Peace. I want peace finally.

"You cooked me delicious meals." I hold to the good despite the odds.

"You made me want to be a better man."

"You gave me many fantastic orgasms."

"I've never had such chemistry with anyone."

Though I should have run out of tears by now, more stream down my face. I wipe my cheek. "You unearthed some of my hidden parts and made me feel free. I'll be forever grateful for that."

As soon as I say the words, I hear their finality. We both hear it at the same time. And Finn shakes his head. "No, no, no."

Another sob rakes through me.

Grunting, Finn pushes to standing. The momentum propels the wheelchair backward and he sways.

I'm on the move, losing the blanket as I dash to him. I slide my arm under his and my other hand goes to his waist. He grabs onto me, steadying himself, and we both freeze.

The contact is not really a hug, but after missing him with every fiber of my being, my body reacts immediately. And it pulls my heart with it, and I melt into him.

Finn wraps his arms around me, balancing on one leg. Something rattles through us, reverberating every nerve into recognition.

It's like coming home, but someone rearranged all the furniture, so you're not sure yet if it's still your oasis.

I bury my face in his chest, soaking his T-shirt. He kisses my hair. "I'm so sorry, kitten. Please don't cry."

His words make me cry harder, so we stand there until I calm down. I don't look up, because I'm not sure where we should go from here.

I know I'm not ready to let go of him, his body so perfectly caressing mine, and I'm too exhausted to continue the conversation.

"Let's go to the sofa. You're heavy." That's the safe, shallow line of talk my mind can manage right now. "You're supposed to engage the brakes before you stand up, you idiot."

I turn, letting him gently sag into the backrest of the sofa. I bring his wheelchair around.

He grunts as he sinks into it, and my heart constricts. How did we get here?

In an almost comical choreography, I wheel him around the large sofa and help him sit down there.

Throwing a pillow on the coffee table, I assist him to lift his cast leg onto it. Before I collapse beside him, there is a gentle knock on the door.

"Who the hell—"

"Oh, it might be Cal." Finn shakes his head.

I sigh, not really understanding what's going on, but I go to open the door.

"Hey." Cal shrugs with a boyish grin. "We were wondering if we should keep waiting." He points over his shoulder.

There is an ambulance with three people standing haphazardly around. "Hey." A young woman in scrubs waves.

Cal leans in the doorway and my eyes dart between the two brothers.

"Is this your ride?" I ask.

"He bribed the doctor to let him out so he could see you, but we should get him back. He only woke up from a coma yesterday—"

I gasp. I don't know if this is the most romantic or the stupidest thing ever done.

"Just fucking wait, Cal," Finn snaps.

"Okay." Cal snickers, raising his arms in surrender. "But Carly needs to use the bathroom."

Finn groans, hitting his head on the backrest.

"I don't know who Carly is, but sure." I open the door wider, and the woman runs up the stairs.

"Thank you." She wiggles her shoulders to her ears, and I point to the powder room under the stairs.

"So..." Cal fidgets when nobody fills the silence.

"How are you?"

"I've been better." I'm not being the most gracious hostess here, but for fuck's sake. Perhaps this is one of those situations that will make me laugh later. Much, much later.

One flush and sound of water later, Carly saunters out and stops by Finn, lifting his hand. She frowns, staring at her watch, while holding her fingers on his pulse.

"Your heart rate is elevated. We should head back." She tries to sound strict. I think.

"Carly, I mean it in the most respectful way, but get the fuck out, my heart rate is elevated for non-medical reasons right now. One of them is yours and Cal's untimely presence."

I don't see Finn's face from the door, but I can hear the glare in his voice. Carly scrunches up her face and, shaking her head, she pads across to Cal.

He wraps his arm around her. "Thanks, guys. We'll be outside."

I close the door and lower my head to the wooden surface. It gives me no strength, so I return to stand by the sofa.

Finn pats the spot beside him, his eyes soft with adoration. But I can't have him touching me because it wipes my mind blank every time. I sit across from him on a love seat.

"Maybe you should go back to the hospital, and we'll talk later."

"No."

I sigh. Stubborn bastard. "Finn, I'm exhausted, and you need to go back before you have another stroke or something."

"I'll have one if we don't finish this conversation."

"I don't think this is a conversation we can have in a few minutes or hours. We have major issues. And we'll have a baby soon. And you irresponsibly endangered yourself. Go back to the hospital, Finn."

He stares at me, a war brewing in his blue eyes.

The floor creaks upstairs.

The light starts changing outside.

Water drops tap in the powder room.

"I resigned," Finn says finally. "That day when everything happened... it started with my resignation. My father didn't react at all. I should have known he would channel his displeasure somehow, somewhere. Turns out he was dating one of the dancers."

She has some new sugar daddy and is hoping he comes to watch her. Celia's words from that night come to me. I sag further into the soft cushions, blowing air from my cheeks.

Finn was planning to leave the firm, but I didn't know... "You didn't say you were planning to resign that day."

He sighs. "I wanted to take you to the gala on my arm, sit at your table and propose. After we talked that morning, I realized my loyalty is with you, so I didn't see a reason to wait any longer. Pa tried to ruin your reputation because he believed you encouraged me to resign."

"And you took his side."

"Paris, that's not—"

He shakes his head and I curl my legs closer to me.

"Kitten, it was out of habit. Pleasing my father is like muscle memory. I was disappointed he showed no emotions when I resigned, and then he called me and I had to defend you to him and it... I don't know, I wanted him to accept or recognize my decision. I was mad at you for blindsiding me."

God, I hate his father. For what he's done to us. But mostly for what he's done to this confident, dominant, smart man who turns into a little boy under his father's influence. But I'm barely ready to have one child, I can't have two.

"Have you been illegally racing?"

He bows his head, letting out a long, loaded sigh. A few endless beats of time pass before he looks back up. "Not since I found out that I'm going to be a father."

"But you never told me about this hobby."

He closes his eyes. "Paris..." There is a plea in his voice. And I wish so much it wasn't there. That we didn't need to have this conversation, because if I hoped for closure tonight, I'm not getting it.

For weeks I longed so much to see him, to talk to him, to be with him. And now, all of that has come true, and I'm more broken and conflicted than ever.

"Do you see the irony in blaming me for my hobby? Of accusing me of not trusting you enough to tell you about it? I suspect I dance burlesque for similar reasons you race, but the degree of risk varies widely."

"What are you saying?"

I stand up and go to the front door. "That you need to go back to the hospital and focus on your recovery." I open the door. "He's ready," I call to Cal and the medical staff.

"Paris, don't do this." Finn tries to push up, but stumbles back to the sofa. "Fuck."

Cal dashes in to get him while Carly moves the wheelchair closer. Once he's settled, they move, but Finn stops beside me and takes my hand.

"I love you, Paris. This is not over. I don't know how to make you trust me, trust in us again, but I know one thing. You're it for me. I've just had a brush with mortality, and there is no way I'm going to let the best thing in my life slip away."

I put my free hand on my stomach. "Go and get better, Finn. I'm not telling this baby their father died from irresponsibility."

Chapter 30

Finn

I stare at the message for so long, it blurs in front of my eyes. It's been two days since my ill-conceived escape from the hospital. I've been trying my damnedest to give her space. To plot how to fix this mess once I'm out of here.

Is she informing me out of duty? As the father of the child? Or is this a shy wave of a white flag? Not that I deserve it. But fuck, I'm taking it.

PARIS

I'm exhausted.

Fuck. That's not much of a conversation opener, but then the dots dance by her name and I wait.

PARIS

I don't want to cry anymore.

Fuck.

Kitten, do you want me to tell you a
really bad joke?

When I get an eye roll emoji back, I take it as a win.

Okay, I have no jokes, but I'm happy
both of you are doing well.

PARIS

What about you? Paying the price for
your nocturnal escapades?

I'm good. A week or two more here
and I'll be as good as new, building
the crib.

PARIS

Look, you do have jokes.

Are you mocking my carpenter skills?

PARIS

I might need some proof. Good night, Finn.

I don't want her to get off the line, but I don't have the moral ground here. As much as I want to rewind back to the night before the shit show exploded, I need to rein in my desire and let her lead.

If there is anything I've learned about this woman who drives me crazy in all senses of the word, it's that Paris can't be rushed. Or bullied, as she'd put it.

Good night, kitten.

We keep texting every evening.

PARIS

Brook is driving me crazy.

That's my job.

PARIS

That's right, she has no chance against you.

How was your day otherwise?

My phone rings and I almost drop it when I see her name.

The cuff tightens around my arm as the nurse makes her evening rounds, taking my vitals.

"Try to relax, because they'll keep you here longer with this blood pressure and heart rate."

"I'll relax the moment I'm out of here," I growl.

I'm only human, and the past ten days have been pure torture. I'm certainly not winning any patient of the year awards. They are probably discharging me early, just to get rid of the grumpy, complaining asshole I've been.

But right now, on the eve of my last night here, I'm edgy because I don't want to miss the call.

I glance at the nightstand. The screen is still black.

"Are we done?" I urge as the nurse slides the monitor's sleeve off.

She shakes her head. "Good night, Mr. van den Linden."

Finally. I grab my phone and stare at the screen like I can make it ring sooner. I don't dare dial myself. Paris has been letting me back in slowly. It gives me an unreasonable heap of hope.

My phone lights up and I exhale a long breath before I answer, feigning nonchalance.

"You couldn't go to bed without hearing my voice," I drawl, but tense immediately.

Where the fuck is she? Eighties pop blares through

the phone. Is she clubbing? That's not safe for her. Who is she with?

"What's the loud music?"

"Brook," Paris sighs.

I relax. Why am I always so worked up around her? Second-guessing, misreading. It's fucking exhausting. But it's like until I'm with her for real, one hundred percent, I can't calm down and be assured she's okay.

"I don't think your sister is good for the whole resting and no stress thing."

She chuckles. "It's only seven o'clock, and we agreed she can enjoy this once a day for an hour without headphones. She's going through some things because of her ex, and I guess dancing it out helps."

"While losing hearing?"

"I'm actually listening to you through noise canceling headphones." She giggles.

It makes me ridiculously happy that she isn't broken and crying anymore.

"How long is she staying? Our baby will grow up a rocker if this goes on."

"I think she hasn't decided yet, and I don't want to push it. She was... I wouldn't have made..." She stumbles over her words, and I regret tainting the conversation with memories of the pain I caused.

Paris sighs. "She's been very helpful over the last

few weeks. Besides, she's been living across the pond, so it's nice to have her closer. Though, yeah, this is a bit too close."

We don't speak for a few long moments. It's not uncomfortable. It's the most pleasant stillness. There are topics we've been avoiding, but we don't rush to fill the quiet. I never could have imagined that finding someone to be silent with would be this peaceful.

"Are you excited about tomorrow?" Paris asks.

Her voice, soft and gentle, twists my guts. I wish she were here with me. Our evening communication has been the highlight of my hospital stay. But I really need to see her.

When she first texted me, it felt like an olive branch for the sake of the baby, but I'll take whatever I can get. It feels like more now, but I'm trying to curb my enthusiasm.

"I'm ready to get out of here, for sure."

We're hanging in limbo. Talking every evening, but not seeing her is my version of hell on Earth. It's like we're having a long-distance relationship, but I'm not even sure if we are still together.

And I'm a fucking coward, grateful for any crumbs, so we both tread carefully, avoiding the subject of us.

"I'm sure all the nurses will be devastated." She chuckles.

"More like relieved." God, I miss her. "How was your day?"

I turn to my side, sick of this bed, of this view, of the fucking owl, of the stench, but hanging on to the only light—the sound of her voice.

"We had a very productive meeting at Quaintique," she says.

"Yeah, that's good, tell me more."

"Our creative vision is aligning perfectly. It's so exciting to work with a client who knows what they want, but they don't micromanage. And Barry is managing the internal work and blossoming in that role, so it gives me time to focus on the creative, which... It's like I've found this space in my company where I finally feel right. I don't know how to explain it."

"I understand."

And I do. I love how alive she comes when she talks about her work. I can listen to it for eternity. And not only because I'm bored out of my mind here. Because her passion gives me hope. Ignites something in me that has been buried under all the frustration of working for my father.

"But I'm still hesitant because they have new leadership, but they haven't announced anything. It's all hush-hush. It's almost like their last CEO has left and they haven't found a replacement, so they are pretending there is a boss. It's all weird. I hope he or she won't be a pain in the ass, or it won't be one of those people hired to clean house and slash budgets."

"You got the contract, kitten."

She chuckles. "But you know I have to overthink it."

I grin like I'm being paid for it. "I miss you."

The silence on the other side stretches into a painful moment. Why the hell did I go there? I've been so careful to do things on her timeline—however fucking long it is—and now I freak her out.

"Finn—"

And here goes nothing. I brace for the cold shower.

"I miss you too."

* * *

"You're in a good mood." Cal hands me a cup of coffee.

It's the same brand Paris stole from me this summer, and I've forced Cal to get me one every single day. Under the guise of hospital coffee tasting like boiled socks—which it does—I have been nursing memories. And hope.

I'm not even ashamed of it. Hope is the only thing I have left at this point. That and a whole lot of stubbornness.

Paris Lowe is mine.

Her *I miss you* last night gave me an unreasonable jolt of confidence.

And while she's overthinking our relationship, I'm going to sneak in and steal her heart again. That's the plan, anyway.

Along with the other plan that might end my career in the industry, or make me the most important player. Dealer's choice, really.

"I'm leaving this bleach jail. Of course I'm in a good mood. And it will improve once you tell me how your meeting went last night."

He purses his lips, staling. The little fucker.

"Spill it, Cal, this is not a fucking game," I growl.

"Jesus, you're intense this morning. Scratch that, you're always intense—"

"Spare me the psych analysis and report."

"Will you be like this when we work together?"

"We've been working together." I smirk. "Don't pretend you don't know what an excellent leader I am."

He snickers. "More like a tyrant. Wait, you do have something in common with Pa."

I give him my best killer look and he chuckles. "Okay, okay." He feigns a dramatic curtsy. "By the close of business on Friday, we'll have forty percent."

A smile tugs at my lips. "Good. If my meeting tomorrow morning goes well, we get another twelve."

"Yeah, but I'll wait to celebrate until that happens.

This meeting is too important for the success of this. Otherwise we'll end up with forty percent and no influence. And disinherited."

"Well, I, at least, have a job. You can learn some skills and get one too," I tease him, but if I'm honest, I couldn't have done this without his help.

The door opens and Cal scrambles to hide behind it. What the hell?

"Mr. van den Linden, here are your discharge papers. Have you spoken to the physical therapist yet?"

The male nurse hands me an envelope and I nod.

"Good, then I'll get a wheelchair and you can go. Is someone picking you up or do you want us to arrange a car?"

"I'm good. And I don't need a wheelchair."

He looks at me skeptically, seeing through my lie, but takes pity on my self-esteem and shrugs. "Sorry, it's hospital policy. I'll be right back."

"What was that?" I shake my head at Cal's loud sigh after the nurse leaves.

He fidgets, glancing at the door as if it might attack him. "I don't want to run into Carly."

I bark out a laugh. "But you were getting along so well."

"Yeah, she's hot, but she got clingy." He shudders.

"A nice, sweet girl accepts an idiot like you, and you get scared," I mock him.

"Not everyone needs to walk through life pussy-whipped."

"Fuck you. You haven't tried it, you can't comment."

"Sure, Romeo."

The nurse rolls in the wheelchair and I finally leave the fucking room behind me.

"I got a surprise for you outside." Cal grins in the elevator while checking out a doctor who looks tired enough to fall asleep standing. He's depraved. I shake my head.

"Will I like the surprise?"

"I'm pretty sure you will." He looks too smug. It doesn't give me much confidence.

"Did you get my Porsche fixed?" I guess, but frankly I'm not even sure I'd enjoy that kind of a surprise. That car has lost its shine, and not only because it was probably totaled by the crash.

"That car is safely buried in the junkyard. We couldn't have saved even your stupid license plate."

"That's okay. It's not like I need it anymore. I'm going to get a Volvo."

"You've become a sensible sedan guy? What was in those drugs?"

The doctor looks at us, her eyes meeting Cal's, and he abandons our conversation to hit on her.

I didn't realize this hospital was the tallest

skyscraper in NYC, but the ride down surely feels like that, especially watching the idiot flirting.

He gets her number at the end. "Score." He raises his arm to high-five me.

"I'm sure she takes her meals in the staff cafeteria with Carly." I stand up and snatch the crutches he's been holding for me.

"Fuck."

I laugh and limp outside, practically dragging my cast leg behind. The shy fall sun hits my face and I close my eyes, enjoying the fresh air.

When I open them, I'm hit with a cocktail of emotions and almost stumble. Paris leans against a white SUV. Her stretchy black woolen dress hugs her curves like a second skin.

My eyes land on the outline of a small bump, a first visible confirmation of her pregnancy. My throat constricts and my heart rate goes haywire. I blink a few times.

She pushes her sunglasses into her—it's chestnut today—hair. Our eyes meet, and I think I'm having a heart attack. But not a shitty one that will send me back to the building behind me, but some sort of arrhythmia that makes my chest swell.

Fuck, she is beautiful.

And she's here.

I don't even want to think about what that means,

because suddenly that hope I've been nursing seems scary.

"Okay, bro." Cal pats my shoulder and I stumble forward, still unable to look away. "You got a ride, so I'll leave you to it. We'll talk later about the strategy for tomorrow morning."

I nod and say something unintelligible, and then my good and my battered legs move, dragging me to the woman who is the center of my universe.

Not the center. She's the entire fucking universe.

"Hey," she says, and opens the passenger door.

"Hi yourself. Did you get a new car?" My heart is breaking some sort of record. I want to grab her and kiss the hell out of her, and it takes all my effort to focus on the trivial conversation.

She leans with her arm against the open door and smiles. "Yeah, someone told me my car wasn't sensible for the baby." Her other hand goes to her stomach.

"So I'm just a someone?" I want to sound light, but my voice is hoarse. Finn van den Linden, choking with emotions. This truly is a new beginning.

Chapter 31

Finn

"Someone important. Get in." She beckons to the passenger seat.

"I like the bossy Paris."

"And I've yet to see an obeying Finn. So get in because I'm parked illegally here, and we both know that my badassery ends at stealing coffees."

I chuckle and get in, trying not to wince because it's enough that she has to help me with the crutches. I don't need my balls cut off completely.

She rounds the front of the car and I admire the lithe movement. God, how does she get more attractive every day?

When she gets in, her scent hits my nose and I groan.

"Are you in pain?" She looks at me alarmed and the pathetic idiot in me rejoices at her concern.

"You're showing." I glance at her stomach to divert attention from my pubescent reactions to her.

She smiles and takes my hand and puts it on her stomach. I stare at her, and then drop my eyes to where my hand rests, and I swallow around the growing lump in my throat.

All my resolve to respect her schedule goes down the drain and I shift, ignoring the pain in my leg. Fisting her hair, I pull her to me and kiss her.

She tenses but doesn't pull away. Her soft lips on mine are like a lifeline I've been missing. Like a breath I haven't been able to draw for way too long.

It's like coming home.

And for a moment I fear she'll shut the door in my face, but then she moans—my kitten—and leans into the kiss.

Our mouths fuse with all the emotions we've been harboring and hiding, while our tongues dance in the choreography that we both know so well. One that was written by us, for us. One of a kind. Just me and her in perfect harmony.

Until the kiss turns desperate—and I'm not even sure who loses their mind first—and Paris pulls away.

Her lips are slick and swollen and her eyes glimmer with hunger, but she looks away and fidgets with the car keys, trying to find the ignition.

"Kitten, I don't think the car needs a key." I'm

disappointed she broke the kiss, but ridiculously pleased with the effect it had on her.

"Oh, right." She pushes the start button and shifts into drive. "We have a doctor appointment if you want to come, but I thought I might treat you to a proper meal first, after the hospital food."

Her voice trembles a bit as she white-knuckles the wheel. We drive in silence, but this time it's not the usual comfortable one. It's charged with sexual tension, and all the conversation we need to have but don't want to.

Because at the end of the day, no matter how many times we fuck up, we will end up together. There is no doubt in my mind about that. The only question is how well we learn to navigate the storms, so we'll always come out of it stronger.

We arrive at Casa Cassi and take a seat at a reserved table. The chef himself comes over before we order drinks.

He kisses Paris. "You look good. Is Brook driving you crazy yet?"

She snorts. "Why? Are you volunteering to host her next?"

He rolls his eyes. "Don't fucking joke about that." He turns to me. "We haven't met officially. I'm Massi, Paris's older brother." He says it with that you-better-treat-her-well-because-I'm-watching-you way brothers do. I know because I've used that tone with Saar's boyfriends before.

"Finn. Nice to finally meet you."

"The jury is still out." He glowers.

"Massi—" Paris urges, color spreading around her cheeks.

He smiles at her—a one-eighty turn from the expression he gave me. I like the guy. Anyone who has her best interest in mind is my favorite person.

"Do you have any special requests, or can I treat you to the chef's choice?" Massi turns to Paris.

"I always trust your choice, if that's okay." She smiles at me, and I nod. I won't be picky. By the looks of it, I'm getting laxatives served with my meal regardless.

"He's not a fan," I say once he leaves.

"He's just being a big brother."

We stare at each other. We've been talking on the phone, but facing her now makes me nervous. And turned on. I've been sporting a semi since that kiss in the car.

"Finn." She bites her bottom lip, fidgeting with the napkin, and my heart rate spikes again. "We haven't been talking about us, and I don't want to talk about it anymore because it's not words, it's actions that matter."

"Okay." I reach for her hand on the table, and she lets me hold it.

"But there is one topic that we need to talk about. One external influence that has been coming between us directly, or often indirectly, because the pressure from your father often influences your behavior."

She pauses, looking at the table, and I wonder if it's my turn to talk, but I feel there is more she is bracing for.

She licks her lips, and I lose my mind for a moment. "You said that pleasing your father is like muscle memory."

"I retrain. For you, for us, I retrain. Because you're the only person I want to please, Paris. Only you. I want to make you happy. If dancing half naked makes you happy, then that's what I support."

She snorts.

"I mean, I might have to kill every motherfucker who enters that club and lays their eyes on you—"

"Finn." She tries to look stern, but there is a mischievous smile ghosting her face. So fucking gorgeous.

"I'm not even kidding. You're mine."

The air bristles with electricity between us as we stare at each other, drunk on emotions.

"I'm not dancing at the club. It was a one time thing. Celeste, my dance teacher, needed help, and I helped. I enjoyed the freedom and loved the courage it took, but dancing in public is not what I want to do."

I let the air out through my cheeks. "Thank God."

She shakes her head.

"It's not what you wanted to talk about though," I point out.

She opens her mouth, but I stop her.

"Everything that happened, and the fucking endless staring at the ceiling in the hospital, got me to understand a few things. My whole life I've been trying to please my father. I've competed with his lovers, his work, his hobbies, his everything, just to have that pat on the shoulder.

"He never pushed me for my own good, only for his gain. I know that now, and I assure you, our relationship is over."

"But he's your father, and—"

"Paris, there is something I need to tell you, and believe me, after tomorrow my father will probably never speak to me again."

She widens her eyes.

"I resigned, which you know. But Cal and I, we have been buying shares of the company. We now own forty percent. Tomorrow Quaintique will hopefully negotiate another twelve with another shareholder."

"Quaintique? How can you negotiate on behalf of

them?" But then her eyebrows jerk up and, fuck, I love how smart she is. "You're—"

"I'm the new CEO of Quaintique."

"But my contract—"

"I wasn't involved in the decision. You got it on your own merit. I disclosed our relationship and remained hands off, so no one can question that you deserved the contract."

"I don't know what to say..."

"Quaintique has been trying to poach me for a while. After the way my father treated you during dinner at their house, I took the call. If everything goes well, Cal and I, along with Quaintique, will own van den Linden resorts. With me at the helm and chair of the board."

"A hostile takeover of your family company?"

I nod. "Something like that. I'm going to keep my legacy but do it on my terms. Not my father's."

She leans back, shaking her head and smiling. "That is... that is... I don't even know what to say."

"Don't say anything yet, because it might all go down the drain tomorrow."

"And you never said anything." She keeps shaking her head.

"I was going to, that night. I'm sorry I stormed out. I knew it was a mistake as soon as my head cleared, racing. I was going to find you right after, but I didn't get a chance."

* * *

"I'm sorry, but the doctor has been delayed with another patient who went into labor. You can either meet with another doctor in the practice or wait. Or I can have you rescheduled." The receptionist shrugs in the exam room's doorway.

"How long will he take?" Paris asks. She's in the gown already, sitting at the edge of the exam table.

"Half an hour, tops. I'm really sorry."

"We'll wait. Don't worry about it. One day he'll be delayed because of me, so I guess it's the least we can do." Paris smiles.

"Okay. If you need anything, just let me know."

As soon as she leaves, Paris pads barefoot to the door and locks it. All my blood rushes into my cock as I squeeze the crutches, trembling.

"The doctor is delayed," she drawls and sits back at the edge of the exam table. "Maybe you need to examine me." Her innocent tone contrasts the hunger in her eyes.

"So there is no sex ban this time?" I tease. I'm breaking any and all bans she might try to impose.

She sighs, dangling her feet. "London reminded me

the other day that I'm too focused on 'should haves,' so I'm trying to do less of that. I should have met my Prince Charming, fallen madly in love, had a huge wedding like a princess, started a family. Instead, I got you."

Fuck. I'm her consolation prize. And not even by choice, but by circumstances that led us to this room. But then she continues and I drop the crutches, my hands collapsing on each side of her hips.

"I got you, and you're my Prince Charming." She leans back, stretching her arms above her head. Beautiful.

"So much better than my dreams. I'm madly in love with you. We started a family already." She puts her feet into the stirrups, and the sight of her soaked pussy has me hard so fast it's painful.

She licks her lips in a deliberate, slow torture. "All the other pieces will settle down in one way or another. So I won't bring the 'should haves' into what we already have. But I suggest you fuck me right now before I overthink it."

Epilogue

Paris

"Finn," I scream, shuddering with pleasure into a blissful morning.

This man.

"Good girl, kitten, let the world know who you belong to." He grins from between my legs, his face glistening with my arousal.

The after effects of my orgasm have me trembling as he climbs up to me. And let's face it, by now the climb is real.

And I get to wake up to this daily. Finn hasn't officially moved into my house, but he's somehow ended up living here anyway. We don't discuss our future, aside from baby preparation.

It's fine though, because neither of us wants to feel

that decisions about the future are being forced by circumstances. So we just go with the flow.

Gently, he flips me on to my side, my swelling belly resting on a pillow. He gets behind me, massaging my breast and nibbling on my shoulder. His erection digs into my lower back as he continues trailing kisses, eliciting goosebumps in the wake of his lips.

"God, I love this baby just for the tits it's giving you," he murmurs, the warmth from his skin spreading through me and pooling at my core.

I chuckle. "You're such an idiot. Does it mean you won't like my body when I'm back to normal?"

"Oh, kitten, your body is the reason I wake up in the morning."

I swat at him. "And here I thought you were with me for my brain."

"What brain?"

"Hey." I try to push him away, but of course I have no chance. Not only is he strong like a bull, I'm at the stage when moving swiftly reaches turtle speed at best.

He squeezes me tight. "I love your tits and your wits. And your talent, your sense of humor—or apparently the lack of it." He bites my earlobe. "I love how you shudder when I kiss you here." He moves my hair out of the way and kisses the crook of my neck, and of course a jolt of pleasure rakes through me.

"I love how your eyes brighten every time I cook for

you, and how you defy me all the time when I want to take care of you, how you roll your eyes at me, and all your mewing and purring, kitten."

I sniffle, tears welling in my eyes. Stupid hormones.

He takes my chin between his thumb and index finger and forces my face to his. "But I fucking hate the tears. What did I do now?"

"They're tears of joy, you idiot." I kiss him. "I'm such a mess," I weep.

"Jesus, woman, let me fuck it better."

I sob-giggle as he lifts my leg and slides into me, filling me to the hilt. We both groan. Finn moves, his tempo slow.

It's maddening how he takes his time when I want the opposite. I can't even complain, because him delaying my instant gratification only prolongs the pleasure, but still...

"Finn—"

"Yes, kitten." His voice is strained with effort.

"You said you'd fuck me."

"My cock is deep inside you."

I groan. "Harder please," I whimper.

"Not a chance. Just relax and enjoy the ride." He pinches my nipple and I arch my back, gasping.

This has been the only point of friction between us. Since we reached the third trimester two weeks ago,

Finn has suddenly turned into a gentle lover. And no amount of seduction can change that.

"Eyes on me, kitten," he growls, and I turn my head.

He captures my lips and stops moving. I groan against his lips, but he holds me in a position so I can't pull away. I try to buck my hips, desperately seeking the connection I need.

But there is no point, he is in charge. Even for the gentle lovemaking, he's in charge. And I might feel I want something different, but in the end, I get exactly what I need.

He resumes thrusting, and when he has me all riled up, teetering on the edge, he stops again.

I whimper and he chuckles. "Patience is a virtue, kitten." His voice shakes. The comment might be cocky, but he's losing control as much as I am.

He continues with his stop-and-go, slow approach for so long, I forget about everything else. I'm putty in his hands, and when he finally lets us fall over the edge, I shatter into a million pieces.

And yet, never have I felt so complete.

After my shower, I waddle to the first floor and find him cooking my breakfast. A content sigh tickles my body as I stop to watch him.

Finn van den Linden, the majority owner, CEO and the Chair of the Board of Quaintique-Linden—

they could have been more creative with the name—cooks for me every single day. And bullies me into praising him for it.

Every boy needs recognition, and his isn't coming from the two people who should have supported him from birth. They no longer talk to any of their children because of the betrayal.

The betrayal that came in the form of a publicized hostile takeover. It came in the form of innovation and successful rebranding unprecedented in the hospitality industry. Especially on such a short timeline.

Charles van den Linden might lament the family legacy, but his two sons are working well together to remodel it for future generations.

"I'm nervous about the evening." I rub my huge belly while I stand by the counter, watching him move around.

"Don't be. It will be great. You did an amazing job with the space, and your designs will be sought after in no time. And Mila and her team took good care of today's opening." He kisses my temple and carries the plates to the table.

"Besides, I'll be there with you." He shrugs theatrically as if I'm being completely unreasonable to worry about the opening night of The Light Oasis.

"Don't be cocky, because I'll remind you again who owned the building before you."

He glowers at me. "You're lucky I can't spank you properly."

"But that's where you're wrong. You can." I sigh and sit down.

"A few more months and I'll punish you for everything, and fuck you so hard you won't walk for days."

"Promises, promises." I huff and dig into my omelet.

Finn stares at me, but I know it's no longer about our banter. He watches me chew. I swallow with a stoic face. It's hard because these eggs are divine. But I like to mess with him.

Without a word, I smile and take another bite. Finn clears his throat and starts fisting his hand.

I stifle a giggle. "You added something new. Whatever it is, this thing is the best omelet you've ever made."

He lights up with pride, his ego barely fitting into the large space of my ground level. "Love is the key ingredient, kitten. Enjoy."

"I don't know how you can outdo yourself every single time," I praise, because my man deserves it. And because he reciprocates tenfold every single day. With his every single—at times annoying—action.

"Congratulations, my dear." Bianca, my stepmother, smiles at me, squeezing my dad's wheelchair handles. "What a wonderful evening. This space is so you."

"I'm very proud of you, darling." Dad grips my hand and I lean down to kiss his cheeks. The last round of radiation damaged one of his vertebrae and walking has been a challenge.

"I'm so happy you could be here with us."

"Sorry to interrupt." Mila gets my attention. "I think it's time you address the guests."

I step aside with her. "I won't talk. I spoke with almost everyone in person. They all know about the vision for this place and everything else. I'm enjoying tonight, and I don't want to spoil it for myself."

The Light Oasis opening night has been a success, with the media, influencers and a who's who list in the world of design milling around the space Finn and I brought to life.

It's not just a designer lighting boutique, but also a beautiful workshop space where anyone can come and create something.

I've hidden my art for so long, creating my pieces in the obscurity of my workshop, but I've had resources to feed my passion. Many talented people struggle to get started.

Here, they can try to create. But also, we'll be able to identify those with potential and get investors for them to start their line of designer decor. This is where Finn comes in, getting capital for startups.

"I love what you've done with the space." Gina hugs me.

"You're not mad you didn't get to work on it with me?" I bite my lip.

"This would have been another restaurant in New York. Okay, mind you, the second best, but still, now it's something special, so no, I'm not mad. I'm proud of you."

"Thank you. This means so much." My stomach is in knots. It's hard to receive praise. Especially for someone who tried to hide from it for so long.

"Well, sis, you did it." Andrea squeezes my shoulder and kisses my temple. "It took you long enough, but—"

"Andrea." Gina gasps. "Give a compliment and shut up."

He laughs. "Okay, I wanted to congratulate you. Vivid is on her way. I might force her to test the workshop." His young girlfriend is talented in her own right, and he can't be prouder of her, judging by the puffed-up chest every time he mentions her.

"I love what you did with the interior," he continues. "I mean, you planted a tree in Massi's shower, so I shouldn't be surprised you brought nature into this space. The way it spills into the waterfront is something else. I'm proud of you." He nods.

Another person. I was nervous before the opening, but I didn't expect all the praise would cause such a riot inside me. It's delicious and scary at the same time.

"I'm so glad I stayed around for this." Brook joins us.

"It's great to have you here." I kiss her cheek.

"If Baldo showed up, the family would be complete for the first time in years," Andrea says.

Brook flinches, but I don't get a chance to interpret her reaction before Mila joins us.

"Finn decided he'll speak," she says.

I whip around, and my eyes collide with Finn's. He's wearing a navy three-piece suit, and his hair is messed up into a perfect and effortless-looking style.

Cal is telling him something, but his entire attention is on me. His hungry gaze somehow has a direct line to my core, and desire swarms me immediately.

How is it I stand across a room full of people, and yet the moment his eyes land on me, everyone else disappears? It's just the two of us, and the echo of my heart.

A cocky grin lights up his face, and he crooks his finger to beckon me to him. And it's like he casts a thread, my legs move and I walk to him. It almost feels like people part to make a path for me.

"Hey, gorgeous." He kisses my forehead.

"Mila told me you want to speak. I should leave you to it, then," I whisper.

He grabs my hand and squeezes. "No hiding, kitten."

I want to protest. Having everyone stare at me is only a shade better than having to speak in front of them. But before I can voice my concern, Finn's voice silences the room.

"Ladies and gentlemen, thank you for your attention." He clears his throat and gives me one of his blinding smiles. He waits for a moment while everyone turns to stare at him. At us, really, and I squeeze his hand hard.

He lifts that hand and kisses my knuckles. "Breathe," he whispers to me, and then faces the audience, our friends, family and everyone else.

"This space, all its raw beauty and natural energy, was designed by Paris Lowe. She spearheaded the idea, and I stood behind it, lending my support from the get-go. Okay, remembering when we were here the first time, it wasn't from the get-go, but that's a different story.

"This space brings together her passion for design, her talent, and my desire to support good ideas. I believe many wonderful ideas will be born here. Or many of you will just get a piece of this amazing woman to light up your home. But this will always be a space, that, against all the odds, brought us very close."

The crowd sighs in unison, and Finn turns to Cal and snatches a handkerchief from his breast pocket. He hands it to me, and I pat the corners of my eyes.

Jesus, he knows how emotional I've been due to the pregnancy, and he makes me cry in a room full of people.

I shake my head, but he shrugs and continues. "But here is something you don't know about Paris. She stole from me."

I gasp. I can't believe he's going to tell that story. London chuckles somewhere in the crowd and Brook tuts. I glare at him, trying to stop him.

"She stole my heart."

Another collective sigh from the crowd accompanies the relief that floods me.

"Last summer, I met this woman who was so beautiful, charming and alluring, she was impossible to miss. And yet she was hiding. She gave me a different name, constantly changed her hair color, was always nice to every impossible client. Lucky for me, meeting me was on her bucket list."

He winks at me, and I giggle through my tears.

"Only she didn't expect that I'd stick around. She fought me on that for a while, but I'm stubborn. Perhaps as stubborn as she is."

Everyone laughs now, and I keep hoping Cal's handkerchief is absorbing my mascara without turning me into a raccoon.

"I stuck around to see her. The real her." He turns to me.

"Paris, you're talented, gorgeous, kind, and such a fucking gift not only to me, but to everyone around you. Just like your lamps, you bring light to my life.

"In the process, I lost things and people I no longer needed, because they were feeding my anger. With you, I found my peace. And I'll spend the rest of my life trying to bring peace to you. I love you, Paris Lowe. Will you marry me?"

I plaster my hand over my mouth, but the mixture of a gasp and moan and a strangled cat cry escapes anyway.

The room goes completely silent, and it only speeds up my hammering heart. It takes me several beats to realize everyone is waiting for me.

"Oh my God." I sob. "Yes."

"Finally." Finn pulls me into an embrace, and I cry into his lapels. Well... it's not the first suit we've destroyed.

"Fucking waterworks, kitten." He grins and steps in front of me, allowing me to compose myself without all the onlookers staring at us. The room cheers while I blow my nose and finally get it together.

"Bro, you forgot the ring," Cal yells, and everyone laughs.

"Oh, shit, yeah, the ring." Finn reaches into his breast pocket, but I pull him to me.

"Fuck the ring, kiss me."

Baldo Cassinetti

Two weeks later

My childhood house looks just like I remember it. It's a strange feeling to walk up the paved path to the manor that holds so many pieces of the past me. Pieces I left behind and never cared—or was too much of a coward—to revisit.

Ridiculous déjà vu sweeps over me as I climb the fence to visit my mother, but I don't want her to see me on the camera.

Why?

Fuck if I know, but being here after nine years is unearthing way too many memories and a whole load of feelings. And I can do without them.

So here I am at twenty-seven, in my three-thousand-dollar suit, behaving just like the brat she remembers.

Why did I even come? Or why didn't I come

sooner? I have appropriate answers for these questions, but walking up to the house, I can't remember them.

Fuck this shit. I'm here, I might as well say hi to my mother and hopefully remain civil around my stepfather, drink some of Mom's lemonade and get out of here.

I ring the bell, and it doesn't take long before the formidable Bianca Cassinetti opens the door.

She blinks a few times, swallows hard, and I swear I'm mimicking her actions. I didn't expect the reunion to overwhelm me this much.

As right as all my reasons to stay away have felt over the years, I should have come sooner.

"Baldo," Mom breathes, her eyes rimmed with tears.

My legs move and I wrap her in a bear hug, her petite figure lost in it. She fists my lapels and sniffles, and then she pounds on my chest. "I'm so mad at you. You've stayed away for so long."

She steps back. Assesses me, tears and a smile mixing on her face. Then she shakes her head and wraps her arms around my waist, holding me for a moment.

Voices from the kitchen reach me. I recognize London's cackle. Shit. Is the whole family here? I couldn't ignore Mom during my unplanned business in

New York, but I'm not ready to jump into the full family dynamics.

"Maybe I'll come back at a different time." I kiss the crown of her head. Maybe she could meet me in the city for lunch. That's safer. Coward. "You have company."

She swats at me, shaking her head. "Nonsense, it's just the girls." She grips my hand and pulls me behind her.

For a woman of such a small frame, she's strong like a bull.

"Oh my God, it's a day of ghosts." London laughs and comes to hug me. "Welcome home, bro. Look at you, all grown up." She pats my biceps.

I squeeze her a little tighter, surprising both of us. I missed her. The sentiment rolls in my stomach undigested.

Sydney comes to kiss me on both sides of my face, shaking her head but grinning. She pats my cheeks as if making sure I'm not a ghost. "Massi would approve of the man bun."

Paris—a very pregnant Paris—wipes tears and comes to embrace me next.

I missed them all. I missed them so much. The Lowe girls, my stepsisters. Fuck, I was such a brat to them when we were growing up together, I had forgotten how much I love them.

And then my eyes land on the youngest of them, and the blood drains from my face. The voices around me fade, my heart thudding loudly in my temples.

Brook slides down from the counter, her face rigid, her jaw set, and walks to me. Elegant like a panther, her long legs glide across the floor. She's wearing a short skirt and some skimpy T-shirt and a floating cardigan.

As if she senses I'm taking her in, she wraps the sweater around her before she reaches me.

If wine gets better over time, the theory is nowhere close to how the girl I lost has blossomed into a gorgeous woman.

And if I'm not mistaken, there is a lot of hate in her eyes.

"Tokyo," I rasp, my nickname for her coming from the deep crevices of memories I kept hidden.

She hated it openly, but I know she loved it secretly. Always upset her parents didn't bother to find a glamorous metropolis to name her after, like her sisters.

I wrap my arms around her.

"Welcome home." Her tone could freeze lava. She goes rigid at our contact, and then steps back and turns to the patio doors, as if she can see anything in the night's darkness.

I watch the reflection of her. She's blinking rapidly

and I think she's just shaken her head. Or I'm seeing things.

Seeing her was never the plan. Fuck. She lives in England. Why is she here?

"Do you want help with that?" Sydney asks.

The commotion of the kitchen snaps me back to the here and now.

"No, I'll bring it to him." My mom picks up a tray with tea.

"Ask if we can come to say good night," Paris pleads. There is sadness across each of their faces.

"If he is up for it, I'll call for you, girls."

Then she looks at me with her sad eyes. "Don't go anywhere," she urges, and beside sadness there is also a glimmer of hope, of joy, of belonging in her gaze.

And if nothing else comes out of my unexpected visit, I know I've made Mom happy.

"Dad is sick," London explains. "So, what brings you here after all these years?"

"Okay, it's ironclad." A tall stranger comes from the sitting room, followed by two other men. "The old lady was sharp like a blade."

He throws some documents on the large square kitchen island and goes to London. She leans into him and he kisses her temple.

"Why would she do that?" Sydney shakes her head, and one of the other men pulls her to him.

The third one wraps his arms around Paris's shoulders, and she rests her head on his chest.

I'm half expecting a fourth douchebag to step in and claim the last sister, and the pang of jealousy that sears me is unexpected, but more importantly unwarranted. What the fuck?

"I'm Dominic Cressard." London's man extends his arm to me.

"Baldo Cassinetti." I shake his hand.

"Oh, the lost brother. Nice to meet you." Sydney's man extends his arm. "I'm Hunter Stuart."

"Finn van den Linden." The last dude introduces himself.

"I'm sorry to interrupt the joyous reunion, but can we go back to this nightmare?" Brook points at the documents on the counter and marches to the island.

She grabs her wine and then glances at me like she wants to throw up. And as if standing in my vicinity is punishment, she moves to the opposite side of the island.

What are we, eighteen still? That's what I tell myself, but I'm annoyed by her cold shoulder. She was the one who severed our relationship before it had a chance to start. What the fuck is her problem?

"Is there a clause about how quickly we need to comply with the conditions?" Sydney asks, squeezing Hunter's—or is it Finn's—hand?

I guess I'd better catch up on all the new dynamics. Yeah, it's Hunter and Sydney, Finn and Paris, and London with Dominic.

What was I expecting? To walk back into the same house and family I left when I was eighteen?

Of course, they are all married now. Mom hasn't mentioned any of it on my too-sparse calls.

"You have three months."

Sighs and groans follow Dominic's statements, but I mostly notice Brook lowering her head and shaking it. So beautiful and so lost. And angry.

"What's going on?" I ask, wondering why no one else is drinking but her. I really want to join her in that endeavor.

"Our maternal grandmother died, and we stand to inherit a shitload of money," London explains.

"My condolences. I'm sorry." There must be more to this story. I wasn't paying much attention when I was younger, but I know their mom's family didn't really like their father, Micah, and they were estranged.

"In order to get the money, we have to be married for a year."

I laugh, but none of them do. "What the hell? How is she going to police that from beyond the grave?"

"It's a long story, but she put a lot of thought into her scheme." Dominic, who must be a lawyer since it looks like he was reviewing the merits of the will, runs his hand through his hair.

Mom returns and looks at me, smiling. Then something I don't understand passes through her face and she says, "Your father was too tired and fell asleep. But he seems much better."

Micah truly is sick. Shit. I really should have just scheduled a lunch meeting with Mom. This is too much to process. I feel like a stranger here.

And something tells me Mom hasn't been completely honest and tried to spare me. To delay my meeting with my stepfather. Or maybe she was protecting him. That's certainly a meeting I'm not looking forward to.

Mom stands by Brook and strokes her back. It feels almost like she's choosing sides. Like she stays on the other side of the island, comforting the woman who is currently shaking with frustration.

"I'll come to visit him tomorrow," London says, and then she looks at Dominic. "Anyway"—she turns to me —"Granny dearest conditioned the inheritance. If we don't marry, the money goes to different organizations."

"Like charities?" I ask.

Finn snorts. "That would have been a no-brainer, but the old lady was clearly set on marrying off her estranged granddaughters. The money would go to different political and economic groups that are involved in an array of causes, including criminal activities, destruction of natural resources, cheap labor, the list goes on."

"Holy shit." I can't even believe what I'm hearing. "Why would she do that?"

"To force their hands," Finn says, shrugging. "She would have been good friends with my father."

"Can we stop yapping about her motivations? It's not like we can ask her. What the hell are we going to do?" Brook grabs the bottle and refills her glass, gulping down half of it.

I look around the room and it dawns on me. She is the only one without a partner present.

"Well, Cressard, we better schedule with the city clerk." London shrugs.

"I got us in for tomorrow at ten." He winks at her, and I'm shocked to see my aloof stepsister melting under his gaze.

"Can we wait for me to have this baby first?" Paris huffs.

Finn kisses her temple. "You'll have the wedding you always wanted, even if I have to contest the fucking will."

"I'd suggest that you"—Dominic looks at Paris, and then at Sydney—"since you're living together anyway, get hitched at the city clerk's office now, to comply with the paperwork, and then have the weddings you planned later."

"Great, and now that we've resolved the issues that weren't pressing since you were going to get married anyway, can we finally focus on me?" Brook sounds a tad desperate, and a bit drunk.

And so lonely.

And something in me snaps with the need to protect her, to make the situation—her life—better for her.

And before I consider the implications, I blurt, "I'll marry you."

Holy shit, what were you thinking, Baldo?
While you're waiting for his story in **Reckless Vow***, I have a delicious enemies to lovers for you, Chosen by the Billionaire.*
*The socially awkward hacker brings trouble to a coffee shop manager, but their love story is "**an excellent read from beginning to the end**", according to a reader's review.*

Bonus Scene:
Not everything is peachy after Paris and Finn's baby is born. Read all about it and a glimpse of their life five years later in the bonus scene here:
www.maxinehenri.com/recklessbond or scan:

Author's Note

Dear reader,

Thank you for reading Paris and Finn's story. The theme of feeling you're not enough, you're not seen is close to my heart.

I attempted to write a love story where, despite being annoyed and frustrated with their situation and each other, Finn saw Paris for her talent and strength and she saw and encouraged his potential.

So if there is nothing else, dear reader, remember this: you're wonderful, you matter and I appreciate you.

Love,

Maxine

Also by Maxine Henri

Reckless Billionaires Series

Reckless Fate (Massi and Gina's Second Chance Romance)

Reckless Desire (Sydney and Hunter's Single Dad Romance)

Reckless Dare (Lo and Dom's Fake Relationship Romance)

Reckless Deal (Gio and Mila's Grumpy/Sunshine Bosshole Romance)

Reckless Hunger (Andrea and Ivy's Age Gap Romance)

Reckless Bond (Paris and Finn's Accidental Pregnancy Romance)

Reckless Vow (A Marriage of Convenience Romance)

Untamed Billionaires Series

Tempted by the Billionaire (A Fake Relationship Romance)

Chosen by The Billionaire (An Enemies to Lovers Romance)

Chased by the Billionaire (An Age gap/Innocent Heroine Romance)

Stolen by the Billionaire (A Forbidden Love Romance)

About the Author

Maxine Henri is a contemporary romance author who infuses her stories with steamy passion and complex characters. When she's not crafting stories that will have you swooning, she can usually be found sipping on a cup of black tea while reading a good book. Or traveling to new destinations.

Maxine believes that stories matter. They facilitate emotional journeys, inspire and entertain. And when it comes to books and fiction, stories are a great escape and probably the most beneficial addiction on this planet.

Her billionaire romances are the perfect escape, offering a taste of luxury and adventure. Maxine introduces heroes who may have a dark past, but are always balanced by a lighter side. And her leading ladies? They're strong, independent women who may be a little broken, but always find their way in life.

You can connect with her on any of these platforms:

facebook.com/maxinehenriromance

instagram.com/maxinehenriromance

bookbub.com/profile/maxine-henri

amazon.com/author/maxinehenri

www.ingramcontent.com/pod-product-compliance
Lightning Source LLC
LaVergne TN
LVHW091655190726
843493LV00001B/13